RANK & FILE

ANCHOR POINT, BOOK 4

L.A. WITT

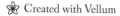 Created with Vellum

ABOUT RANK & FILE

Senior Chief Will Curtis is as straitlaced as they come. While his fellow Sailors have partied their way through their enlistments, he's had his eye on the prize—making master chief and retiring after thirty years of service.

Lieutenant Brent Jameson is a Navy brat turned Annapolis grad. He's lived and breathed the military his whole life, and he knows he's destined for great things—once he's done paying his dues at the bottom of the ladder.

When their paths cross, both men know better than to give in to temptation, but that doesn't stop them. It also doesn't keep them from coming back for more, even though being discovered would sink their careers. Something has to give—Will can retire, Brent can resign, or they'll both face court-martial.

But there's also the option neither wants to acknowledge: jump ship and walk away from each other instead of ending their careers over a fledgling relationship. And they should probably decide before they fall in love.

Except—too late.

This book was previously published.

CHAPTER 1

WILL

I HATED DOMESTIC CALLS. Most cops did, even if they hadn't witnessed—or experienced firsthand—the things I had. Driving like a bat out of hell into base housing, I was nervous not only for myself, but for my younger masters-at-arms who were already on the scene. Who'd already called for backup.

I held the wheel tighter and gave the accelerator some more pressure. The MAs who'd called hadn't given much detail over the radio. They'd requested assistance, and since I'd been in the area—closer to their location than the watch commander or anyone else—I'd headed their way.

Sometimes calls like that meant the MAs on scene were in over their heads. Domestics weren't easy to defuse, and both patrols involved were relatively young and inexperienced with this type of call. MA3 Harvey hadn't sounded panicked on the radio. Just uneasy. Like things hadn't gone to shit yet, but he had a feeling they would and didn't quite know what to do. That could mean anything from a pair of spouses who would not, despite repeated requests, calm down, up to and including someone getting violent. There'd been no mention of a weapon, so presumably we were just dealing with belligerence. Still, I went in with the assumption there was actual danger to my MAs, the people in the house, and myself.

Of course we were trained for this, but nothing ever quite prepared you for a domestic. Too many variables. Too many ways things could go south in a hurry. MA3 Harvey and his partner, MA2 Lee, were both levelheaded. If they needed help, this could be bad.

I slowed enough for my headlights to illuminate a street sign, and when I'd double-checked this was the right street, I hung a fast left. There was no need to check the address beyond that—base housing was row upon row of identical blue-trimmed white duplexes that were especially hard to distinguish from one another at night, but the patrol car parked on the curb was a dead giveaway.

I parked outside, radioed the watch commander to let her know I was on scene and heading inside, and cautiously approached the front door, which was wide open. Voices—a lot of angry, loud voices—spewed out onto the porch.

There was no point in trying to shout over them, but the MAs would hear their radios, so I told MA3 Harvey I was there. He responded that they were in the living room, and confirmed there were no weapons and everyone was accounted for.

With my hand on my Taser and the other close to my pistol, I went inside.

As soon as I saw the scene in the living room, I didn't need anyone to explain what was going on.

A woman in a T-shirt and not much else was screaming at a man in blue digicam utilities, who was right in her face and giving as good as he got. Behind her was another man in a pair of jeans—only a pair of jeans—dabbing blood from the corner of his mouth. Another day, another cheating spouse in base housing. My favorite.

MA2 Lee and MA3 Harvey alternated between exchanging uneasy glances and trying to verbally defuse the situation. They both looked at me with *dude, we've got nothing* on their faces. The guy with the bloody mouth noticed me and watched me, eyebrows up in a look I recognized as someone who simultaneously hoped I'd intervene, and hoped I'd walk away and pretend I didn't see anything. He was visibly rattled, and probably scared shitless that he was going to wear some handcuffs too. I couldn't get a look at the husband's face to confirm my suspicion, but it was rare for one guy to take a swing and the other to just sit back and take it. If the wife's paramour had gone hands-on, he was getting his rights read too. Company policy.

I shifted my gaze from him to the couple, who were lighting into each other so viciously, they didn't seem to be aware there was anyone in the room, never mind that another well-armed MA had entered the scene.

I cleared my throat, and when I spoke, the cop voice I'd honed for the better part of twenty years came out: "Sir. Ma'am."

Two words, and the shouting stopped. The silence was so sudden, my ears rang. The couple stared at me, slack-jawed. The guy with the bloody mouth drew back a bit too.

While the shock was still raw and no one had had a chance to start shouting again, I took over the scene. "I'm separating everyone to give statements. Anything that comes out of anyone's mouth from this moment on is going into a report. None of you"—I gestured at each of the non-MAs in the room—"so much as looks at each other, talks to each other, or goes into the same room as each other until I say so. Am I clear?"

Silent nods all around.

I turned to the husband. "Sir, I'm going to ask you to step outside with MA3 Harvey."

"Outside?" He made a sweeping gesture. "Why should I leave my own house so they—"

"*Sir.*"

His teeth snapped together.

I turned to MA3 Harvey. "Take him outside and get a statement."

Harvey nodded and motioned for the husband to follow him. There was some more grumbling and a withering glance at his wife and her lover, but the man went outside.

"MA2 Lee." I gestured at the wife. "Take her into the bedroom and do the same."

Lee and the wife disappeared in seconds.

Leaving me with the paramour.

He sank into a chair, dabbing his lip again, and kept his gaze down.

Now that things were quiet, I studied him, trying to get a bead on him. He'd seemed kind of timid earlier, but I supposed anyone would in his situation. The husband had already slugged him after presumably catching him in bed with his wife. There were cops on the scene, tempers flaring, and—if he was military like his girlfriend's husband—careers on the line. He had plenty to be nervous about.

My cop voice would be the opposite of helpful right now, so I shifted it down to something softer. "What's your name?"

He didn't meet my gaze. "Brent."

"Brent...?"

He swallowed. "Jameson. Lieutenant Brent Jameson."

No wonder he was nervous. I hadn't had a chance to look at the scorned husband's uniform, but this was enlisted housing. Not a good look for an officer to be busted in the bed of anyone's wife, but there was *just* enough animosity between officers and enlisted that one nailing the other's wife was insult to injury.

I cleared my throat again. "You want to go to medical and have that lip looked—"

"No. It's fine." Eyes down, he shook his head. "It's one of those cuts that isn't bad but bleeds like a motherfucker."

I opened my mouth to ask how he got it—not that it took a rocket scientist to figure it out—but my radio crackled to life. The watch commander getting a status update while she was still en route. MA3 Harvey responded, so I turned down the volume on my radio and faced Lieutenant Jameson again.

He was already nervous and shaken, so having six feet of armed cop looming over him probably wouldn't help. I took a seat on the sofa, sitting close enough to him that we didn't need to raise our voices to hear each other, but keeping a comfortable distance between us.

I took my tiny green notepad out of my pocket and rested it on my knee. "I need you to tell me what happened."

He swallowed, dabbing at his lip again. The bleeding had slowed, though a little had started to dry at the corner of his mouth. "I swear to God, I had no idea she was married."

I tightened my jaw to keep from calling bullshit. Just because my ex-boyfriend's last couple of side pieces had insisted on not knowing about me didn't mean this guy really didn't know he was the other guy.

At least he didn't claim that she'd fed him the line about being in an open marriage. That was the oldest lie in the book for cheaters on base, and the oldest alibi for side pieces. Especially since there really *were* a lot of open marriages—on the down-low, of course, since that could get somebody court-martialed—but also plenty of *not* open marriages.

The second oldest lie was *I'm not married*, accompanied by the second oldest alibi—*I didn't know she was married*.

Tone flat, I said, "You thought she lived in base housing by herself?" Which wasn't necessarily out of the question—she could've been a single mom or something—but it was unusual.

He glared at me. Then he shifted uncomfortably, wringing his hands in his lap. "I *didn't* think about it, okay? I was thinking with my dick, and..." He sighed. "Look, you don't have to tell me I was an idiot. I know I was. Thing is, she told me she was single, and I didn't think anything of it. I didn't pay attention to where we were, and I didn't think anything was wrong until he came home and she freaked out. Then they started fighting, he wouldn't let me leave, and—" He rubbed the back of his neck. "Fuck. I... This was not what I signed up for."

"How did the two of you meet?"

He fidgeted again. "Tinder."

"This your first time seeing her?"

He nodded.

My gut told me he was telling the truth. And, well, we saw this a lot. If we'd caught them in the middle of the day, then I'd have expected him to be at least suspicious that she had a husband who was at work. Then he'd have had the daylight to take in the evidence that was all around him, including the large framed wedding photo that currently hanging on the wall about a foot above his head. But if they'd found each other on a hookup app, gone straight from the front door to the bedroom, and not paid attention to anything else, then yeah, I could see him being genuinely startled when her husband showed up.

So maybe my perception of him had been colored by my own past. He was nervous and shaken and probably more than a little humiliated, and he was not my cheating ex or one of the men he'd taken into our bed. I wasn't being fair.

"What happened to your face?" I knew but needed him to tell me so it could go on paper.

He sucked his swelling lip into his mouth as if he'd forgotten it was bleeding. Color bloomed in his cheeks. "Uh..."

"Even if you hit him first," I said quietly, "I need to know what happened so I can—"

"No! He didn't hit me."

I watched him calmly. It wasn't unheard of for someone in his position to try to downplay what had happened. Sometimes out of a macho need to make sure no one thought he'd had his ass handed to him. Sometimes out of fear he'd be arrested too. "Did you hit him?"

"No. No, it was nothing like that." He lifted his chin and met my gaze, his expression sheepish. "It was her. And totally accidental."

I blinked. "Come again?"

"We..." He covered his face with his hands, but not before the red in his cheeks got even brighter. Then with a sigh, he dropped his hands to his lap again and looked at me with that resignation that meant he was tired of bullshitting and was about to tell me the truth. "When he came home, she panicked, and while we were, uh, getting untangled, she clocked me with her elbow." He motioned toward his mouth. "Like I said, it was an accident."

"Oh." That was actually a hell of a relief, assuming her

story lined up with his. If it did, then there'd be no assault charges. Less paperwork. Nobody leaving in handcuffs. It could also mean the husband hadn't laid a hand on him *yet*, though that could change the second we let them back in the same room.

Brent sat back in the chair, pressed an elbow onto the armrest, and kneaded his temple. "Fuck."

I studied him again, and admittedly, caught myself taking in more than his defeated posture. When I was at work, especially on a call, I never checked people out, but… Jesus. How often was I sitting across from someone this hot? It was probably because he was shirtless, and his light-brown hair was still tousled enough to make sure I was aware that he'd been in bed with someone very recently.

He was a bit young for me—probably mid-late twenties or so if he was a lieutenant, and with a slight baby face to go with it—but I could make an exception for someone with his smooth stomach and broad shoulders. No six-pack, which was actually my preference anyway, especially with my forties looming and time beginning to take its toll. I didn't need an underwear model in my bed to remind me of everything I wasn't.

I shook myself and tore my gaze away. The guy was straight, and I was here as a cop. Clearly I needed to go out and get laid ASAP, but now was not the time.

"This is going to get back to my command, isn't it?" His voice was still filled with resignation.

"The responding patrols will file a report that there was a domestic dispute. And yes, a copy of that will be sent to your command."

He flinched. "Shit."

"But assuming no one requests a protective order and

no charges are filed, that's the extent of it. More of an FYI than anything."

"Ugh. Great." He wiped a hand over his face, then let his head fall back against the chair, and while he stared at the ceiling, I absolutely did not steal a look at his stretched neck.

Christ. I really do need to get laid.

I pulled my focus away from his throat, and glanced down at my notepad. Outside, I could hear agitated voices. "Will you be all right for a minute?"

Eyes closed, he nodded.

I got up and went out to the porch. MA3 Harvey stood at the foot of the steps, and the husband sat on the top one, shakily smoking a cigarette. The husband twisted around to look up at me, and in the warm light coming from the hallway behind me, there was some extra moisture in his eyes. His face was a little red too, and probably not for the same reasons Brent had changed colors a few times.

I met MA3 Harvey's gaze, and lifted my eyebrows. *You got this?*

He nodded.

I responded with another nod, then went back inside, but I didn't rejoin Brent. Instead, I followed the soft sounds of female voices to the bedroom, where I found MA2 Lee sitting on the edge of the bed. Beside her was the wife, who'd put on a pair of yoga pants, and like her husband, had also gone from screaming and angry to quietly crying. MA2 Lee and I had the same silent exchange I'd had outside with her partner, and I left the bedroom.

In the living room, Brent looked at me. "So, what happens now?"

"When my patrols are finished getting their statements, everyone will be free to go unless there's a reason we should arrest someone." I paused. "I would recommend that you not stay here after—"

"Ten steps ahead of you," he muttered. "Just need to figure out how—" His features tightened. Then he closed his eyes again. "God, I am so stupid."

I eased myself onto the sofa where I'd been earlier. "Something I should know?"

Brent laughed humorlessly. "Besides how much of an idiot I am?" He turned to me. "She wanted to meet up for drinks first. Soon as I got there, she said we should go back to her place, and insisted we take her car." He rolled his eyes. "And there I was, thinking with my dick and not realizing she didn't want my car in their driveway in case he showed up." He gestured sharply in the general direction of the husband. "Fuck. You'd almost think she's done this before."

I bit back an unprofessional comment. I'd been a Navy cop for almost nineteen years. The cheating that happened within military marriages was eye-watering, and yeah, this particular wife probably had enough experience to know how to cover her tracks. Or, at least, to *try* to cover her tracks. In fact, I'd have bet money that the only reason she and Brent had been busted tonight was a nosy neighbor tipping off the husband. Wouldn't be the first time, and wouldn't be the last.

Brent drummed his fingers on the armrest and looked right at me. His blue eyes were so intense, it took me a second to realize he'd spoken.

"Sorry, come again?"

He eyed me, but didn't seem annoyed. Curious, if anything. "I asked when I could get out of here."

"Oh. Let me check in with my MAs again and see if

they're finished." I pushed myself back to my feet. "Sounded like they were wrapping things up."

I ordered the spouses to stay put. Nobody put up a fight. The husband lit another cigarette, and the wife buried her attention in her phone.

I took my patrols in the kitchen, and everything checked out. The wife corroborated Brent's story, and the husband had come home after a neighbor had texted him. Damn. Either I was getting good at this, or it was just another case of base housing déjà vu. Nobody wanted to press charges. Nobody needed to go to medical. The husband was going to go crash at a friend's house. The wife was going to stay here. Neither she nor Brent had any desire to speak to each other, which led me to believe their story really did check out. They were strangers, not lovers who'd finally been caught.

MA2 Lee took the wife into another room so her husband could pack an overnight bag, and she handed me Brent's shirt, shoes, and jacket.

While Brent was tying his shoes, the husband suddenly walked into the living room, MA3 Harvey hot on his heels.

"Wait," Harvey said. "He's not ready for—"

"Sir." I put a hand up and put myself between Brent and the husband. "I need you to wait a minute."

The husband sighed heavily. "Look, I don't..." He made an exhausted motion toward Brent. "I just want to get my shit and go. I don't have any beef with him."

Brent and the husband's eyes locked; there was no hostility. They both seemed tired, defeated, and more than a little humiliated.

Softly, Brent said, "I'm sorry. I had no idea."

The husband nodded. "Yeah. I know."

They exchanged a look. Then Brent got up, moving like it took all the effort in the world, and stepped away from the chair so the husband could continue toward the bedroom without them rubbing elbows. The husband walked past without another word.

"Sorry," MA3 Harvey said. "He got away from—"

"It's okay." I paused. "Can you and MA2 Lee take it from here?"

He nodded. "Yeah, we've got it. Thanks, Senior." He followed the husband.

I turned to Brent. "Where's your car?"

He swallowed. "By McCade's. Outside Gate 4."

I motioned for him to follow me. "Come on. I'll drop you off."

CHAPTER 2

BRENT

THERE WAS a cop car on the curb in front of Jenna's house, but the cop who'd offered me a ride continued toward a black pickup parked next to it. Government issue, probably with a light bar hidden in the grill or the bottom of the windshield, but not quite as conspicuous as the patrol car. Fine by me.

As I buckled my seat belt, I said, "I, uh, never caught your name."

"Senior Chief Curtis."

I faced straight ahead and tongued the sweet spot where my tooth had sliced into the inside of my lip. Curtis wasn't terse about his introduction, just businesslike. Which made sense. He was a cop. He wasn't here to be friendly. But right then, with as raw and stupid as I felt, it would've been nice for someone to do one better than cool professionalism.

As he drove out of the cul-de-sac and into the maze of base housing, I stole a few looks at him. Not that I could see much in the glow of the streetlights or the faint blue from the dashboard, but I'd memorized quite a bit of his face while we'd sat there in Jenna's living room. It hadn't been the time or the place, but drooling over the hot cop had been a step up from wallowing in how much of an idiot I was or how thoroughly I'd fucked my career.

He was a bit young for a senior chief. Maybe midthirties or so? Most senior chiefs were in their forties. Maybe he just looked younger. He had a few lines and a few grays, not to mention sharp features and eyes that were perfect for a cop —hard when he was ordering a room full of screaming people to shut up, soft when he was talking to someone who was nervous and shaky. God, he was hot. And the blue digi-cams looked ridiculously sexy on cops anyway. The uniform itself was kind of generic, but add a police belt and a side arm strapped around the thigh, and... whoa. Too bad he was enlisted.

And a cop. A cop who'd come to calm shit down before Jenna's husband tore my throat out or something, and who was taking me back to my car because I'd gotten my dumb ass into that situation to begin with. Pretty sure it didn't matter that I was an officer and he was enlisted.

"You gonna be all right tonight?" His voice startled me enough I actually jumped. When he glanced my way, his brow creased with palpable concern, and I wondered if he thought I was just rattled from everything that had happened. I was good with that. Better than him realizing he'd nearly caught me ogling him.

"Yeah. Yeah, I'm..." I focused hard on the street in his headlights. "It's been a hell of a night."

"Sounds like it." Silence fell, and I thought that might be the end of the conversation, but then he went on. "For what it's worth, you're not the first and you won't be the last."

"Huh?"

Curtis tapped his thumbs on the wheel. "Getting duped

into thinking someone is single. Finding out the hard way that they're not." His eyes flicked toward me for a second. "Everyone always feels like an idiot, but it happens a lot."

"Doesn't make us any less stupid."

"I'd say you're more deceived than stupid."

"I should've figured it out, though."

He was quiet again, this time for almost a minute. "At my last command, I responded to a call that was a lot like this one. Only difference was the guy in your role had been seeing the woman for months. I have no idea how she kept the wool over his eyes that long, but you've never seen a more shocked face than when her husband came home from deployment."

I stared at him. "Seriously?"

Curtis nodded. "It really does happen. A lot. Only way it could be completely avoided would be to do a thorough background check on every person you want to hook up with." He glanced at me again. "I'm a cop, and even I don't do that."

To my surprise, I actually felt better. No less shaken up, and still pretty stupid, but... better. If nothing else, because *he* didn't think I was stupid. For some reason, that was important right now.

Neither of us said anything for the rest of the drive, which wasn't all that long. The entrance to that particular section of base housing was pretty close to Gate Four. Housing was under Navy jurisdiction, but this section of it wasn't physically on the base. It was a development about half a mile away, and there were a shitload of bars and clubs in between. There were bars and clubs clustered around every gate on every base, but the seedier meat market ones always seemed to be closer to base housing. Couldn't imagine why.

"You said McCade's, right?" he asked.

"Yeah." The bar's familiar red and green neon lights came into view, and I gestured toward it. "Right there."

Curtis put on his blinker even though there was no one else on the road—such a cop—and pulled into the parking lot.

"Here is good," I said. "I can walk the rest of the way."

He stopped gently beside a couple of other cars. "Take care, all right?"

"I will." I turned to him, intending to thank him for the ride, but my tongue suddenly stuck to the roof of my mouth. I couldn't decide if it had just been a long time since I'd looked at him, or if there was something about the way the parking lot lights picked out his blue eyes, but Jesus Christ, I didn't want to look away. He really was hot. Like... *hot*.

He was also enlisted, as the stripes and anchors on his lapels made very clear. And he was probably straight. He probably also needed to get back to work instead of sitting here with the idiot lieutenant who was just horny because he'd been interrupted before he'd had a chance to get his rocks off.

I cleared my throat. "Thanks. For the lift. I really appreciate it."

"Don't mention it."

I smiled, and let myself steal another second or two of drinking in his features. Weirdly enough, he didn't seem to mind. He didn't look away either.

He started to say something, but then his radio sputtered, startling the fuck out of both of us. I didn't understand what the voice on the other end said, but Curtis scowled, pressed the button, and responded, "Copy that. On my way." He looked at me again, an apologetic grimace on his face. "I gotta go."

"Right." I reached for the door. "Thanks again."

"You're welcome, sir."

Why was it so weird to hear him call me *sir*? He didn't have to when we were out of uniform, but it...

Well, whatever. I couldn't think anymore tonight. I opened the door and went to step out, but it turned out that isn't very effective with a still-buckled seat belt. Feeling like an idiot for the fortieth time tonight, I unbuckled it, tried again, and made it out of the truck this time.

Senior Chief Curtis left, and I stared at his taillights until they'd disappeared down the road. Then I headed for my car.

I made it as far as the driver's seat and got the key into the ignition, but that was it. I leaned back in the seat like I had in that chair at Jenna's while Curtis had questioned me. Funny. I'd never really felt like he was interrogating me. If anything, he'd seemed more concerned that I was all right. Yeah, he'd wanted to find out what happened, especially since he'd thought her husband had hit me, but he hadn't made me as nervous as I'd expected a cop to. Or maybe I'd just been so relieved that Jenna and her husband had been out of the room.

I closed my eyes and exhaled through my nose. Tonight had turned out to be such a fucking disaster. All I'd wanted was to get laid, and Jenna had apparently been on the same page. Hell, desperate as I was tonight, she probably could have been wearing her wedding ring, shown me that gigantic wedding portrait on the wall, and introduced me to her husband, and it still wouldn't have registered because my little brain had been running the show.

Thinking about that, I cringed. I wasn't a pig who saw women—or men—as holes to put my dick in, but I'd been stressed and horny lately. I'd been upfront on Tinder that I wanted sex and nothing else so there would be no false expectations, and when the hot brunette had responded, I'd been sold.

Should've known she was too good to be true.

And then, because I wasn't frustrated enough—Jenna had gotten off, but I hadn't—the cop that showed up had turned out to be Curtis. Gorgeous Curtis. Maybe I should've been on Grindr tonight because apparently I was in the mood for a man. Or, at least, I was now. Christ, one look at that hot cop, and now I was seriously jonesing for a guy.

Pity that hot cop was probably straight, definitely on duty, and absolutely enlisted. He couldn't be any more off-limits if he tried.

Son of a bitch.

I'd been at the office five minutes the next morning when I got called into my commander's office. Base security worked quickly, apparently—they hadn't wasted any time getting that report to the powers that be.

Might as well get it over with, so I put my jacket and coffee cup in my office, then walked back up the hall. I knocked on my boss's door.

"It's open."

I paused to pray that this wasn't a career-ender, then stepped inside and closed the door. "You wanted to see me, sir?"

Commander Wilson eyed me over a printout of something, but his voice was mellow. "Have a seat, Lieutenant."

I did.

He put the printout on his desk and folded his hands on top of it. "You want to tell me what happened last night?"

I met an insanely hot cop and really wish I'd invited him home and—

Wait.

No, you meant the other part.

I gulped. "I, um..." There was no point in trying to play stupid or bullshit Commander Wilson. And, really, I didn't want to. He was about the most relaxed person I'd ever met in the Navy. Completely cool with letting people do their jobs, and only getting in their faces if they made it clear they'd not only fucked up, they had every intention of continuing to fuck up until someone gave them an attitude adjustment. A few people in the department had learned the hard way that Wilson's bad side was not a place you wanted to be.

So I cleared my throat and sat a little straighter. "I met a woman online, and we met up for..." The heat in my cheeks made me wince. "Anyway, I didn't realize she was married until her husband came home."

Wilson gave a slow single nod of understanding. He skimmed over the report. "There's a note on here that you had blood on your mouth."

I absently tongued the cut, which was closed now but distinct. "It... wasn't because anyone got violent. She bumped me with her elbow, and I..." I motioned toward my mouth.

"I see. Why was base security called?"

"I'm not sure, to be honest." I tried not to fidget in the chair. "The couple got into it, and wouldn't let me leave, and—"

"Hold on." His eyes widened. "They wouldn't let you leave?"

"Uh. Well." My face must've been bright red. "I don't think they'd have physically forced me to stay, but at the time, I was scared, and he was pissed, and..." I waved a hand. "I guess I kind of froze." I summed up the rest as best I could, from the part where the two young cops couldn't quite get Jenna and her husband to cool it, and when Senior Chief Curtis had shown up and gotten a handle on the situation. I left out the part where I'd shamelessly checked out the senior chief at the most inappropriate moments. Commander Wilson was openly gay, married to another officer who worked right down the hall, but he'd probably look askance at my lapse in military bearing.

When I'd finished giving him the most professional explanation of everything that had gone down, he nodded. "All right." He pushed the printout aside. "You're good. I just wanted to hear it from you so I knew what was going on."

Thank God. He dismissed me, and that was the end of it.

In fact, to my surprise, it really was the end of it. I didn't know how many people had heard about last night, but as the week continued, no one said another word about the domestic at Jenna's house. Security didn't follow up on anything. Navy legal didn't get in touch. Commander Wilson didn't mention anything. I didn't hear so much as a rumor around the watercooler.

Jenna's husband didn't knock down my office door either, though I really hadn't expected him to. After that exchange right before I'd left, the guy had seemed more devastated than angry. Like the screaming and shouting with Jenna had kept him going, but as soon as everything had quieted down, the truth had sunk in. His wife had cheated on him in his own bed. Maybe he'd suspected it for a while. Maybe he'd been blindsided. Either way, now he knew, and it was painfully obvious that the truth hurt. Somehow he'd had the presence of mind to understand that I honestly hadn't known and that I was genuinely sorry for the role I'd played.

I felt for the guy. I thought about him a lot over the next week, and wondered if he was all right. For all I knew, he'd been an utter dick to Jenna and deserved every cum stain that wasn't his on their sheets, but I didn't think so. It might've just been my guilty conscience, but my gut said no.

Whatever had happened, though, I didn't see or hear from either of them, and still, no one said a word. Which meant I needed to move on, forget it ever happened, and figure out what to do about this simmering sexual frustration.

Only problem was I couldn't get that night out of my mind. Every time I drove past base housing or saw a patrol car, my mind went straight back to that night.

Not the part where I'd had my head between Jenna's thighs, going to town on her and making her crazy right up until the sound of a key in the door had turned it all into a frenzy of panic. Not the part where I'd gone home, horny as hell and on the verge of blue balls, and couldn't even rub one out because I'd been too frustrated, not to mention irrationally sure that some angry husband would come crashing through the wall like the Kool-Aid Man.

No, I kept going right back to the ride to McCade's. To the cop who'd driven me. And with him almost constantly on my mind, I was *way* hornier than I'd been the night Jenna and I had hooked up.

I hadn't been with a guy in a while. Maybe that was it. I'd been with plenty of women recently, but guys... it had been at least three or four months since the last one, and a good six months since I'd driven up to Seattle and spent the weekend with various dicks down my throat. Maybe that was what I needed. Not another weekend of debauchery—that had been fun, but in that exhausting, once-in-a-blue-moon kind of way. Just someone to get naked and sweaty with for a night.

And with Senior Chief Curtis still firmly planted in the front of my mind, especially whenever I got myself off, apparently I needed to get naked and sweaty with a guy.

No apps, though. No websites. I wanted to meet someone. Size them up face-to-face. Get a good look at their left hand in case there was an incriminating tan line on the third finger. With any luck, we could find someplace private, get what we both came for, and walk away happily without any disgruntled partners in our wake.

There were a handful of clubs in town that were fairly gay-friendly, but only one that was really a gay club. All the rest were down in Flatstick, which was way too fucking far to drive tonight. So, not a lot of options. After work, I'd grab a shower, put on something reasonably hot, and take my ass over to the High-&-Tight.

And hopefully I wouldn't be spending tonight alone.

CHAPTER 3

WILL

WHAT THE HELL am I doing?

I looked around the club. Most of the guys here in the High-&-Tight were years younger than me. The music was geared toward their generation, not mine, though it was catchy. The beers were all right even if I hadn't heard of most of them. It wasn't a bad place by any means, but I wasn't sure if coming here was such a good idea. My best friend, Noah, had sworn by this club. Anchor Point finally had a gay bar, and according to him, it was a damn good one. So if there was a place to get laid in this town, the High-&-Tight was it.

Being close to the base, and with a name like that, it was no surprise the place was crawling with military. First termers, mostly—guys who probably hadn't been able to legally drink for more than a few months. Guys I had no business touching.

Christ. I didn't know what I expected to find here. Someone barely over half my age who was game for a hookup in the men's room, maybe. Younger guys weren't exactly my thing, but I didn't see many alternatives in this club. And the high-and-tight haircuts at least let me know who to stay away from. I didn't relish the idea of being called into Captain Rodriguez's office to explain why someone had a photo of me making out with some E-3 I hadn't recognized out of uniform.

I played with the label on my beer bottle. Ultimately, I wasn't here because the men in this crowd were what I was craving tonight. They were a distraction from what I hadn't been able to get off my mind for the last several nights. I'd given up on fooling myself into believing I could get Lieutenant Jameson out of my system if I thought about him with my hand on my cock enough times.

I took a deep pull from my beer and rolled the ice-cold liquid around in my mouth until my teeth ached.

You're an idiot. No two ways about it. Getting hung up on a straight guy? Yeah, because that had worked out so well in the past. Not that getting hung up on queer guys had worked out any better. As it was, I hadn't been laid in almost a year. Not since my ex had left with his side piece.

What the fuck is wrong with me? Why am I so depressed tonight?

It was probably because just this week, I'd agreed to help Noah's boyfriend move in with him when they finally had all the logistics sorted out. There was nothing I wouldn't do for Noah—and by extension his boyfriend—but I wasn't looking forward to helping them unload that U-Haul. It'd be like a reverse of what Noah had helped me do earlier this year, when we'd been taking boxes *out* of my house and putting them *into* a truck. His boyfriend was coming to live in Anchor Point. Mine had been getting the hell out of town with someone younger and more limber.

Fuck. Even now, the better part of a year later, something came along every so often and reminded me that

Vince was gone. I was over him, and wouldn't take him back if he were the last man on earth, but after six years together, it had taken time to get used to being Will, and not one half of Will and Vince.

So that was it. I'd been raw after agreeing to help Anthony move because apparently I was more of a wreck than I'd realized, and I'd zeroed in on an attractive man. He'd been a distraction from my ex, and from how wound up I always was when I had to respond to a domestic, so I'd run with it. I'd let myself memorize him. I'd ogled a half-naked man with just enough bedhead to make my mouth water, let myself wish I could be the one messing up his hair, wondered if he liked it pulled, or if—

Stop it. You're going to make yourself crazy.

Yeah, he'd had messy hair after getting out of bed *with a woman*. The guy was straight. End of story. That long look before he'd gotten out of my truck? My imagination. The way he'd kept watching me while I drove—which I'd noticed because the rearview had been tilted to let me steal glances at him—had also been my imagination.

He was gone, and even if he wasn't, he was out of my league, so I needed to get over my ridiculous fantasies and find a guy who actually played for my team. I could either spend the night hunched over the bar and staring into my beer, or I could pull my head out of my ass and start looking for someone to distract me for a while.

So, I turned around, leaned against the bar, and—

Froze.

You have got *to be kidding me.*

If I'd thought Brent was gorgeous in a pair of jeans and nothing else with sex-ruffled hair... Okay, I stood by that, but Christ, tonight he was really abusing the privilege of being sexy. His tight jeans clung to his ass, and something about the way the black belt sat made my skin tingle. He had on an unbuttoned black shirt, and under that a skintight white tee. And instead of his hair being disheveled from sex, or hastily finger-combed into place, it was meticulously styled now. Like a lot of officers, he didn't cut his hair as severely as enlisted guys often did, and he had enough length on top to style it and give it that "neatly messy" look.

Fuck.

And he was here. In the High-&-Tight. A gay bar.

I couldn't tell myself that maybe he'd stumbled in here. Sometimes that happened. A guy had enough drinks in him, or wasn't paying attention, and suddenly found himself in a club with conspicuously few women. You couldn't mistake the High-&-Tight for anything that wasn't a gay bar. The rainbow flags in the windows were a dead giveaway.

And, anyway, Brent was standing close to another guy, exchanging flirty grins and *almost* touching.

Yeah. He knew where he was.

Well shit. That would lighten my mood—watching the man of my fantasies hook up with another man. Fucking sweet.

Cursing to myself, I turned back toward the bar and debated ordering something stronger after I finished this beer. I was hesitant—Noah had been enough of a problem drinker to make me hyperaware of my own habits—but decided I could get away with *one goddamned night* of really drinking. Especially while Brent was right over there, probably charming his way into the pants of that other guy. Fuck.

The barstool next to me had been occupied for a while, but the cute blond wandered off around the time I was ordering my second drink. I focused on the bartender, on watching him uncap the bottle, and as I picked it up, I barely noticed when someone took the blond's place.

"I thought that was you."

I turned and nearly tumbled off my own barstool. Shit. He was *right there*. Looking at me. Waiting for me to respond, since he'd... he'd said something, hadn't he? Hell if I could remember what, so I just went with, "Oh Hey. Uh. What are you doing here?" As soon as I'd said it, I winced. God, what a dumb thing to ask. Like running into someone I knew at the commissary and asking them that, as if they might say they were buying a car or performing brain surgery.

Lieutenant Jameson didn't miss a beat, though. "I'm guessing the same as you—looking to get laid."

My new beer almost slid out of my hand. "Oh. Uh."

He chuckled and shifted a little, and when he settled again, he was a fraction of an inch closer to me. When I'd met him the other night, he'd obviously been subdued by his own nervousness. Now, the side of him that was probably the real Brent—fueled by the drink in his hand—was out in full force.

I gulped. "I... thought you were straight."

He smiled. No, grinned. No, something somewhere in between. "I'm bi."

"Yeah, so I'm gathering."

"Bi, and perpetuating the stereotype that we're all complete and utter sluts." He winked.

Holy fuck, this beer wasn't nearly cold enough.

He held my gaze. "I never caught your first name."

I took a deep pull to wet my mouth. "Will."

"Brent." He extended his hand.

"Yeah. I remember." But I shook his hand anyway because I couldn't resist. And I let him hold it a second longer than necessary because... fuck, why wouldn't I? As I withdrew it, though, reality washed over me, killing the moment like someone had dumped a buck of ice-cold bilge water on my head.

Lieutenant. He's a lieutenant. Off-limits, idiot.

That wasn't to say I hadn't fucked plenty of men back when DADT had made them *all* off-limits, but banging an officer took a special kind of stupid. The UCMJ did not, unfortunately, make an exception for the "Can't you see how fucking hot he is?" defense.

Brent had to have known that as well as I did, and he seemed sober enough to have his bearings, but he didn't back down. "So can I buy you a drink?"

I hesitated. "I've..." I held up my mostly full bottle. "This will probably do me for the night."

"Fair enough." He paused. "So *are* you here for the same reason I am?"

I nearly choked.

You are the reason I'm here.

Somehow I managed to look him in the eye. "Can't imagine why anyone else comes to this place." Damn it. Not the right answer. "I—"

Brent's hand slid over my leg, and I jumped like he'd shocked me. He grinned, and God, he definitely wasn't that shaken-up guy I'd driven back to his car the other night. I could see how he'd charmed his way into the woman's bed, that was for damn sure.

"I'm, uh..." Since when did I get this tongue-tied around men? "I'm going to go hit the head."

"Sure. I'll be here." He didn't wink, but something told me he almost did.

I left my beer on the bar and shouldered my way through the crowd to the hallway that led to the men's room. As soon as I was around the corner and out of the crowd, I paused to gather my thoughts and catch my breath. So much for coming to this club to get him out of my head. Now he was here, and bi, and flirting with me, and...

An officer. Absolutely not someone I need to put my hands on.

I leaned against the wall and let my head fall back. *Fuck.* First man to defibrillate my libido since Vince left, and he was bad news. Career-damaging, promotion-killing, court-fucking-martial bad news. Career-*ending*, if I was brutally honest with myself. I hadn't busted my tail for almost twenty years just to literally fuck it away.

Except after so long without having sex—hell, without *wanting* to have sex—I liked this attraction. I *liked* being drawn to someone and wanting to know what his skin might taste like and what he sounded like when he came. Maybe there was some cold comfort in knowing I still had the ability to be attracted to someone, but right now I was frustrated as fuck that someone had this magnetic pull on me and we couldn't act on it.

After a cheating boyfriend and being depressed to the point of sexual numbness for this long, couldn't a guy catch a fucking break?

A set of footsteps broke rank from the noise inside the club, heading my direction, and I knew before I looked that it was him. It wasn't rational to assume that, but it didn't matter. I *knew* it was him.

And I was right. Oh shit.

Brent stopped beside me, arms folded loosely across his chest, and pressed a shoulder against the wall. "I'm almost getting the feeling you're trying to get away from me."

"I probably should be." I tried to ignore the way that posture made his hips look narrower and his shoulders broader, but I was already looking, so apparently I was failing. I stared up at the ceiling. "I know I should be. But..."

He came a little closer, almost enough to let me use his body for support instead of the cold plaster. "You should be, but do you want to?"

Absolutely not.

I dropped my gaze, which was a mistake. Now I was looking straight down into the narrow sliver of space he'd left between our chests. And our belts, for that matter. As if I wasn't already struggling not to get hard just by being in the same room with him.

I cleared my throat. "If I'm avoiding you, it's not because I want to."

That brought the most deliciously satisfied grin to his lips. Like he had me right where he wanted me now. Maybe he did.

And damn him, but he narrowed that space between us by a fraction of an inch, which made the air in the hallway a hundred times harder to breathe. Against my better judgment, I turned so I was facing him. He was shorter than me —not by much—and lifted his chin a bit as if to make up the difference.

His expression shifted, and while the lust was present and accounted for in his eyes, there was something else too. "Listen." He glanced over his shoulder. "I'm not gonna lie. I came here tonight because I can't stop thinking about you."

I stared at him, disbelieving that my own words had come out of his mouth. "But... you're an officer."

"And you're enlisted. I know." He looked down at himself, then at me. "I don't see any uniforms. Do you?"

"Doesn't matter."

"No." Brent stepped closer, eyes locked on mine, and

that something else gleamed hotter now. "But it's just us. No one has to know."

I bit my lip.

"Please," he whispered, and the faint raggedness of his tone made my knees wobble. His brow pinched slightly, and his expression shifted from cocky to... not. Oh God. It was need. Pure, primal, irresistible *need*.

My cock was definitely on board.

Brent swept his tongue across his lips, and when he spoke again, his voice shook with desperation. "The only thing I know right now is that I'm never going to concentrate on anything again if we don't—"

I kissed him, both to taste all that desperation and because, damn it, I couldn't wait.

And I didn't think I'd even startled him. The second our lips met, his arms were around me. A hand slid up into my hair, the other down over my ass, and he tilted his head as he probed at my lips with his tongue.

In some weird way, I'd almost hoped he was a terrible kisser. At least then I could bow out and move on because there was no point in staying. If a guy couldn't kiss, then I wasn't interested.

Dear sweet Mother of *God*, this man could kiss. He was forceful without overdoing it and knew how to tease my tongue with the tip of his until my knees turned to liquid and my cock was painfully hard. He wasn't all tongue, either—his lips moved with mine so perfectly, so skillfully, I couldn't help wondering what other talents they had.

The best part? He kissed with his hands too. He stroked my hair. Teased his fingertips along the shaved sides of my head. Curved a hand around the back of my neck. Let it slide down my chest. They were never still, at least not for long, and left goose bumps in their wake.

Abruptly, Brent pried himself off me and met my gaze. We were both breathing hard, and I thought he was shaking. God knew I was.

"Let's get out of here," he panted.

"No."

Brent pulled back, eyes wide with confusion. "What?"

I nodded down the hall toward the men's room.

He glanced that way, then looked at me again, and a grin slowly formed. "You didn't seem like a blowjob-in-the-restroom kind of guy."

"Who said anything about a blowjob?" I wrapped an arm around him and half growled, half moaned in his ear, "I want to fuck."

Brent exhaled as he wavered on his feet. "Jesus..."

"Is that a no?"

"It is absolutely *not* a no."

CHAPTER 4

BRENT

WILL DIDN'T JUST STEER me into a bathroom stall—he shoved me in. Roughly. Like he was manhandling someone in cuffs.

As if I wasn't already on the verge of coming in my pants.

The stall door banged shut behind us, and Will stopped long enough to turn the latch. Then he was on me again. Kissing me. Forcing me up against the brick wall. Hell *yes*.

He'd been so hesitant at first, I'd had to talk myself into following him into the hallway. I didn't want to play games, so I'd decided to take the direct approach, and if that failed, I'd... well, whatever. It was a moot point now.

And so was his hesitation. Now that we'd crossed the line and were well on our way to racking up all kinds of charges if anyone caught us, he didn't hold back anymore. He was aggressive and hungry, kissing me and groping me like he didn't care who caught us. Well if he didn't, then I didn't either, so I gave as good as I got, curling my fingers around handfuls of his shirt and grinding my crotch against his.

Will grabbed my hair, pulled my head back, and started on my neck. I let out a string of curses and didn't care who heard. His stubble burned my skin, which made the softness of his lips drive me even wilder. Being pinned to a brick wall by a rough, horny man whose lips and hot breath were on my throat? Oh, fuck yeah.

Somehow, I managed to say, "Get the feeling you're a top?"

"Can be." He kneaded my ass and nipped my earlobe hard enough to hurt. "Depends on which way makes you moan the loudest."

"Oh God." I shuddered, gripping his shirt and squirming between him and the wall. "You got condoms?"

"Mm-hmm. Lube too."

"You really *did* come here to get laid."

Will lifted his head and met my gaze. "How else was I going to get you out of my head?" Right then, he slid a hand between us, down over my cock, and I made a strangled sound. As tightly as we were pressed together, he was rubbing himself too, and his low growl was too fucking hot for words. He kissed me again, briefly, before he said, "So you tell me—am I a top tonight? Or am I—"

"You're damn right you are."

He groaned, pressing his dick against me. I slid my hands over his ass and encouraged him to press harder. As if he needed any encouragement.

"I should probably give you some warning." He kissed my neck, and I swore I expected teeth. "When I top, I do it hard." *There's the teeth. Oh fuck.* "Can't promise you'll be sitting comfortably or walking straight tomorrow."

A whimper slipped past my lips as I tilted my head to expose as much of my neck as possible. It had been a while since I'd been with a man. It had been way too long since I'd had sex this frantic and dirty. In fact, I didn't think I ever had.

Tonight's a good goddamned time to start, though.

"Sounds... sounds exactly like how I want to be fucked tonight." I wasn't sure if the words came out in the right order, but apparently the message made it across.

Way too easily, Will turned me around and pushed me chest first against the wall. With his knee, he shoved my legs apart, and because I wasn't already coming unglued enough, he released a ragged breath against the side of my neck.

"I'm going to fuck you right here," he growled in my ear. "Then we're going to back to one of our places, and I'm going to do it again."

"Ungh. Yeah."

"Get your pants off."

That was easier said than done, but at least I hadn't worn a button fly or something today. The belt came loose, and as I worked my jeans down over my hips, apparently Will was taking care of his own clothes. The jingle of a buckle had never sounded as dirty as it did in that moment, coming from right behind me and echoing through the restroom. His zipper opening with a quick, sharp pull? *Fuck.*

Foil tore. I closed my eyes and pressed my forehead against the cold bricks. God, yeah. As horny as I'd been lately, and as much as I'd been fantasizing about him, I needed him to fuck me right now before I turned into a pile of ash.

The slick sound of him stroking lube onto his dick made me shiver.

And... panic.

"W-wait."

He froze. "What?"

"It's…" I gulped. "It's been a while. Just, uh, go easy. At first." I almost expected him to get irritated or plow into me anyway, but his grip on my hip softened.

"Glad you said something now." He kissed right below my hairline. "I don't want to hurt you."

"Thanks." It sounded dumb, but I was pinned up against a bathroom wall with a hard-on and a man about to fuck me, so I cut myself some slack for not being very articulate.

A finger teased my hole. As he pushed it in, my head spun, and I was sure my knees would drop out from under me any second. The wall didn't offer much to hold on to, but I found a little bit of purchase between the bricks, and dug my fingertips in.

For as eager as Will had been, he took his time now. With slow, smooth strokes, he stretched me gently until he met no resistance at all, and even then he didn't quit. I started rocking my hips to encourage him, fucking myself on his hand until my vision blurred. Christ, it wasn't like I hadn't taken *anything* recently—I had a couple of toys next to my bed that were thicker than his fingers—but I was still losing my mind just from this. Maybe because of the whole scene. I'd never been roughly fucked in a men's room stall by a guy I'd been fantasizing about for days, and now I was going to do exactly that, and I was so turned on that everything he did was ten times hotter than—

"I think you're ready for more," he purred.

"Uh-huh." I closed my eyes as a shiver ran up my back. "Yeah."

He slid his fingers free, and I bit my lip.

Yes, yes, yes. More. Please. I want—

Oh yeah. That.

Good God, you're thicker than I thought.

Oh yeah. Yeah. Fuuuck...

He exhaled as he eased himself in. I touched my forehead to the cool wall again, holding on to the brick edges for dear life, and moaned.

"Goddamn, you're so tight," he murmured, and pushed in again.

I didn't bother trying to talk. Something about Will—about every fucking thing he did—melted my spine. He was the perfect size, and it was like he knew exactly how much I could take at a given moment. When I started to yield to him, he picked up speed. When it was suddenly more than I could handle, he backed off before I could say anything, and gave me a moment before he continued.

And then we were fucking. Really fucking. Deep and hard, knocking me off-balance every time he thrust, and dear God, it was awesome. No wonder I hadn't been able to get him out of my mind—it was like my body had known from the start that this was a man who could plow me until I cried.

I clawed at the wall for balance. "Oh fuck..."

"You all right?" he asked.

"Uh-huh."

"Want it harder?" His fingers twitched on my hips, and I was pretty sure I really did hear a note of *please tell me you want it harder* in his voice.

I widened my stance and braced my forearms against the wall. "Hard as you can."

Will groaned. A hand slid up my back and over my shoulder, and apparently that gave him some extra leverage. His fingers dug in. He drove himself into me so hard it hurt, and I hoped the sounds I was making translated to *more*. They must have, because holy fuck, he gave me more.

"Oh God, yeah," he panted. "Can you... can you come when you're... being fucked?"

"If I couldn't before, pretty... pretty sure I can now."

The low, sexy growl told me that was exactly what he'd wanted to hear, and somehow, he managed to fuck me even harder. Or maybe I was too far gone to keep track. Whatever. He had me pinned to the wall, his dick slamming into me, and yeah, yeah, I was absolutely going to come from this.

I squeezed my eyes shut and surrendered. I didn't try to hold back my orgasm, or whatever sounds came out of my mouth, or anything—I let him unravel me and ride me through every single shockwave until even the wall and his body could barely keep me upright.

Will wrapped an arm around me and let me melt against him, and he kept thrusting, groaning in my ear as he took those last few erratic strokes before he grunted, shuddered, and came inside me.

I pressed my forehead against the wall. He pressed his against the back of my neck. We both panted for a minute, up until he started going soft. Then he pulled out and stepped back, probably to get rid of the rubber.

His clothes rustled, and his fly zipped. "I'll be right back."

"Kay."

He left the stall, and I did the best I could to pull myself together. I had never in my life had so much trouble zipping and buttoning a pair of jeans before. My belt? Fuck. Forget it. It could dangle and jingle. Wasn't like it was going anywhere.

With my pants on, I looked at the spot where we'd fucked. There was cum... basically everywhere. So, I wadded up some toilet paper and wiped it off. As I was flushing it, Will came back into the stall and latched the door again. He stood right in front of me, eyes locked on mine as he buckled my belt for me.

It was funny how he'd been kind of shy when I'd come up to him earlier, but now he was taking charge. Apparently I'd woken up the sleeping dragon.

"So were you serious?" I wrapped my arms around his waist. "About going back to one of our places and doing this again?"

Will nodded, licking his lips. "You better believe it."

"My apartment's about two blocks away."

"Closer than mine." He leaned in for a short kiss. "How thin are your walls?"

I shivered. "They're thin. But with as much as I hear my neighbors fucking, I'd say they owe me one."

Will laughed. Wow, he had a gorgeous smile. Or maybe it was because he was flushed and had a little bit of sweat along his hairline. Whatever. I wanted more of him.

I nodded toward the door. "Let's get out of here."

He grinned, and I knew I wouldn't be walking right tomorrow.

CHAPTER 5

WILL

I COLLAPSED on my back next to Brent. We were both drenched in sweat, both shaking and panting, and neither of us moved or spoke for a good long time. He didn't bother wiping his cum off his stomach yet—I wasn't sure he had the coordination at the moment.

Not that I was much better. I'd come so hard I was surprised I hadn't blacked out, and anyway, I was still trying to get my head around the fact that we were even here. That I'd fucked Lieutenant Jameson not once, but *twice*, and it had blown my damn mind.

God, but he was hot. In uniform, he probably presented as clean-cut and perfect—every inch an officer. In the neon glow of a half-lit bar, he'd been a man who needed to be pinned down and thoroughly debauched. He'd been all but begging for it, and I'd happily given it to him.

Fucking him up against the wall in the bathroom had been ridiculously hot. And here, when I'd put him on his back? The picture laid out before me had been beyond sexy —Brent, open and needy and pleading, sweat plastering the hair on his chest and glistening across his forehead as he'd shamelessly taken my cock and jerked himself off. Just the thought of him coming all over his smooth, quivering abs and his broad chest had made my balls tighten and sent me right over the edge with him.

A pleasant shiver raised goose bumps all over my body. My head was clear enough now that I could stand without winding up in a heap on the floor, so I got up to get rid of the condom and get him a washcloth. With some effort— neither of us was very steady yet—we cleaned ourselves up, and once again dropped onto his rumpled sheets.

"Fuck," he finally murmured.

I chuckled, trailing fingers along a crescent-shaped welt I'd left on his shoulder at some point. It was probably going to bruise tomorrow. In the moment, I hadn't realized how hard I'd bitten him, but I was pretty sure there was enough detail to match my dental records. And holy hell, he'd clenched around me when I'd done that, and moaned like he'd been about to lose his mind.

I traced the distinct bumps from my teeth. "You like it rough, don't you?"

"Ya think?" He draped himself partway over my chest and kissed me. "I've been laid a lot in my life, but I swear to God it's never been as dirty as it is with you."

"That a good thing?"

His delirious grin answered before he spoke. "Yeah. Yeah, it's real good. You want to fuck me like that again, say the word."

I laughed, sounding about as delirious as he looked, and smoothed his sweat-dampened hair. "Might have to give me a few minutes." Three times in one night? We'd see about that. I wasn't exactly twenty anymore.

Then again, Brent was the first man I'd touched since my breakup. I hadn't realized how long overdue I'd been for some sex until now. It was entirely possible my body was going to rally so I could make up for lost time.

Fortunately, Brent didn't seem to be in a big hurry. He was still practically boneless against me, and with as slow and steady as he was breathing, he might've been dozing. I let him. I'd missed this feeling. It had been way too long since I'd had someone cuddled up next to me while we savored the achy satisfied afterglow of an enthusiastic fuck.

I tried not to mentally compare him to Vince—mostly because I didn't want to think about my ex at all—but admittedly, the contrasts made me grin. Vince hadn't been bad in bed, but he'd been kind of... boring. Even from the start. He'd always been affectionate, which I'd loved, but never terribly adventurous. Hair-pulling, bruising, border-line-violent sex had not been part of that man's repertoire. I'd tolerated being somewhat bored in the bedroom because I'd loved Vince. And we certainly had had plenty of sex.

It just hadn't ever been the kind of sex that'd landed us in a sweaty, tangled heap of trembling muscles and bite marks.

And, I realized with a sinking feeling, it hadn't ever been the kind of sex that could get one or both of us court-martialed.

The forbidden aspect had been a thrill—I couldn't deny it—but like most of the dumb things I'd done in my career, it wasn't something I could justify doing twice. Not that I'd done a lot of dumb things, especially not since my first enlistment, but I was as human as the next Sailor.

I'd slept with a shipmate onboard a carrier while we were underway during DADT. *Once.*

I'd drunk myself stupid during a port call, passed out in an alley, and barely dragged my hungover ass back to the ship before I'd been reported UA. *Once.*

I'd spent an entire night having a threesome with two insanely hot Marines, had less than an hour of sleep, and staggered in the next morning to take the advancement exam. *Once.*

And I'd had sex with an officer in a public restroom a block away from a tiny base in a small town where everybody knew each other. *Once.* Technically twice, and once was in his bed, but whatever. The whole night was one of those things that absolutely couldn't happen again.

As much as it killed me, I gently freed myself from Brent's lazy embrace and sat up. "I should probably go." I brushed a bead of sweat from my temple. "If I stay, we'll end up falling asleep." *After we fuck again.*

Brent sighed but nodded. He ran a hand through his damp hair, which made it all spiky and— *Goddamn it, why can't I stay for* one *more round?*

Because of our careers. End of story.

It wasn't easy, but it was the way it had to be.

I wanted to kiss him one last time, but I knew damn well if I did, I'd never leave. Not before daylight, anyhow.

"I really wish you could stay," he said.

"Me too. But..."

Our eyes locked, and neither of us finished the thought. There was no point. Instead, we got up and started to pull ourselves together. I got dressed, and he put on his jeans. Of course that didn't do much to minimize the temptation—he looked almost as good shirtless as he did naked. Especially with the bite mark on his collarbone.

I tore my gaze away before I changed my mind and dragged him back to bed. I doubted it would take much dragging, either. Brent was the most enthusiastic lay I'd had since long before Vince. I would've loved to find out everything he was into. As aggressive as he was when he kissed, he probably gave one hell of a blowjob. And dear God, if he ever topped me—

Fuck. I made as subtle a gesture as I could of adjusting myself.

"Still thinking dirty thoughts, eh?" Brent's teasing tone didn't help at all.

I shot him a glare, but the grin on his lips made my pulse speed up again. Despite my better judgment, I hooked a finger in his belt loop and pulled him closer. "With as much of tonight as I've spent balls-deep in you? You better believe it."

He bit his lip and shivered. Crap. This was a mistake. I should've kept us an arm's-length apart. At *least* an arm's-length apart. I hadn't, though, and I wasn't doing such a hot job at fixing the situation either.

Brent inched closer. Enough that his body heat radiated through my shirt, but we didn't actually touch aside from the finger I still had firmly hooked in his belt loop.

"You know," he said. "The longer we stand here, the less convinced I am that you're actually leaving."

You and me both.

"I should leave, though."

"Mm-hmm." He lifted his chin to narrow the space between our mouths. "You should. But are you?"

"I'm..."

We hovered in that space between kissing and not, like we were each daring the other to cross the line.

"If this is the only night we can do this," he murmured, almost brushing my lips, "don't you think we should make it count?"

"Doesn't it already count?" God, why couldn't I get my hands off him? Or keep my mouth away from his?

"Yeah." He shrugged, and when he grinned, we were so

close I could almost feel his lips move. "But if we get caught, we'll get in as much trouble for fucking three times as we will for doing it twice."

Damn. He made a good point.

I slid my hand up his back, drawing his body in closer until those low-slung jeans grazed mine. "You're not going to be able to move tomorrow."

"I'm counting on it." He pressed against me, and yes, he was definitely getting hard again. "I'm also curious if you're as good with your mouth as you are with your dick."

A groan escaped the back of my throat. "Fuck..."

Brent laughed softly—wickedly—and kissed me.

So much for leaving.

CHAPTER 6

BRENT

WILL TOOK off around two in the morning. I slept until almost noon before I managed to roll out of bed, stumble into the bathroom, and let a hot shower ease the full-body ache. Fortunately it was Saturday and I didn't have to work. Spending all day in that too-hard chair in my office would've been... unpleasant.

By tomorrow, I'd be fine. I wasn't that bad today—just tender in a few places.

I'd have been useless at work too, and not only because I'd have been focused on getting comfortable. The sex we'd had last night was the stuff they made pornos out of. Knowing that would be the first and last time? So not fair.

Where are the men like him who aren't *enlisted?*

Probably not in this godforsaken little town. Maybe I'd get lucky and wind up at one of the bigger bases as my next duty station. At least then there'd be more options. More elbows to rub, more friends to make in high places. More guys to hook up with, ideally *not* on the sly.

For now... Anchor Point. NAS Adams. Shit job.

I made it through the weekend on autopilot, slept like the dead on Sunday thanks to an orgasm inspired by Friday night, and woke up cursing when my alarm went off. My mind immediately went to Will. Probably because I'd been dreaming about fucking him on the flight deck of an aircraft carrier. I shook my head and rubbed my eyes—the Navy really needed to get the fuck out of my dreams. I could think of a lot better places to fuck than on a ship, for God's sake.

Couldn't think of a better guy, though. I shivered as I got out of bed.

There was one epic downside to having really hot sex—not just the morning after, but the Monday after. Waking up and going back to my real life... *Fuck.*

I'd felt amazing when I'd been in bed with him.

And now I felt like shit.

It wasn't that I regretted my hookups. Aside from accidentally diving into bed with a married woman, I didn't have any regrets where sex was concerned. The problem was that the better the sex and the hotter the night, the more it seemed to emphasize how much the rest of my life sucked.

I'd tried to stay positive and optimistic. I really had. I was paying my dues before I got to the good parts—commander, captain, and upward—and if I could get through these slow, boring years, the rest would get better.

But it was getting harder and harder to convince myself of that. In fact, I was getting dangerously close to a breaking point. *Something* had to give. I was miserable. I'd been depressed for months. Probably the last year or two if I really gave it much thought. Three times, I'd made it to Fleet and Family Services to see about an appointment with a therapist, but I'd never actually followed through. What could they do besides tell me the same shit my dad and grandfather always did?

"It's going to get better."

"Everyone's career sucks at first."

"Once you make lieutenant commander, you'll be golden."

Right. Because I'd never seen a miserable lieutenant commander. And "at first"? Counting Annapolis, I was *nine* years into this shit. I was damn near halfway to retirement eligibility.

I shook myself and headed out to the car. I was just bored. After spending my formative years being groomed for my future as a captain or—God and Congress willing— admiral, I was understandably restless as a paper-pushing lieutenant. I'd get there. I'd be fine.

Clinging to my coffee cup, I headed to the base.

Every time the gate came into view, something sank in my stomach. Today was no exception, but damn if it wasn't more noticeable than usual.

Will was probably already at work, and had been for a while. The masters-at-arms kept eye-watering hours that made my nine-to-five shifts look pretty damn nice by comparison. At least I couldn't complain about that part. Just... the rest of it.

Like I did five days a week, I parked outside the admin building. Every parking lot on base had several spots reserved up front. They were marked with painted-on letters, and I let my gaze drift from one space to the next, same as I did every morning. Command master chief. Executive officer. Commanding officer. Some departments had additional spaces for people like the security officer or whatever. The admin office had one for our Officer-in-Charge, and that spot was currently occupied by Commander Wilson's car.

I scanned over the ranks on the reserved spaces, and like I did every day, I reminded myself that I'd get one eventually too. I wasn't there yet, but I *would* be.

For now, my job title might as well have been Admin Bitch. I did the work my commander didn't have time to do. Had it been any other boss, I'd have said I did all the things he thought he was too good to do, but in this case, that wouldn't have been fair. Commander Wilson really did pull his weight, and he did plenty of paperwork that he could've pawned off on me. Busy as he was, he needed a secretary. And that was basically what I was—a secretary.

At least I had my own office.

Well, sort of.

I sat down at my desk—an old metal thing with a stack of sticky notes shoved under one foot to keep it from wobbling—and looked around my office. *Office* was being pretty generous. It was more like a glorified storage closet where someone had shoved a desk, and then decided to shove a lieutenant behind said desk. I'd personalized the place as much as I could—a few pictures, some framed certificates, the GI Joe my brother had given me as a gag gift when I'd graduated high school—but it was still a closet.

My degree from the Academy looked ridiculous wedged into the tiny sliver of badly painted wall between the crooked supply cabinet with the broken door and the drab gray shelves that were bowing under the weight of overstuffed procedural binders. Graduating from Annapolis was supposed to be a huge thing. A foot in a lot of doors that led to a lot of prestigious positions. And it was. I just hadn't realized there'd be this long interim as a peon before those doors actually opened.

I'd busted my ass to get into the Academy. Then I'd busted my ass *at* the Academy. I hadn't graduated at the top of my class, but I'd been up there. High enough to bode well for future promotions. In fact, I'd be up for lieutenant commander in the not-too-distant future, and Commander Wilson was confident I'd be a shoo-in.

At this stage of my career, I was exactly where I needed to be. Everything I'd been doing since high school—before that, if I counted all those years in Sea Cadets—had been leading up to this.

Or, rather, it was all leading up to when I became a senior officer. That was the endgame. I was still at the dues-paying stage now, and there was no way around it. With each promotion, there'd be more opportunities to advance my career and move me toward my own ship. Maybe even my own region.

All of that assuming, of course, that I played by the rules. Made the right friends. Did the right favors. Kissed the right asses.

And didn't sleep with the wrong people. I'd heard plenty of stories about officers who'd given up their careers in the name of love. Hell, Commander Wilson was good friends with the former CO of the base, and he'd told me once that the guy had made it all the way to captain, then retired so he could be with his now-husband. Like me, he'd gone to the Academy. He'd had his eye on admiral. But then he'd retired. I didn't know the full story, only that for what-ever reason he couldn't have both his career and his man, so he'd hung up his uniform and called it a day.

Not me. No way. It was tempting sometimes because

this job sucked right now, but I wasn't throwing away my job for a man or a woman. I *would* get through this phase of my career, and I *would* get to the top where I belonged. Just like my dad and my grandfather before him. I *would* get there.

Eventually.

Groaning, I let my face fall into my hands. I just hoped the next several years weren't as long as the last several. I wasn't sure how many years I could spend at a job where I had to give myself a pep talk just so I could get through the day.

On the bright side, at least I wasn't on a boat right now. I couldn't stay ashore forever—and I'd need to spend a fuck-load of time at sea if I wanted to be taken seriously—but a couple of years at Anchor Point wasn't the end of the world. Ships got claustrophobic after a while. I needed some time on shore to catch my breath and have my own space. My tiny one-bedroom apartment was cavernous compared to that damn stateroom I'd slept in for months.

Especially that queen-size bed.

Without anyone else in it.

Fuck.

My mind kept wandering back to the other night. Even if I'd been more depressed than ever the morning after and still felt like shit now, I was glad I'd done it. I'd needed it. I had never been with a man who'd thrown me around like a sack of laundry, told me *just* how hard he was going to fuck me, and followed through with gusto.

Good thing we'd gone three rounds too. Might as well get as much as we could out of the one and only night we dared to spend together. After all, he was the last man I should be sleeping with, and in the daylight, he'd probably come to his senses too. While I was kicking myself for not convincing him to stay until morning, he was probably kicking himself for being in my bed in the first place.

We hadn't exchanged numbers because there'd been no point. We hadn't made any promises to do this again because they would've been empty. We'd fucked, we'd walked away, and that was the end of it.

But, damn, I wanted *more*.

CHAPTER 7

WILL

CONCENTRATION WAS NOT HAPPENING.

There was a mountain of paperwork on my desk, and it was probably still going to be there tomorrow. In fact, it would be higher because, from the radio chatter, my patrols were staying busy today. By tomorrow morning, there'd be a whole new batch of reports for me to look over. With any luck, my brain would be back on the rails by then.

Not likely. Not unless something came along and erased that hot, insatiable lieutenant from my memory.

It had been almost a week since we'd hooked up, and I was still glued to last Friday night.

On the bright side, nineteen years of pushing past insane amounts of fatigue had taught me to do most of my job on autopilot. Just this morning I'd been able to focus enough to deal with a couple of young MAs who'd been sheepishly herded in front of me by their LPO. By the grace of God and coffee, I'd put on my Senior Chief face, read them both the riot act, and made sure they knew that if I heard their names and *insubordination* again, they'd be taking it up with the CO. By the time they'd scurried out of my office, red-faced and rattled, I was satisfied they knew I wasn't kidding.

The minute they were gone, though, my mind went right back to the other night. Again.

I'd known, of course, that sleeping with Brent wouldn't do a damned thing to get him out of my head. Though I supposed on some level I'd thought that I could fuck him, realize he didn't measure up to my fantasies, and move on.

Except it was my fantasies that hadn't measured up to him.

Leaning back in my chair, letting my police belt press into a few still-tender muscles, I indulged in a happy sigh. Sex with Brent had been a terrible idea, but I'd be lying if I said I hadn't needed it. What a way to welcome me back into the realms of the sexually active.

I kept telling myself that was the explanation right there —I was hooked on the first piece of ass who'd come along in a while—but it wasn't that. I knew I could get on an app or go to a bar and find someone to swap orgasms with.

Someone like Brent, though?

I whistled into the silence of my office, and shook my head. They didn't make guys like him very often. I'd never be able to look at him without being acutely aware that I had a solid decade on him, but it hadn't been like being with a kid. Ten years and too many ranks apart, and I'd still felt like we were on level ground. Like I'd met my perfect sexual match.

A shiver ran through me. He'd been rattled the night we'd met, so he'd been understandably subdued. At the High-&-Tight, though? And in the bedroom? He was some-thing else. He had an air of certainty around him that made my skin tingle. There was none of that second-guessing that came with inexperience. Wherever he put his hands, his mouth, or his cock, he meant to do it, and he knew what he was doing. I'd been with younger guys before who'd had a certain innocence about them. Like everything was new, and what we'd been doing had been an exploration. That could be fun in its own way, but nothing in the world turned me on like a man who knew what he wanted, knew how to ask for it, and wasn't afraid to demand it.

That was Brent to a T. Holy fuck.

Now I regretted not switching with him at least once. He'd been such an enthusiastic bottom, and if I ever had to choose, topping was absolutely my preference. But how often did I get my hands on a man who pinged as aggressive enough to top me the way I liked it?

Well, if he existed, Brent couldn't be the only one. So what if it had taken me until damn near forty to find him? There had to be more guys who could do what he did to me without also putting both our careers at risk.

I'd walked away in the wee hours of Saturday morning without looking back because I valued my career, so I needed to get *back* to valuing it. And *doing* it. That stack of paperwork on my desk wouldn't shrink itself, and the Navy frowned on burning things like that.

So, bound and determined to be a goddamned adult and do my job, I took the first folder off the stack, opened it, and got to work.

I made it through three reports. One was a minor car accident with no injuries or damage. The second, a DUI involving one of the Sailors from the supply ship moored at Pier Two. That one would be turned over to his chain of command, but we kept it on file here too in case witnesses were needed.

The third file was another domestic dispute in housing. No charges had been filed, but reading between the lines, I suspected we'd better keep an eye on that particular couple. There'd been broken glass on the kitchen floor and a dent in the living room wall. Both parties had insisted the glass had been knocked over while one of them had been gesturing carelessly, and the dent in the wall was from when the movers had misjudged the size of a bed frame they'd been maneuvering into the hallway. MA3 Harvey had noted that the husband had what looked like recently bruised knuckles, but he and his wife had both insisted it was from his job as an aircraft maintainer.

It was plainly obvious there was a problem in that house, but at this point, there was nothing we could do.

"Nothing we can do sometimes," an old chief had said back when I'd been an MA3, *"except wait until it's too late."*

He hadn't meant it as a joke. He'd been as frustrated as we all were that our hands were tied. To this day I sometimes wondered if he was still as haunted as I was by the incident he'd been commenting on. The older I got, the more I decided he had to be—no amount of time or training ever completely prepared a cop to walk into a scene like that. Especially when it was the fifth call to the same house, and you knew it really would be the last. As far as I knew, the husband was still at Leavenworth and would be until he was dead.

I shuddered and took a deep swallow of coffee to quell the nausea. The coffee was getting cold, but it kept my stomach in place. When I was reasonably sure I wouldn't get sick, I sent an email to the training department to see if we could get a refresher course on working with potential domestic violence scenes. If my people were better trained in asking the right questions and looking for the right signs, maybe we could be more effective at intervening.

After I'd sent the email, I signed off on the report and put it on top of the other two I'd finished. Something always felt kind of weird about putting a file like that into the business-as-usual stack, but such was the job.

I moved on to a much more benign report about price tag switching at the Navy Exchange.

For fuck's sake. This again?

I rolled my eyes, perused the report, signed it off, and dropped it on top of the domestic. Then there was a fistfight at the E club after a couple of Seabees had had too much to drink. Because *that* never happened.

As I was reaching into the pile to see what other excitement NAS Adams had to offer, a familiar voice came from a little ways down the hall and made my heart stop:

"Is Senior Chief Curtis around?"

You have got to be shitting me.

"I think he's in his office," MA2 Hill said. "You want me to check?"

"Sure. I've got some forms for him from admin."

I gulped, staring at my open door. Since when did admin send a lieutenant to do their bitch work?

Footsteps came down the hall. Then MA2 Hill leaned into the doorway. "Senior, there's a Lieutenant Jameson here with some paperwork from admin. Do you want me to send him in?" It wasn't a rhetorical question. If I was genuinely busy or just plain didn't want to deal with whoever was asking for me, I had no compunction about asking her to get their information so I could put it off until later.

If ever there was a time to let my MA2 run interference, it was now.

But I cleared my throat and reached for my cold coffee. "Yeah. Send him in. Thanks, MA2."

"Will do." She left my office. I listened to her footsteps. Then the exchange of words. Then another set of footsteps that were sharper and much more determined.

I held my breath.

And there he was.

"Hey." He stood in the doorway, a drab green folder under his arm. "You have a minute?"

I hesitated, but then put my coffee cup down and folded my hands on my desk. "Sure. Yeah. What do you need?"

Brent shut the door behind him so gently, I barely heard it click. In his hand, he had that file folder, but in his eyes there was something decidedly less professional.

I gulped. "You have something for me to sign?"

He chuckled. "Nope." He held up the folder and winked. "Call it a forged hall pass."

I didn't laugh. "Brent..."

Sobering, Brent swallowed as he set the folder down on my desk. "Listen, I'm not gonna lie. I can't stop thinking about..."

My stomach somersaulted. "You know we can't, though."

"Yeah. Yeah, I do." He ran a hand through his hair, and my fingers twitched at the memory of combing through it, grabbing it, pulling it...

I cleared my throat. My alternately bored-horrified-annoyed mood evaporated along with any concentration I might've mustered up for my job. "So what are you doing here?"

"Because this is killing me."

I blinked.

A set of boots and voices went by outside. My neck prickled—if I could hear them, they could hear us. So, in an effort to be a little more discreet, I got up and came around the desk. At least now we could speak more quietly.

Except... it also meant we were closer.

A lot closer.

And then Brent took a step, and...

Fuck. We were eye to eye now. When he shifted, the toe of his boot nudged mine. He didn't pull away. Neither did I.

"You know we can't do this," I said.

"I know no one can know about it." The stubbornness in his eyes did weird things to my pulse. He knew as well as I did what a risk this was, and he was determined to do it anyway? That should've reminded me that we were being fucking idiots, but instead, it was flattering. And hot. What the hell did I do for him that made this a risk worth taking?

"You do understand what's at stake here, right?"

"Yes," he said, barely whispering. "But what we did was the first thing that's felt that good in..." His eyes lost focus. Then he shook his head. "I don't remember how long."

That hit somewhere under my heavy police belt. "Yeah. I know the feeling."

"Right? And the thing is, I'm a million miles from everyone I know. I'm fucking miserable at my job." He locked eyes with me and swallowed hard. "Regs be damned —I want to feel that good again."

The raw need in his eyes did me in. Not only because I felt for him—I'd sure as fuck been there in the early days of my career—but because now that he'd put it into words, I felt the same way. I'd been treading water emotionally for way too long. Everything had been stagnant and cold since I'd caught my ex cheating. I was hardly in love with Brent, but damn if there wasn't *something* between us that I needed right now, even if it was nothing more than physical.

I reached for his waist, and he stiffened when my fingers brushed his blouse. "You're not sure about this, are you?"

"I'm..." Avoiding my gaze, he exhaled. "I am. Kind of. I mean..." He shifted his weight, then blurted out, "I don't know what this is, and I don't know *you*, but it doesn't feel like something I want to walk away from."

I blinked. Now that he'd said it, I couldn't argue. We were strangers for all intents and purposes, but there was some chemistry here that I'd never experienced with anyone. Alone in my office, I could tell myself all day long that I needed to ignore this and move on, but now that I had him here—now that I was touching him—that internal lecture was long gone.

"Yeah, I don't want to walk away from it either." I glanced down at my hand on his waist and didn't pull it back. "But there's a lot on the line. If we do this and get caught, we're both done. You know that, right? They'll dismiss you and force-retire me."

Brent nodded. "I know." He looked in my eyes again. "No one has to know but us."

"No one *can* know but us."

"I won't tell anyone if you don't."

"Good." And against my better judgment, I pulled him to me and kissed him.

Fuck, *yeah*, this was a good idea. Keep it a secret? Fine, as long as this kept coming.

I cradled the back of his head, and he opened to my kiss. He wrapped his arms around me, and damn that police belt for getting between us. I had no way of feeling if he was hard or well on his way there, but if his ragged breathing and needy kiss were any indication, his uniform was getting as snug as mine was.

He touched his forehead to mine, breathing hard against my lips. "So, I'm going to take that to mean you're in?"

"Yeah. I'm in." I stroked his face and stole another brief kiss. "I know what you mean about needing to feel good for once. After my breakup..." Fuck, I was not going there. Not now. So I reeled him back in and kissed him harder, and that soft whimper almost sent me up in flames.

I was the one to break away this time, and panted, "You busy tonight?"

"You better believe it."

I chuckled. "One thing, though."

"Hmm?"

Letting our lips brush, I murmured, "Don't expect me to call you 'sir' in bed."

Brent pulled back, and he grinned so wickedly, my pulse went haywire. "I don't know." He slid a hand up the middle of my chest. "Might be kind of hot if you do it while you're fucking me into the mattress."

"Oh... God."

The grin got impossibly more evil, and he let his fingertip drift along my collar. "So, I'll see you tonight."

I gulped. "Yes, sir."

Our eyes locked, and we both shivered. Much more of this, and I was going to take him right over my desk.

I cleared my throat and let him go. "I should get back to work."

"Yeah." He glanced at his watch. "Shit. Me too. But we're really on for tonight?" He lifted his eyebrows.

I nodded. "Definitely. I'll, um, text you when I leave."

"Might need my number first."

"Good point."

We took out our phones and quickly exchanged

numbers. He also put in his address, which was good because I doubted I could remember how to get to his place. I gave him mine too.

Then he headed for the door. For the hallway full of people who worked with me and for me. People who, so far, had no idea I'd slept with—and was going to sleep with—an officer.

Panic knotted in my gut. "Brent."

Hand on the doorknob, he turned around.

"I'm dead serious—no one can know about this."

He nodded. "I know. I've got as much to lose as you do."

We held each other's gazes for a moment, and then he was gone, leaving my door open the way it had been when he'd come in.

I sank into my chair and stared at the open doorway, absently tracing my fingers along my lower lip. God help me if there were any major calls or incidents today.

Because my brain was already where my body needed to be—in Brent's bed.

CHAPTER 8

BRENT

AS IT ALWAYS DID, my day ended at five o'clock sharp. Being an MA and a senior chief, Will's shift apparently ended whenever he'd put out whatever fires had started throughout the day.

At seven thirty, the text finally came through: *On my way*.

If I'd been restless before, I was this close to losing my mind now. I paced by the door, listening for footsteps. He was probably fifteen minutes away, depending on how thick the bottleneck was at the gate. In theory, I could use this time to get dressed—I'd showered, but hadn't bothered to put on more than a pair of jeans—but what was the point? He'd probably have me naked before we made it to the bedroom anyway.

I did try to keep my mind off him, though. It didn't really help, but being this painfully hard wasn't doing anything to make the time go by faster.

I adjusted the front of my jeans. How I'd made it through the day without wedging a chair under my "office" door and jerking off at my desk, I'd never know, but I was kind of regretting it now. Turned on as I was, it wouldn't take him more than a lick or a couple of strokes to set me off.

Then again, the sooner he got me off, the sooner I'd recover so we could start all over again. I shivered at the thought, and instead of adjusting myself this time, I gave my dick a slow knead through my jeans. Not much longer. I could wait. Hell, maybe I should strip off my jeans while I was at it so he could get right to getting me off. Maybe—

The door at the end of the hall opened, and I froze.

Is that him?

There were footsteps in the hall. Approaching fast. Boots. Were those *boots*?

My apartment had an interior entrance, so at least that gave us a little bit of cover. Someone might see him coming into the hallway, but they wouldn't necessarily see that he was on his way into my apartment. There were civilians and enlisted guys on my floor, so his destination would be anyone's guess. We were good as long as we didn't linger in the hallway, and I doubted that would be an issue.

It wasn't.

Within seconds of him knocking, he was in my apartment with the door shut behind us, and... ahh. Finally.

"Do you have any idea," he murmured between kisses, "how hard it's been to concentrate since you came into my office?"

"Mmm, I think I can guess." I teased the corner of his mouth with my tongue. "I didn't get a damn thing done after I left."

"Neither did I." Using my hair, he pulled my head back and started kissing my neck. "Oh God, I want you."

I couldn't speak. I was too busy breaking out in goose bumps and trying to stay on my feet as his five-o'clock shadow burned all the places his soft lips had brushed.

He'd ditched his uniform in favor of jeans and a T-shirt, though he still had on boots. Changing clothes had probably cost him five minutes or so that he could've been here and kissing my neck like this, but it was prudent. Showing up at my door in his uniform would be a hell of a lot more conspicuous than civvies. Irony that camouflage would make him stand out more than not.

And, dear God, what I wouldn't have given to rip that uniform off him, even if it and all its insignia were blatant reminders of why he shouldn't be here at all.

I tugged at his T-shirt. "The fact that we're not supposed to do this, and we could be in seriously deep shit if we got caught..." I licked my lips. "Is it just me, or is that kind of hot?"

Will's grin turned me inside out. Or maybe that was his hands sliding up my bare back.

"No," he whispered, brushing his lips across mine, "it's definitely not just you." Then he pushed me up against the wall and went to his knees. It took him a few seconds of fumbling to undo my jeans, but his fingers touching me through denim sent heat rushing through my whole body, curled my toes into the carpet, made my breath catch like I was already fucking his hot, talented mouth.

And then I was. He groaned as the head of my cock slipped past his lips. When I started rocking my hips, he encouraged me with his hands on my ass, and I stared down at the most gorgeous man I'd ever touched swallowing me and moaning with pleasure.

He paused to lick the head and looked up at me. "I've been dying for this all day."

"M-me too. Can't stop... thinking about you fucking me."

Will shuddered, his ragged breath rushing past the wet skin of my cock, and I damn near melted to my knees too.

He stood, and as he kissed me, he started stroking me. "You know how tempting it was to just push you over my desk and do you right there?"

Oh. *God*.

"Don't know. But I think you need to take me in the bedroom and—"

"Good idea. Now."

My legs weren't quite cooperating, and my head was so fucked that I had to actually think about where my bedroom was, but I stayed upright and didn't take him into the kitchen or something stupid like that.

As soon as we were in my bedroom, I kicked off my jeans and helped him out of his clothes—not that I was very helpful when I was kissing and groping him the whole time. Somehow, though, he went from dressed to naked, and the heat of his skin against mine was mind-blowing.

I dragged him down onto my bed. He settled between my legs as his lips skated all over my neck.

"Swear to God," he breathed against my throat, "I'm gonna fuck you so hard, you won't be able to move tomorrow."

A long moan escaped my lips as I arched under him. "Yeah. Please."

He growled something and kissed my neck again.

From where I was happily pinned beneath him, I reached for the nightstand drawer, but it was too far away. Damn it.

He lifted himself up, and his gaze followed my arm. Grinning, he said, "Need something out of there?"

"You think?"

Will chuckled. He leaned down and flicked his tongue

across the inside of my elbow. That should *not* have been hot. It had no right to be. How the— Oh fuck, it was.

I shivered under him. "Condoms. C'mon."

He gave that spot another lick, grinned when I moaned, and then reached for the drawer.

Just like when he was getting undressed, I was probably more hindrance than help. He didn't seem to mind, though —as he fumbled with putting on the condom, he didn't object at all to my kisses, or my hands all over him, or me teasing his balls. His breathing was more rapid now, and I swore his skin was getting hotter, but he made no move to stop me.

Not until—

"Turn over," he ordered, and lifted himself up to give me room. "Now."

My bones had turned to something a lot less sturdy, but somehow, I managed to get onto my elbows, then my side, and—

And Will shoved me the rest of the way onto my stomach. I landed with a grunt. His knee roughly pushed my thighs apart. I grabbed the sheets. Oh yeah. Yeah, this was what I'd been fantasizing about.

C'mon, c'mon, more...

His weight wasn't on me, but it was over me. I could feel him—the warmth of his skin, the sheer presence of him— and it was hot and addictive and not nearly enough. Not even when he slid his thick lubricated cock between my ass cheeks.

I spread my legs farther, willing myself to be patient as he eased himself in. He teased a little until I was taking the head without resistance, and then he slowly slid his entire length inside me. Holy fuck. No wonder I couldn't leave well enough alone. As if everything he did wasn't already mind-blowing, his cock was the perfect fit for me. Big enough to feel it, without being so big that he had to be extra careful not to bruise something vital. He was thick enough to take my breath away without feeling like he might split me in half. He could thrust all the way in, slam that thing home, and it would hurt, but not *hurt*. Exactly the way I liked it.

Then, once I was taking him easily, he used his weight to encourage me down onto my stomach. My favorite position. I loved this. Loved nothing more than a man stretched out over me, as much skin touching skin as possible, while he fucked me.

He found a slow, smooth pace, not pulling out more than an inch or two before pushing back in, and I closed my eyes and enjoyed the ride. And the way he kissed my neck and shoulder? How his strokes made my dick rub against the mattress? The hot huffs of breath across my skin? There was apparently some reason we shouldn't have been doing this, but hell if I could put my finger on it right then.

"God, yeah," I breathed. "M-more."

A soft growl vibrated against the back of my neck, and then he thrust hard, knocking the breath out of me. "Like that?"

"Uh-huh."

Another deep thrust. I braced for more, but he stopped. All the way inside me, hips planted firmly against my ass, he whispered, "Beg for it."

"Will..." I tried to rock my hips, but couldn't go anywhere. "Ungh..."

His lips and breath brushed my ear. "Beg for it, *sir*."

A strangled moan slipped past my lips. When I'd joked about that earlier, it had sounded kinda hot, but now that he actually did it—now that he'd called me *sir* in bed while he was making me beg for his dick—my brain went haywire.

"C'mon, sir," he purred, letting his stubbled chin graze my neck. "You want it or not?"

I managed to untie my tongue enough to speak, but before I could, he withdrew a little and thrust in again. Everything blurred. Holy hell, I was going to come if one of us so much as *breathed* the wrong way. Right way? Whatever. I let go of another choked sound—something between a whimper and what might've been a curse if I'd still been able to form words—and clawed at the sheets.

He laughed and pressed a long kiss to my neck. "Tell me you want it or I'll stop." As if to prove his point, he started slowly pulling out.

"No, don't stop!" The words tumbled off my tongue. "Please don't stop."

He eased back inside. "Then tell me what you want." He flicked his tongue against my earlobe. "If you want it, *sir*, you're going to have to beg for it."

"Can't... talk."

Another laugh, one I felt more than heard. "Can't talk?" He moved his hips just enough to draw my attention to the thick cock buried in my ass. "Why not?"

"Feels... too good."

"Oh, that's what I like to hear." The husky voice gave me goose bumps. His hips started rocking a little more, keeping all those nerve endings stimulated and me frustrated. "But I really want to hear you—"

"Please," I whined. "Fuck me."

"How do you want me to fuck you?"

I squeezed my eyes shut. "Hard. Please, fuck me *hard*."

He took his sweet time pulling out, and panic shot through me.

"Don't pull out," I pleaded. "C'mon, please, I want—"

He forced himself back in, sending a shockwave of pure bliss right through me, and before I could reclaim the breath I'd lost, he did it again. And again. And again.

Every thrust knocked another single word out of me. "Please. Yeah. More. *Fuck*."

"Oh God," he breathed. "You like that?"

"Fuck yeah."

"You like it, *sir*?"

The sound that escaped my throat was barely human, but he must've understood the emphatic yes it had tried to be, because he kept right on fucking me while I gripped the bed for dear life.

"Look at yourself," he purred, pulling my head back. "In the mirror."

I forced my eyes open. I'd all but forgotten the closet doors in here were mirrored, but damn, there we were. And, holy shit, he was beyond sexy like this.

He was so collected and professional in uniform. Hell, his soothing demeanor had calmed *me* down when I'd thought Jenna's husband might try to smash in my skull. Like this, though? When lust took over and he was riding my ass? He turned into a wild animal. One whose single-minded goal was to fuck, deep and hard, until he came. Until we *both* did.

I could seriously get hooked on that.

Fuck, who was I kidding? I *was* seriously hooked on it.

"Oh God," I moaned. "I'm gonna come."

"Yeah, you are." Eyes locked on mine in the mirror, he kissed the side of my neck, and my vision blurred. I shuddered. Whimpered. Tried to breathe if only because I didn't want to pass out. And—

Came.

Hard.

My eyes rolled back, my body tensed and released at the same time, and Will groaned in my ear as he pounded me until he shuddered too. That groan became a strangled "*Fuck*" before a hot huff of breath rushed past my neck, and he relaxed.

When the dust finally settled, we were sprawled next to each other. I didn't know when he'd gotten rid of the condom, or when I'd wiped the cum off myself and the bed, but somehow, here we were.

My whole body throbbed, and the epicenter of that throbbing was my ass. I would feel this tomorrow. Absolutely. Just like I had the first time.

Will panted beside me, sweat dripping down his face. His chest hair was plastered to his flushed skin, and his lips were a little swollen. With the way we'd been kissing earlier, mine probably were too. And, dear God, he was gorgeous.

"I'm pretty sure they don't know who I am," he slurred after a while, "but it's a safe bet your neighbors know someone's doing you."

I laughed. "Yeah. I'd say so."

We turned to each other and laughed. He found my hand between us, and once we'd made that connection, I needed more, so I slid closer to him.

As I draped my arm over him, he kissed my temple. "For the record, I don't only top. You ever want to switch, say the word."

I wriggled against his hot skin. I loved being on top, but bottoming for Will was addictive. "Maybe eventually. If *you* want to switch, say so." With a wink, I added, "So you don't think I'm hogging all the good stuff."

He laughed. "The good stuff? Oh, I'm getting plenty of

that." His fingertips drifted up my thigh. "I am more than happy to fuck you into next week anytime you want."

Any witty response I might've had disintegrated into a little moan.

"And if you give me a few more minutes," he murmured, "I am definitely planning to fuck you like that again tonight."

All I could manage was, "Yeah."

This was going to be one *long* night. And tomorrow was going to suck.

I grinned.

Bring it on.

CHAPTER 9

WILL

DURING SLOW DAYS, it wasn't unusual at all for me to kill time with Noah. He was a chief whose office wasn't far from mine, and we both probably spent as much time in each other's offices as our own. It was frequently work related since we worked in the same department and I was his supervisor, but there was a lot of shooting the shit too. Rank had its privileges sometimes.

Today, we were in my office, lounging after he'd dropped off some vehicle reports and an update on the harbor patrol boats that were still malfunctioning despite the "best" efforts of Port Ops. Fucking idiots. We sipped our coffee and caught up, pausing whenever the radio on my desk crackled to life in case it was something we needed to address. Not that there was much going on. The only radio chatter so far had been routine check-ins from watch commanders and one FYI about a fender bender in the Navy Exchange parking lot, but that could all change in a heartbeat. Only took a second for a major wreck, a gate runner, or a domestic to have us on our feet and out the door.

So far, so slow.

As we talked, I took a moment and just looked at my friend. Some days, I still couldn't believe it, but he was a different man than he'd been in all the years I'd known him. He'd finally stopped drinking earlier in the year, and he was so palpably in love with Anthony that even the guys around the precinct had noticed. That man had saved Noah's life too. I'd tried for years to get Noah to control his drinking, and even issued him an ultimatum after I'd busted him post-bender one too many times.

It was really Anthony who'd driven it home, though. When Noah had realized his career had been on the line *and* the man he loved had been gone, he'd pulled himself together faster than I'd imagined possible. There'd been bumps and setbacks, but I was pretty sure he hadn't touched a drop of booze in months. A few weeks ago, when a nasty cold had dropped him on his ass for almost a week, he'd refused to take any of the good stuff for it because of the alcohol. That was when I'd known for sure he was in this for the long haul. When he'd rather suffer through days on end of not being able to breathe than risk a single shot of Nyquil, he was serious about staying clean.

Now, his eyes were clear and he seemed healthier— especially since he'd been using the gym as an outlet—not to mention happier. Being sober and in love was a damn good look on him.

"So how goes the move?" I asked.

"Slow, but it's coming along. Anthony's got a couple of job interviews this week, so hopefully something will pan out."

"Really? He found some nibbles in this town?"

Noah shook his head. "Portland, mostly, but they all allow telecommuting. The one he's really hoping for requires him to be there one week out of the month, but they'll pay some of his moving expenses to Oregon so he doesn't have to fly back and forth from Denver. The salary is more than he's making now too."

"Wow. Sounds like a sweet deal."

"Very." Noah held up his hand, his fingers crossed. "They really like him, so we'll see how it goes."

"Tell him I said good luck."

"Will do." Noah sipped his coffee. Then he kicked back in his chair and rested his boot against the edge of my desk. "Somebody got laid this weekend."

I nearly choked on my own breath, which he'd probably hoped for. "I don't know what you're talking about."

He rolled his eyes. "Bullshit."

"What makes you think I got laid?" I looked down at my blue camouflage blouse and tugged at my lapel. "I have a cum stain or something?"

Noah snorted. "Please. Like you'd ever let someone come on your uniform."

I lowered my hands. "Well, it must be something."

"I don't know." He shrugged. "You just seem different. I was starting to think you'd lost interest in the entire male species after that dick-wad left, but you look... different this morning than you have in a while."

"Maybe I've been getting more sleep or—"

"Stop it, Will. You're not fooling me."

I grinned to hide the nervous pounding of my pulse. "Okay. Maybe I am getting laid. Doesn't mean I'm divulging the details, though."

His eyebrows arched impossibly high. "You're doing someone you shouldn't be, aren't you?"

Oh, you could say that.

He stared at me, and he was about to say something, but then our radios came on, making both of us jump.

"Charlie one, this is Alpha eight."

Noah scowled, then pushed the button on his radio. "This is Charlie one. Go ahead."

"Yeah, we need some assistance down on Pier Three. Dispute with shipboard security."

Of course. The never-ending dick-waving contest between landside and shipboard MAs.

"Copy. On my way." Noah released the button and scowled at me. "Well, damn." As he stood, he wagged a finger at me. "This isn't over. I'm going to figure out what—or who—you're doing." It was playful, but there was a note of concern too. Like he was genuinely worried I'd gone off the deep end.

Maybe he was right.

I had a meeting with Commander Wilson this morning to go over some changes to our admin procedures, so at around eleven, I strolled over to his building. On the way, I tried to ignore the fact that this was the department where Brent worked. No one would see us and magically put the pieces together, but we couldn't be too careful.

I didn't see him, fortunately, and made it to Commander Wilson's door. I knocked, and when he let me in, I said without thinking, "Good morning, sir."

Sir.

Oh God.

I suppressed a shiver. When had *that* word become electrically charged?

Around the time I started using it as dirty talk in the bedroom, that's when. With my officer fuck buddy. Crap.

Wilson apparently didn't notice. "Good morning, Senior Chief." He gestured at a chair, and I took a seat.

Our meeting wasn't terribly exciting—they never were—but I couldn't shake that squirmy feeling that had shown up after I called him sir.

Throughout the meeting, I slipped in a few casual *sir*s to desensitize myself again. By the time Wilson dismissed me, I managed a professional "Thank you, sir" without any kind of embarrassing response. Maybe I could get used to "sir" again after all. Maybe.

I stepped out of the office to head back to the precinct, and—

There he was.

In blue camouflage, focused on something another officer was telling him, the man I'd spent last night riding like he was the last man I'd ever fuck.

He looked so official and put-together. His uniform was as squared away as I'd expected—he'd struck me as someone who, despite breaking all those regulations last night, was as by the book as I was.

I shivered and kept walking before he noticed me. Seeing him like this made the sex we'd had a hundred times hotter. It was no longer the high school equivalent of cutting class with one of the football players to make out under the bleachers (something I'd done more times than I could count during my teenage years). More like sneaking off with the class president and fucking over the principal's desk—wilder, hotter, and a lot more dangerous.

I grinned to myself and stole a glance over my shoulder before I turned the corner. It was stupid to get this turned on by doing something that reckless. But, hell, maybe after this many years of being a good little Sailor, I needed some rebellion. As long as no one found out, then what was the harm?

Idiot.

All the way back to my office, I couldn't get the image out of my head of Brent in his uniform. Our base hadn't switched over to the green camouflage yet, though several Sailors who'd recently transferred in were already wearing them, so he and I were both still in blue. Not that it mattered if we were wearing green or blue at this point. Ever since the Navy had switched to camouflage utilities across the board, the distinction between officers and enlisted had blurred a little. From a distance, we were indistinguishable from each other. Just generic blue-clad members of the same rank and file. Up close, when insignia were easier to see, it became more obvious. The gold anchors on my lapel signified my rank as a senior chief. The pair of silver bars on his made it known he was a lieutenant. Two tiny pieces of insignia that very firmly established our places on the food chain.

It had always irritated me on some level that an officer like Brent was technically senior to me. I probably had a decade more in the Navy than he did. He was an O-3. I was an E-8. If he'd been an *E*-3, I'd have outranked the everloving fuck out of him. But that *O* not only meant he got paid probably twice what I did, it meant that *I*—with more years, more promotions, and more time at sea—would have to salute to and obey *him*.

I had to admit my chronic annoyance with the officer-enlisted bullshit was significantly placated in this case. Yeah, if we ran into each other outdoors with our covers on, I'd have to salute him and call him *sir*. Yeah, if it came down to it, he could give me orders I'd have to obey.

But that was much easier to swallow when I knew and he knew that he'd been bent over a mattress last night, naked and hard and begging for my dick.

Who's in charge now?

I grinned to myself and suppressed a shiver. A little voice in the back of my head was trying to pipe up and remind me why I needed to stop doing this, but I ignored it.

A few more hours, sir, and then you're all mine...

CHAPTER 10

BRENT

ANOTHER DAY. Another meeting. I'd grown up going to Navy events and listening to the brass drone on about... stuff. I'd learned to tune most of it out by the time I'd been in kindergarten. These days, I actually had to *listen* to it. Today, the three captains—base, carrier, and supply ship—had spent a full hour arguing about whether to move the carrier to Pier Two or leave it at Pier One. Then after that, another thirty minutes hashing out if the move should happen now, or if it would make more sense to wait until the ships went to sea, and switch them when they came back. *So. Boring.*

Plus the supply ship captain's nose whistled when he breathed.

Funny how the instructors at Annapolis never bothered to mention this part of the job. They probably thought us poor cadets had been hazed enough.

Eventually, we were dismissed. I was surprised when I checked my phone and realized the meeting had only gone on for two and a half hours. I legitimately thought I'd been in there long enough for an empire to rise and fall.

Commander Wilson and I walked back together, shooting the shit on the way, and after he'd gone into his office, I continued toward mine. There, I dropped into my chair and stared up at my Annapolis diploma. Not because I thought I'd find some inspiration or motivation in it, but because it was there. In my line of sight. Something to look at besides the gray wall or the paperwork I was supposed to be doing.

Coffee. I needed coffee.

So I abandoned the paperwork and went in search of coffee. When I'd found that, I came back and forced myself to start slogging through the forms and reports and whatever else had been thrown my way.

At exactly twelve o'clock, I wasted no time getting the hell out of the office. For a long time, I'd brought my lunch to save money and be healthier. Then I'd figured out that if I brought lunch, I'd eat it in the break room or at my desk, and it didn't feel like a break at all.

So, more often than not, I hit up the officers' club or the food court over by the Exchange. Today, the latter. I'd have to go for a run this afternoon to make up for it, but that was okay. Good way to kill time before Will came over.

Will. I shivered, hoping no one else in the Subway line noticed. And then, of course, a couple of MAs picked that exact moment to walk by. Everyone on base wore the same digicam uniform, but the MAs were easy to spot. The bulky police belts, black bulletproof vests, and sidearms strapped to their thighs were a dead giveaway.

Normally I'd ogle the hell out of them because why the hell not. Today, I made sure to look anywhere but right at them. I didn't want anyone catching on that I found anything attractive in an MA. After all, that might make them think I found something attractive in one MA in particular.

That was ridiculous. My paranoia was beyond stupid. No one had any reason to suspect Will had ever given me so much as the time of day, never mind some of the most powerful orgasms of my life.

This was a tiny town and even tinier base, but there were still several thousand people here. I didn't know what Lieutenant Commander Bodner did once he left the office. I had no idea what Commander Wilson and his husband got up to after dark. Ensign Green could be teaching French at the community college and doing magic acts at kids' birthday parties on the weekends for all I knew. Once the day was over, that was it.

Which meant none of them had any reason to believe I was burning up the sheets with Senior Chief Curtis.

And somehow... that made everything we were doing a lot hotter.

So much for suppressing that shiver. I was probably blushing too. Whatever. The thought of what I was getting away with—wild sex with a man I wasn't supposed to touch—was way more of a turn-on than it should have been. I took my career seriously. I didn't take regulations lightly.

But this one act of rebellion? This one thing no one had to know about but us?

Is it time to go to his place yet?

Finally, it was five o'clock.

And finally *again*, around seven thirty, Will's shift was over.

But when I walked into his apartment, something in his expression made my gut clench.

"What's wrong?" I asked as he shut the door.

"I..." He sighed. "I was thinking today. About what we're doing. And, my God, it's hot, but..."

"But it's a risk."

Will nodded. "Yeah. It is."

"We knew that going into it."

"Right, and it hasn't changed. One minute, I'm turned on just thinking about it. The next, I start *really* thinking about it, and..." He met my gaze. "Are you sure you're still on board with this?"

"Are you?"

His expression didn't change. "I asked you first."

I gnawed the inside of my lip. I'd been climbing the walls all afternoon, waiting for us to finally be behind closed doors so we could fuck. It'd been all I could think about.

Now that he'd put that thought out there...

It was still all I could think about.

I stepped closer and put my hands on his waist. He didn't back away, thank God.

"Yes, I'm still on board."

He looked in my eyes, and the *Are you sure?* in his expression must've been visible from space.

"If you don't want to do this," I said, "say so."

Will shook his head. "It's not about wanting, believe me. Just... second thoughts, I guess. Or fourth or fifth. Whatever."

"I get it. Don't worry." I sighed. "And, listen, I'm not taking it lightly. I promise I'm not. But the thing is, from the time I was ten and started Sea Cadets, my entire life has revolved around the Navy. Setting myself up for a shot at the Academy. Then graduating the Academy as close to the top of my class as I could get. Now, moving up the ranks and checking all the boxes so I can get to the top." I ran my palms down Will's sides. "This is the one thing I've done for myself in all that time. And I can't get enough."

"Even if it jeopardizes everything you've worked for?"

"It only jeopardizes my career if people know. As long as we keep our mouths shut and do this all behind closed doors…" I curved my hands over his hips. "There's no reason to worry, is there?"

Will's lips pulled tight, but he couldn't hide the way he shivered when I let my thumb brush just shy of his cock.

"I live and breathe the Navy." I stroked him through his pants. "This thing we're doing? I want it for myself."

"So you get off on bending the rules, do you?" The growl in his voice was subtle, but it was there, and it reverberated straight to my balls.

"Not usually. But everything I do with you?" I moved my hands around to his ass and squeezed the firm muscles. "It's hot, and the more we do it, the more I want." I regretted the words as soon as I'd said them. Just what I needed—Will catching the scent of desperation and thinking I was going to be clingy.

He grinned, though, so he must've understood what I'd actually meant. He backed me up a step. Then another. When my shoulders hit the wall, he pressed against me, pinning me there and sending a tremor through my entire body.

"I'm not usually one for breaking the rules." His lips grazed mine. "But I'm willing to make an exception."

"Oh yeah? Why's that?" *God, don't question it. Just go with it.*

"Why?" He kissed me harder. "Because being in bed with you is worth it. Every time."

"Fuck..."

"And now that I have you here, you know what I want to do?"

"T-tell me."

"I want to take you into my bedroom." He breathed between kisses. "I'm going to tear you out of those clothes, put you on your knees, and"—he pressed my hand against his dick—"fuck your mouth until I come. That sound good... *sir*?"

I whimpered against his lips and squeezed his cock, which made him give a throaty little groan. Somehow, I managed to murmur, "Please."

His lips curved against mine, and his tongue darted into my mouth before he claimed a deeper, more determined kiss. Fuck, but I loved what he did with his mouth. Every single time, his kiss turned my knees to water and my nerve endings to pure electricity. All I could think of was how much I wanted him.

He kept me there against the wall, pinning me with his strong, hot body. Still kissing me, he reached between us with both hands and jerked my belt open. The way he undid my fly, I was sure he'd broken the zipper or torn my jeans, but then he was on his knees with my cock deep in his throat, and I didn't care what he'd done to my pants.

He kept both hands on my hips, holding me to the wall as if he thought I might go anywhere. Yeah, right. Not with the way his mouth worked its magic on my dick. Jesus, he even managed to use his *teeth*, letting them slide carefully over the head before he covered the same area with his tongue.

This was... oh fuck. Insane.

I'd never been with a man who could make giving a blowjob seem like an act of domination. As if he were saying, *I'm* going *to suck your dick, and you're* going *to stand there and take it*, and dear God, yes, I was absolutely going to stand there and take everything he gave me.

I'd been with guys who'd taken control in ways I didn't like. Especially those who were taller, broader, and stronger than me. Will had the physique if he wanted to use it, but I'd never once felt like he would. Or, rather, he absolutely did throw me around, pin me down, and force his cock into my mouth or my ass—but it was *hot*.

That, and I was always completely certain he'd stop the second I protested. Even in the very beginning when he'd been a total stranger, he'd never given me any reason to second-guess him. Maybe it was because he was a cop. My first impression of him had been the calm, collected, take-charge guy who'd defused a volatile situation. He'd always radiated *safe*.

So when he let loose in the bedroom, so did I. And right now, with my back against the wall and Will's mouth turning me inside out, I didn't hold back. I swore and moaned and didn't even try to keep myself from coming. I doubted I could have if I'd wanted to—Will was obviously bound and determined to get me off, right here, right now, and there was nothing to do except enjoy the ride.

Eyes closed and knees shaking, I stuttered what I hoped was encouragement. I tried to grab hold of his hair, but it was too short, so I grabbed his hand on my hip. He curled his fingers around mine, and that tight grip anchored me, and I held on for all I was worth as he licked, sucked, teased my cock, and then I yelled something I didn't understand, and the wall kept me upright (barely) and Will kept me coming (forever) and—

"S-stop." I shivered hard. "Oh God…"

Will stopped, and by the time my spinning head had

slowed and my vision had cleared, he was standing again. Though I wasn't anywhere near catching my breath, I grabbed him and kissed him, and the salt of my cum in his mouth made me dizzier.

Finally, I had to come up for air or I was going to black out right there between him and the wall. I touched my forehead to his and took a few gulps of breath. "Thought... thought you said *I* was going to suck *you* off."

"I did." He grinned. "And now you are... sir."

With that, he shoved me to my knees.

And oh fuck yeah, I absolutely did suck him off.

CHAPTER 11

WILL

AFTER NINETEEN YEARS in the Navy, I'd used the word *sir* so much it barely registered as more than a punctuation mark. It was automatic.

What wasn't so automatic—or hadn't been until recently—was saying it and suddenly having my dick get hard.

Ever since that meeting with Commander Wilson, I'd been wary of using the title. Not that I could avoid it, considering I dealt with officers on a daily basis. Thank God for my camouflage utilities, not to mention the bulky police belt. They obscured everything until I had a chance to pull myself together, though the security officer probably wondered why I'd suddenly gotten red-faced and flustered while we'd been standing in the hallway discussing the watch rotation.

This was seriously going to make my job awkward if I didn't get a handle on it.

I'd known a few guys who were into kinky stuff, and the ones who liked to be in charge got off on being called *Sir*. That had never really appealed to me since I wasn't an officer, so I didn't want to be called that, and I sure as hell wasn't going to get on my knees and try any of that *Thank you, sir, may I have another* stuff. Not when I had to use the title at work, sometimes toward officers who weren't worth the cloth their insignia was sewn on.

It had never occurred to me how hot it would be to call a man *sir* while *he* was on *his* knees. I could handle that. Obviously Brent wasn't the only one getting a rebellious thrill out of this thing we were doing. We were both as straitlaced as they came, especially where our careers were concerned. Breaking away from that to disappear behind closed doors for some forbidden sex, and turning our rank difference on its head while we were are it? Oh fuck yeah.

I'll scratch your back if you scratch mine.

Especially if you leave marks like that again.

Oh my God, is it time to go home yet?

I was horny, but also restless and bored, and it was one of those typically quiet days on NAS Adams, so I left my office and wandered over to Noah's. At least we could shoot the breeze and kill some time, which meant I might stay sane between now and when I had Brent naked again.

Fortunately, Noah was there, and his door was open. He had a stack of watch bills on his desk, which he probably needed to sign off by the end of the day so they could be posted to let everyone know when and where they'd be standing watches. As soon as he saw me, though, he put down his pen and sat back, stretching his arms above his head. "Oh thank God. A distraction."

"What's wrong?" I chuckled as I took my usual seat in front of his desk. "Watch bill assignments don't keep you entertained?"

"Ugh." He rubbed his hands over his face, muffling what I guessed were some curses. Dropping his hands into his lap, he exhaled. "So what's new with you? You must not be very busy if you have time to come distract me from my shit."

"Same old, same old. Got a meeting with Port Ops later today so they can fill me in on what's going on with the boats." I scowled. "I can't decide if harbor patrol is fucking up the boats, or if Port Ops isn't repairing them right, but if someone doesn't get my boats up and running this week, heads are going to roll."

"That shit again? Man. Better you than me. I've had it up to here with Port Ops."

"You and me both." Port Operations were notorious for butting heads with security at pretty much every base I'd ever been stationed. All they had to do was keep the patrol boats functioning. Why that always seemed to be too much to ask would forever be a mystery to me.

It was hard to get stressed about it right now, though. Annoyed? Sure. But every time my blood pressure started rising over something work related, all I had to do was shift my thoughts back to Brent, and... well, my blood pressure still rose, but it was a hell of a lot more pleasant.

"Someone's got a dick on the brain."

I nearly choked. "What?"

Noah laughed. "Come on. Don't act like I don't know you." He pointed a finger at me and inclined his head. "You've already tried to deny it once, but seriously, the only time you're this spacey is when you're oxygen deprived from having a dick down your throat for too long."

"Anyone ever tell you how classy you are?"

He shrugged. "Anthony said something about it a while back, but I think he might've been sarcastic. It's hard to tell with him."

"No, it's not. And he absolutely was."

Noah chuckled. "So who's the lucky guy who finally broke you out of the post-Vince dry spell?"

Uh, well, that's a bit complicated.

I cleared my throat. "How do you know it's just one?"

His eyes were instantly huge.

Grinning, I ran with it. "Maybe I've finally been getting out there and getting laid. Been a while, you know? Time to play the field."

"You?" he sputtered. "Playing the field?"

"Hey, we can't all be respectable soon-to-be-married men, so—"

"Whoa, who said anything about 'soon to be married'?" Noah laughed. "I'm shacking up with the guy, not chaining myself to him."

"Yet."

He waved a hand. "Yeah, we'll see."

"So if Anthony took you to some candlelit dinner, and got on one knee with a ring in his hand, you'd—"

"You're changing the subject."

"And you're blushing."

"Fine. If he asks, then yes." A little smile tugged at his lips, and I suspected he was secretly hoping Anthony would ask. Or maybe he was trying to work up the nerve himself. "So with that out of the way." He inclined his head. "Let's get back to your dude. Because I don't believe for a second that you're out there being a manwhore."

"Why not? I spent six years unknowingly taking part in an open relationship and being sexually frustrated while my boyfriend was putting his dick in anything that moved." That all came out with more bitterness than I'd intended. Clearing my throat, I shifted a little, and tried to inject some actual humor as I added, "Maybe I've got some bedroom karma to burn off."

The skepticism in his expression didn't budge. "The fact that you're being so cagey about it is..." Skepticism turned to concern. "You're not doing anything stupid, are you? Because that's not like you."

I put up my hands. "I'm not. Come on. You know me."

"Yeah, I do. That's why I'm weirded out that you're keeping this so close to the vest. I mean, if it's none of my business, it's none of my business, but you're acting really weird about it."

"It's nothing to worry about." I made a big gesture out of looking at my watch. "And don't you have post checks to do?"

He scowled. He could always tell when I was trying to avoid a topic. And it wasn't like he could argue—I'd done the last set of post checks over an hour ago, and one of us tried to swing by and check on our various sentries a few times a day. Partly to make sure they didn't need help, and partly to make sure they weren't fucking off.

"All right, all right." He stood. "Just... whatever you're doing... be careful, all right?"

I nodded as I stood too. "Always am."

But maybe not careful enough under the circumstances.

CHAPTER 12

BRENT

SNEAKING IN and out of each other's apartments had become strangely routine. Whenever we could, we were in each other's beds, and I was getting used to making a quick, stealthy escape in the dead of night. Varying my route. Avoiding any people who were lingering outside at that hour for some reason.

The novelty didn't last long, but neither of us made any noise about changing anything. In fact, our late-night escapes were getting later and later because even after we were physically exhausted, there was never a real sense of urgency to get away from each other.

As much as it was taking its toll at work, I was looking forward to this part as much as I was the sex, and now, here we were again—lying in Will's bed, naked and comfortable, talking about whatever came to mind.

Somehow tonight, we'd landed on the subject of our past love lives. Or, in my case, lack thereof.

"In high school," I said, "I had a boyfriend my sopho-more year and a girlfriend my senior year, but even then, my focus was on getting into Annapolis. So they kind of fizzled out. Since then, I've never really had any relationships."

"You've been out of Annapolis for, what, five years now?"

I nodded. "But it was always something. I had a friend with benefits for a little while, and right about the time I thought things *might* get serious with her, I deployed, and shortly after that, transferred out here. Like I said... always something." *Like meeting someone in the wrong paygrade.*

"You really have lived and breathed the Navy for a long time, haven't you?"

"Yep. I'll probably live and breathe it till I'm dead."

Will's eyebrows rose. "Committed."

I nodded.

He smiled a little and brushed the backs of his fingers across my cheek. "I get it. I'm in for the long haul too."

"Well yeah. You're almost to twenty, aren't you?"

"I am, but I'm sticking it out to thirty. I want to retire as a master chief on seventy-five percent pay."

I grinned. "That does sound like a pretty sweet deal."

"I think so." He returned the grin. "Almost two-thirds of the way there, with plenty of time left to get promoted."

"Nice. There anything you don't like about your job, though?"

"Oh, it has its bullshit like any other. Red tape. Paperwork. Assholes in charge. But..." His expression darkened. "If there's one thing I could really do without? I fucking *hate* domestic calls."

I chewed my lip. "Like... the one where you met me?"

He met my gaze and chuckled softly. "That one ended a lot better than others do. And not only because I met you." The humor faded. "It's just... It's hard, you know? Seeing people rip each other apart like that? Especially since I've, uh, been there."

My spine straightened. "What?"

Will swallowed. "My ex—not the recent one, but the one before him—was abusive. Mostly verbally, but sometimes physically too."

"Seriously?"

"Yeah." His eyes lost focus, and he exhaled. "The violence wasn't as bad as I've seen as a cop, let's put it that way. It was still bad, but my job has sure as shit put it into perspective."

"Still." I couldn't help squeezing his hand. "That's awful."

"It was, yeah." He brought our hands up and kissed my fingers before tucking them beneath the covers between us again. With a bitter laugh, he said, "The irony of it is that if the cops had ever been called, DADT would've killed *both* of our careers faster than any domestic violence charges would've damaged his."

Horror tightened my throat. "Really?"

Will nodded. "We can suspect all we want that there's domestic violence, but until we have indisputable proof—and in most cases, one partner willing to press charges against the other—there's nothing we can do but wait for it to escalate. And, even then, shit could get swept under the rug. Hell, I worked for a master chief who was arrested twice for beating his wife, but knew enough people in high places to make it disappear."

"But under DADT, if they found out you were gay..."

"You were done. Period. I mean, they needed something more than a rumor, but it didn't take nearly as much to convince the military you were gay as it did to convince them you were in danger at home."

"Did you ever..." I hesitated.

"Hmm?"

I searched his eyes, then took a breath. "You're a cop. Did you ever bust anyone? For being gay?"

Will shook his head. "I caught people from time to time. Once, on the ship, I was on watch and caught two guys blowing each other out by the fantail. They saw me, I saw them, but I walked away and never said a word about it. Far as I know, they never got caught." He paused. "The only time I ever intervened was when my buddy went staggering out of a bar in Japan with the ship's XO."

"So, an enlisted guy about to bang an officer?" I asked dryly.

He played with my hair. "That, and about to go stumbling and groping into a taxi in front of God knew how many guys from our boat. So yeah, I stopped him."

"Smart," I said.

"I'd have done that even if DADT hadn't been in effect anymore. For, uh, obvious reasons."

I laughed dryly. "Like I said—smart. So have you been openly gay since it was repealed?"

"Sort of. I never threw the doors off the closet or anything. I mean, I had a boyfriend at the time, and once it was repealed, we just... stopped hiding it."

"That must've been a huge relief."

"God, yeah." Will sighed like he was reliving that relief all over again. "The secrecy was fucking *draining*."

"Yeah. I can, uh, see how that would happen."

Our eyes met.

My stomach clenched. I was sure we were going to go there. Going to address the thing we'd carefully avoided discussing since we'd decided we were doing this.

Instead, he shook himself. "Ironically, it probably

wouldn't have been an entirely bad thing for me if DADT had hung around a bit longer."

"How do you figure?"

"Vince would've left. He didn't like all the sneaking around, and he was at the end of his thread when the repeal happened. It would've hurt, but not as bad as when he really did leave. At least then I never would've known he cheated."

I winced. "Fuck. Yeah, I can understand that."

He shrugged. "It is what it is. And I mean, I probably should've known we were in trouble. When I was up for reenlistment the last time around, we argued for *weeks* over it."

"Really?"

"Yeah. He wanted me to get out, and he was pressuring me hard to ditch my career."

"He wanted you to end your career over him?"

Will's lips tightened, and his voice was tinged with bitterness. "Apparently if I really loved him, I would do it. Instead of putting him through all that hell and..." He rolled his eyes. "Never mind how much my career means to me. If I loved him, the choice would be a no-brainer. Period."

"Wow," I said. "How did he feel when you re-upped?"

"He wasn't happy. Especially because I chose to take orders to a ship since I needed some time at sea so I could make senior chief. Going back to a ship meant deploying, and there was a pretty good chance that when I got off the ship, I'd be moving to another base. He grudgingly made it through the deployment, and he moved here to Anchor Point when I transferred, but things were never really the same between us. Especially when I told him there's about a ninety percent chance that my next set of orders will be overseas." Will sighed. "Or maybe he was pissed because I made him move away from his *other* boyfriend. Or boyfriends."

"What a dick."

"Tell me about it."

"Not that I'm surprised." I rolled my eyes. "We almost always lived in officer housing when I was a kid, and my mom hung out with the officers' wives. So even before I was old enough to know what sex was, I knew who was cheating, who was sleeping around..." I shook my head. "Life on a Navy base, I guess."

"Yeah." He nodded. "It's nuts."

"It is. When we were in San Diego, the wives would come over a couple times a week and have wine with my mom. Once they were all buzzed, they'd start gossiping about who was fucking who. My brother was sixteen then, and he'd eavesdrop in case they started talking about someone's daughter being a slut. Then he'd go try to hook up with her."

Will rolled his eyes. "Seriously?"

"Yep. In fact, my sister-in-law is the daughter of a retired rear admiral. They met in high school, before my brother went off to the Academy. I don't know if they met because he found out she'd sleep with anything that moved, but it honestly wouldn't surprise me."

"Damn. You ever follow in those footsteps?"

"Nah. I probably would've slept around a lot more than I did, but I was too scared."

Will straightened. "Scared?"

"Oh yeah. Thing is, by the time I was in junior high, my dad was a CO. It *sucks*. Believe me, I sympathize with the captains' and admirals' kids who rebel by sleeping around or getting high at every opportunity."

Will scowled. "Yeah. Me too. I haven't been to a single

base where I haven't had at least one experience of arresting some high-ranking officer's kid. Usually for vandalism, or something alcohol or drug-related, or for fooling around in a parked car with someone they shouldn't."

"I don't blame them at all."

"Right? I mean, Captain Rodriguez's twins seem to have their heads screwed on pretty straight. Captain Carter, though? From the supply ship?" Will groaned and rolled his eyes. "His poor daughters are so desperate for attention, they don't even try not to get caught."

"Really?"

He nodded. "Of course he bails them out every time and sweeps it all under the rug, which only makes it worse. I figure they're going to keep doing bigger and bigger shit until he has no choice but to ask them what the hell is wrong."

"Hopefully that'll happen before they do something that'll destroy someone's life."

"No kidding. It wouldn't be the first time, either."

"Believe me, I know."

He arched his eyebrow. "So did you ever get into trouble during your Navy-brat days?"

I shook my head. "Absolutely not. My dad put the fear of God into both of us from the time I was in kindergarten. Said getting busted for doing something stupid would destroy our chances at the Academy."

Will blinked. "He was using the Academy to keep you in line when you were in *kindergarten*?"

"Well…" I pursed my lips. "Okay, the longer version is that when I was five or six, base security picked up my brother and his friends for shoplifting at the Exchange. They were dumb teenagers who ripped off a couple of candy bars. Not exactly a federal crime, you know? But Dad still had to pick him up from security. He read my brother the riot act for... I mean, looking back it feels like hours and hours, but it probably wasn't that long. Maybe two hours. My parents made me sit in on it too so I'd understand how serious this kind of thing was. So when I was right about kindergarten age, I got to listen to my dad tell my brother for two hours about how stealing a candy bar could ruin his life forever."

Will's eyes widened. "Wow. That's crazy."

"Ya think?" I rubbed my eyes, suddenly exhausted by the topic. "You know what the shittiest part about that was?"

Will arched an eyebrow. "Besides browbeating a couple of kids over a candy bar?"

"Yeah." I exhaled, absently running my hand up the middle of his chest. "The thing Dad kept harping on the most was that if we fucked up like that, the only career we could hope for was on the enlisted side."

The other eyebrow came up. "Is that right?"

Cringing a little, I nodded. "As far as my dad is concerned, the only respectable career is as an officer, and the worst thing a person could possibly be is enlisted."

I thought Will might get pissed, but instead, he laughed. Like, really threw his head back and laughed.

"Oh, he's one of *those* officers." Rolling his eyes, he clicked his tongue. "I wonder what he thinks the Navy would be if us lowly NCOs weren't around to do the hard work. He might actually have to get his hands dirty." As soon as he'd said it, he quickly sobered. "Er, sorry. I shouldn't talk shit about your dad. Isn't like I know the guy."

"Actually, you're not far off the mark. And he's well aware the Navy would never function without the enlisted ranks. He just thinks that's for *other* people to do. You know, the unwashed masses."

"Of course," he muttered. "We live to serve."

I laughed, but not with much feeling. "As if officers don't do plenty of shit work. Ask me how I know."

His brow furrowed as he touched my face. "You don't seem very happy with the Navy."

I blinked. "Of course I am."

"Are you?"

"I..." I wanted to get defensive, but... happy? With the Navy? Had there ever been any other option?

Finally, I shook my head and blew out a long breath. "Eh, I'm just at that stage where it's still kind of shitty. Like, I'll be happy once I manage my own McDonald's, but I'm not enjoying the entry-level burger-flipping part."

Will laughed quietly. "You do realize there's still plenty of bullshit at the top, right?"

"Yeah. But that's where I want to be. It's where I've always wanted to be." I sighed again. "I guess I underestimated how long you really have to be part of the rank and file before you get there, you know?"

He nodded. "In my rate, paying your dues means standing at the gate and checking IDs for hours on end. Believe me when I tell you I understand."

I wrinkled my nose. "That... always has seemed like it must be miserable."

"Oh God. You have *no* idea."

"Yeah?"

Will chuckled and propped himself up on his elbow. "Back when I was an MA3 at my first shore command, the CO's wife complained because every time she came through the gate, it was shift change. So then the CO came down on our chain of command, saying that the sentries needed to stay on the gate for longer stretches so it didn't hold up traffic."

I arched an eyebrow. "Does shift change really make that much of a difference?"

"No. But it does take a second for one guy to step out while another steps in, and they might make a few comments back and forth about something. Like that the ID scanner is on the fritz, or whatever. It really doesn't make much difference to anyone but us. There's extra people on the gate during shift change, since the oncoming and outgoing shifts are both there for all of ten minutes." He rolled his eyes. "My best guess is that a sentry was distracted for a second and didn't salute properly, or... who knows?"

"Oh for fuck's sake," I grumbled. "God forbid the captain's wife not get saluted properly."

"You would be amazed how much shit we have to deal with from officers' wives who wear their husbands' ranks."

I snorted. "No, I wouldn't. I worked in an admiral's office when I was an ensign."

"Oh." He grimaced. "Yeah. You get it."

"Uh-huh." I paused. "So what happened after she bitched?"

"We all had to stand longer shifts on the gate. Nothing is better for morale than telling a bunch of kids they get to spend *more* time being bored, bitched at, and exposed to the weather, and that their feet really will stop hurting after they get used to it."

"Do they get used to it?"

"Eventually, but it definitely fucks with morale. When the next set of bullshit changes come along, they're already pissed off, and it gets worse. That's why we had such an awful retention rate at my last command. You had guys in their second terms who had every intention of making a career out of it, and by the time they were up for reenlistment, couldn't get away from the Navy fast enough."

I chewed my lip. "What about the ones who stick it out? Does it get better for them?"

"If they end up at a better command, sure. I've had a couple of people transfer here from other commands, ready to get out at the first opportunity, and then they decide they'll stay after all. Amazing what happens when you treat your people like human beings. And when you don't... well, you can't be surprised when your attrition rate is high."

"Except people leave from the good commands too."

"Well, yes." Will shrugged. "Not everyone wants to stay for life. Not everyone likes it as much as they thought they would."

My heart sped up.

He cocked his head. "What's wrong?"

I sighed. "I just... I can relate to wanting to jump ship. Sometimes it's frustrating, you know? And I know it's a long game. Gotta get through the bullshit before you make it to the better stuff. It really sucks at this level."

"I can understand that. One of my old chiefs—way back in my early days—said Wog Day was a pretty good metaphor for Navy life." He paused. "You been through Wog Day yet?"

I groaned.

Will laughed. "I'll take that as a yes. So you know how it goes. And according to this chief, the first five, ten years of your career is like an extended version of Wog Day. It's bullshit, it's shitty, but when it's over, things get better. And I can tell you from experience that the first half of my career was kind of like going through the Tank of Truth and Wisdom—it sucks, and it feels like it takes forever, but then it's suddenly over, and it's all downhill from there."

That was a pretty apt description for how I felt about my career lately. I shuddered at the memory. Of everything they'd thrown at all of us who were crossing the equator for the first time that day, the Tank of Truth and Wisdom had been the worst. It was an inflatable raft filled with every kind of liquid imaginable that wouldn't create an actual biohazard, plus garbage thrown in. I wasn't entirely sure what had been in it, only that the smell was what finally made me heave over the side of the flight deck. And that was *before* they'd made me crawl through it like the other wogs.

It wasn't fun, but it was a point of pride in the career of anyone in the fleet. When it was over, you were a shellback. Next time you crossed the equator, *you'd* be heckling the hapless wogs on their way through the day-long hazing. No one particularly enjoyed going through it, but you weren't truly a man of the sea until you had. Like every other shellback, I was glad when it was over.

"So at what point do I feel like I'm a shellback instead of a wog still crawling through the Tank of Truth and Wisdom?"

Will smoothed my hair. "It's different for everybody. For me, once I made E-6 and stopped getting shit on, everything was better."

"Everyone keeps saying it'll be better once I make lieutenant commander." I held up my crossed fingers. "Let's hope so."

"Yeah. Let's hope. As long as you don't turn into one of the dicks we've got running my part of the base."

"What do you mean?"

"We just got a new security officer here at Adams, and

he and I have been butting heads for a month." He groaned. "Every fucking SECO is on a power trip, I'm telling you."

"Why's that?"

"Because half the time they're senior enlisted who went warrant officer, so suddenly this former enlisted guy's got his commission, and he's in charge of an entire security department." Will rolled his eyes. "Motherfuckers always seem to forget they used to *be* the guys they're currently stomping on."

"Wow."

"Yeah. And, um, if it's not too weird to offer some unsolicited career advice while we're in bed..." He lifted his eyebrows.

"No, it's fine. I'll take anything I can get."

He trailed his fingers up my forearm. "Do not forget where you came from. When you get up there in rank, remember how miserable you are right now. Your guys on the bottom of the totem pole will have exponentially more respect for you if they think you understand what it's like for them, and you don't treat them like shit on your shoe."

"Good to know. I'll remember that."

"Everyone with any authority should, but they don't. A lot of COs seem to forget that they're only as good as the rank and file they're commanding. If the rank and file respect him? They'll walk through fire for him. If not?" Will shook his head. "They'll do just enough work to stay out of trouble, and that will *not* look good when he wants to advance."

"Duly noted. What do you think of Captain Rodriguez?"

Will shrugged. "I like her. I'd like to see her rein in some of her people, especially jackasses like the security office, but she's one of the better COs I've worked for."

"She does seem pretty chill."

"She is. Doesn't take crap from a lot of people, either. Not that you really can at that level, but I've seen some COs who were doormats, so..."

"I'm amazed they last long," he said.

"Yeah. Me too." Will was quiet for a moment, and I realized he was watching me intently.

I squirmed. "What?"

"Just, uh..." He chewed his lip. "Can I ask you something kind of personal?"

"Sure."

He searched my eyes. "*Are* you happy with your career? I know you're not thrilled with where you are right now, but... in general?"

"Like, am I happy with being in the Navy?"

Will nodded.

"Sure." I shrugged. "This is what I've always wanted to do. I'm impatient and really want the next few years to go by as fast as possible, but yeah. I am."

"So after you've advanced a few more paygrades?"

"Exactly."

"What'll it be like when you get there? On a day-to-day basis, I mean."

"It'll be—" My teeth snapped shut. "Well, sure as shit more interesting than it is now."

Will held my gaze but didn't speak.

I gulped.

He absently caressed my arm. "The upper echelon isn't all standing on the bridge and giving orders. There's a reason most of the admirals are either gray or bald."

I chuckled, but it wasn't enough to shake loose the ball of lead in my stomach. "I don't expect it to be easy. Just... less boring than pushing paperwork, you know?"

"I'll give you that. There's definitely more happening at that stage." He paused. "I'm curious about something."

"Sure."

He ran his fingers through my hair. "If you weren't in the Navy, what would you be doing?"

"I don't know."

"You don't?"

"No." I shrugged. "Never really thought about it. This has been the plan since I was a kid. What about you?"

"I'd probably be a civilian cop."

"That what you've always wanted to do?"

He nodded.

"So you get it."

He didn't seem convinced, but he let it go.

Though I went along with the drifting conversation, my mind kept wandering back to that part. His comments had rattled something in me. How much different *would* it really be when I rose to the top? Sure, I'd have a higher security clearance, and I'd be involved in bigger decisions than ordering supplies for the training classrooms, but the actual day-to-day shit?

Well. I pushed the thought away. I'd find out when I got there.

The only thing I knew for sure? It would be a hell of a lot better than where I was now.

All I had to do was *get* there.

After a while, I glanced at my phone and scowled. "It's getting late. I should probably go."

Will frowned, watching his hand run along my arm. "Yeah. Probably."

Disappointment tugged at me. Just once, I wanted to wake up in the same bed. This was the first time in my life I'd slept with someone beyond a one-night stand and still had no idea what he looked like when he woke up scruffy and disheveled. There was something kind of endearing, maybe even a little charming, about seeing a guy in that frazzled, grumpy, precoffee state.

"You know." I slid my fingers through the graying hair on his chest. "We could always take a weekend out of town. Go to Portland or something."

Will's lips quirked like he was really thinking about it. "Yeah, I guess we could."

"It would be a little risky," I admitted. "But better than going out here in town."

He nodded.

"If we're smart..." I couldn't finish the thought because I didn't want to talk him out of it. Out of going to Portland, or out of doing *this*.

Will sighed. "If we were smart, we wouldn't do this at all."

Damn it. Heart thumping, I said, "Yeah. I know."

"So..."

We locked eyes. His hand was still on my arm. I was still in his bed. Yeah, if we were smart...

But here we were.

I swallowed. "So I should book a room?"

"Yeah. Book a room."

CHAPTER 13

WILL

ON MY NEXT THREE-DAY WEEKEND, I met Brent in Portland. We didn't dare take one car—Anchor Point was a small enough town, someone was sure to see us leave together. In fact, to be safe, he drove up on Friday morning, and I left later in the afternoon.

My cell phone's GPS guided me through the knotted interstates and weird roads that made up Portland, and eventually brought me to a stop in front of a gorgeous hotel. In fact, it was nice enough I had to double-check the confirmation he'd forwarded me to make sure it was the right place.

It was. I didn't know who Brent had blown to get us a good deal on the room—or maybe officers really did make more than I thought—but this was *not* a cheap hotel. It was one of the glass high-rises overlooking the river.

I parked in the parking garage, took my bag out of the trunk, and headed inside. On the way to the elevator, I texted Brent to let him know I was here. When I got to the lobby, my phone buzzed with a reply—the room number.

The elevator took me up to the eighteenth floor. Our

room was at the far end of the hall, and by the time I reached it, my heart was pounding from anticipation. It didn't matter that we'd spent countless nights in his bed or mine. This was different. A little bit dangerous, a lot exciting, and an entirely new place than one of our bedrooms.

I knocked on the door and wasn't at all surprised when I was greeted by a grinning—and stark-naked—Brent.

I dropped my bag at our feet and wrapped my arms around him. "Not wasting any time, are you?"

"Should I?" He lifted his chin for a long, languid kiss. "I only get you for three days. Why waste it?"

"Mmm, good point."

He dragged his lips across mine. "I'm all ready for you too."

"Ready for—" The piece fell into place, and my pulse surged. "You want to get fucked, don't you?"

"So much. Right now."

I wondered how long he'd been winding himself up for me. I pulled him closer, and as I kissed his neck, whispered, "Maybe I want to tease you anyway."

The choked, frustrated groan made me laugh, but it also made my dick even harder.

"Fuck me," he begged.

"Not yet." *Or I'll go off before I'm inside you. God, I want you.* I let him go, gently turned him around, and nudged him toward the bed. "Get on your back."

He did as he was told, and I stripped off my clothes as I took in the view—Brent, naked and flushed and rock-hard, stretched out on the giant bed that was ours for the weekend. He didn't touch himself, so he must've been as turned on as he'd said he was. As close to losing it as I was.

He bit his lip as I climbed onto the bed. When I settled between his legs instead of coming up to kiss him, he gasped, and as I took his hard cock into my mouth, he exhaled, and I swore I heard a ragged "Oh fuck yeah."

Brent stroked my hair and gave soft moans of encouragement as I sucked his dick. When I tapped his thigh, he spread his legs wide, and good God, he wasn't kidding about being ready—my fingers slid easily into his slick, prepped hole.

"I've been waiting all day for you to fuck me," he breathed. "Don't want to wait anymore."

"But it's fun to make you"—I curled my fingers inside him—"squirm."

"Son of a bitch." He arched. "God... c'mon..."

"How bad do you want it?"

He cursed under his breath. "If you'd made me wait another ten goddamned minutes, I'd— Oh fuck. I'd have... taken care of it myself."

"No, I don't think you would have." I lapped at his balls, then took my sweet time dragging my tongue all the way up his cock. "Real thing's worth waiting for, isn't it?"

"So much. But... I was going crazy."

"You don't know what going crazy feels like yet." I flicked my tongue across the head of his cock, and then as I withdrew my fingers, I said, "Stay there. I'll get a condom." I started for the bag I'd dropped on the floor, but he stopped me with a hand on my arm.

"Nightstand."

I turned. Sure enough, he had a brand-new box of condoms and a full bottle of lube ready and waiting. I grinned. "You really didn't want to wait tonight, did you?"

"No fucking way."

I kissed him once more, then pulled a condom off the strip.

As I rolled on the rubber, Brent gestured across the

room. "Should we shut the curtains?" He smirked, but there was a hint of shyness in his eyes. "I mean, we're way up here, but still."

I glanced at the windows. These weren't regular hotel windows. Two entire walls of our room were floor-to-ceiling glass, and from this high up, we had to have a spectacular panoramic view of the city.

Electricity surged through me. "Actually, I have a better idea." I got up and motioned for him to do the same. "Come here."

A scowl flickered across his face, but he obeyed. I led him across the room, turned him around, and pushed him up against the window. He gasped, probably from the chill of the glass, and as I kissed along his neck, I said, "I want to fuck you right here. Where the whole city can see us."

Brent moaned, and nothing about that sound said he objected to the idea. Especially not the way he was rubbing my cock with his ass.

"You like that idea?" I murmured.

"Uh-huh. 'Specially the... fucking me part."

I grinned. "Someone's getting turned on."

"What was your first clue?" He looked over his shoulder. "Just fuck me already. Please?"

"Well, since you asked nicely..." I nudged his legs a little farther apart with my knee. Then, with the city laid out below us, sparkling in the night without noticing us all the way up here, I took him with a long, deep stroke, reveling in his helpless moans as he pressed back against me.

I kissed his neck and gazed over his shoulder out the window. The view sent a delicious thrill through me. After weeks of hiding this behind closed doors, now there was no one within almost a hundred miles who could give a flying fuck that my cock was inside Brent.

No one except me. Except us.

"Been looking forward to this all week," I purred, and fucked him a little harder. I kept an arm around him so he wasn't leaning completely on the glass. I was sure it would hold, but still—no point in taking chances.

"M-me too." He shivered, and a soft, helpless sound escaped his lips.

As I fucked him deep and hard, I kissed the back of his neck. "You like that?"

He made another sound, one that was probably supposed to be "Yeah," and his inability to speak drove me on. I sank my teeth into his shoulder, slammed my cock into his ass, and gave him everything I had. He cried out, voice vibrating against the window, and flattened one palm, then the other on the glass he was already fogging with his breath.

"Christ, you feel so good," I moaned into his hair. "And you look... *so hot*."

He whimpered and shuddered. "I'm gonna come." His hands slid down the glass, squeaking and leaving smears of sweat behind. "God, Will, don't stop."

I gritted my teeth and held my breath, concentrating on keeping my own orgasm at bay until he'd come. I wanted him coming just like this, in full view of the city, so the whole world could see that he was mine and he was getting off to everything I was doing to him.

"Oh fuck." He clawed at the window. A shudder nearly knocked him off his feet, and a hot huff of breath made a cloud across the glass. "Oh fuck, I'm... ungh... *yeah*..." He grunted, clenching around me, and I stopped holding back. I thrust as deep as I could, shuddering hard all the way down to my feet, and the city blurred below us before I had to close my eyes anyway.

With a sigh, his whole body went slack. Then mine did. I wrapped both arms around him to keep both of us upright, and kissed below his ear. "That was hot."

"Uh-huh." He shivered between me and the glass. "Think anyone saw us?" The grin in his voice made my skin tingle.

"I hope so," I growled against his skin.

"Yeah. Me too."

After a shower—and a lazy fuck in the giant stall—we were both getting hungry, not to mention a little eager to venture out in public for the first time. So, once we were both dressed and presentable—and once we could both stand without our hips threatening to dislocate—we went down to the hotel lobby. Neither of us felt like walking very far, and the hotel's restaurant sounded good. This was one of those convention hotels with a gigantic restaurant and a menu with a little of everything. Perfect.

At our table in a far corner, as I skimmed over the menu, I kept stealing glances at Brent, and struggled to keep a poker face. He looked amazing, dressed down in a button-up black shirt and a pair of jeans, his hair still wet and meticulously arranged as always. No one could look at him and know that I'd been riding him against the window or in the shower within the past hour. That was all mine.

But that wasn't the only thing that kept pulling my attention to him. It was hard not to get a little sentimental about this being the first time we'd ever eaten together in public. Some little voice inside my head tried to tell me that was insane since we were friends with benefits, but the thought didn't stick. I couldn't quite define what we were, only that the *friends with benefits* label didn't fit so well anymore, and going out in public for dinner at a restaurant with candles and white tablecloths *did* fit.

I felt too good to try to define it, so I ignored that stupid voice. This was a short trip and a rare opportunity, and I was damn sure going to enjoy the hell out of it.

If we'd taken a chance and done this in Anchor Point, it would have been a disaster. We'd both be checking over our shoulders and jumping out of our skin every time the door opened.

Here, if someone we knew walked in, we could easily brush it off as running into each other and deciding to have dinner together instead of alone. Not technically fraternization since neither of us was in the other's direct chain of command. Just two guys who happened to be in the same place at the same time.

Which seemed ridiculous, since the whole point of coming to Portland had been to take a break from the nonstop discretion. Baby steps.

Well, aside from the part where we'd fucked against a window in plain view of anyone who'd chosen to look, but I doubted anyone would recognize us from that far away. I just loved the idea of someone—anyone—seeing how much I wanted this man.

Brent's eyes flicked up, and he caught me staring. A blush bloomed in his cheeks. "What?"

"Nothing." I cleared my throat and dropped my gaze to the menu I'd been ignoring. "Uh... nothing."

"You sure?" He laid his menu down and reached across the table, and right there in the restaurant, slid his hand over my forearm.

Our eyes locked. We both grinned. Our cover was

blown now. If anyone walked in and saw us, we were busted, and I... didn't pull away.

Fucking above the city had nothing on the electric thrill of a brazen act of affection at a secluded table in a deserted restaurant. Heart racing, I turned my hand over, and we closed our fingers around each other's forearms.

Neither of us had to say a word.

So we didn't.

We just let the moment be.

After dinner, we wandered into the lobby to check out the display of tourist attractions. Being November, a lot of things were closed or not at their peak of attractiveness— apparently roses were a big thing here, and shockingly, they didn't grow so well in the cold. We took a few pamphlets to peruse later.

As he tucked them into his pocket, Brent said, "It's still kind of early to call it a night. You want to go out somewhere?"

"Well, that *is* why we're here, isn't it?"

"Good point." He looked around. "So, what should we do? Go wander downtown, or...?"

"Let's save that for daylight. I think I saw a theater down the road. Maybe we could see what's playing."

"A movie?" Brent grinned. "Almost like a real date."

"Almost?"

Our eyes locked, and his grin turned into a smile.

We walked a block or so to the multiplex, and though there must've been fifteen movies playing, it didn't take us long to settle on the latest comic-turned-action-film. Thank God we didn't compare notes on what ages we'd each been when we'd started reading the comics. I wasn't sure I wanted to know.

We bought our tickets and headed into the auditorium.

It was mostly empty, so we had an entire row to ourselves, not to mention the rows in front of and behind us. Even better, this theater had armrests that could actually be lifted up, so Brent put up the one between us and slid in close to me. I wrapped my arm around his shoulders.

"Man, this is crazy," he said.

"What is?"

"It really does feel like we're on an actual date." He craned his neck enough to look up at me. "Our first real date, isn't it?"

"Yeah, it is." I kissed him softly. "So the question is, do you fuck on a first date?"

He squirmed beside me and slid his hand down my thigh. "Would that make me a slut?"

"Absolutely. Of the dirtiest kind." I guided his hand higher, stopping just shy of my crotch. "My favorite kind."

He looked up again, and when our eyes met in the low light, we both laughed.

"Good thing I like being a slut." He lifted his chin and kissed me lightly. "Because I am one hundred percent planning on fucking on our first date."

"Perfect." I cradled the back of his head and went in for a longer, deeper kiss.

There weren't a lot of people in the auditorium, and nobody within four rows of us, so I wasn't too worried about bothering anyone. And I had to admit, I got a charge out of kissing Brent and talking dirty with him in a public place. There was no one around to catch us, and no reason for me *not* to seize the opportunity for one of those long, languid kisses that had me so addicted to him.

I tugged his hair, pulling his head back, and started kissing his neck. His hand slid up the inside of my thigh, and he teased my cock and balls through my jeans. Neither of us made a sound—not one that could be heard over the ads playing on the screen—but he was practically vibrating with arousal. So was I. Because he was mine. For the entire weekend, the Navy could go fuck itself, and Brent was *mine*.

The music suddenly faded, and I opened my eyes in time to see the lights dim.

"Movie's starting." I drew back. "Don't want to miss it, do you?"

He gave a frustrated little moan but settled against my shoulder, keeping his hand on my thigh and dangerously close to my dick.

As the previews kicked on, I kissed his temple, then whispered, "One more thing."

"Hmm?"

"When we get back? You're on top."

CHAPTER 14

BRENT

THERE WAS no way in hell I was going to remember one single line from this movie. In fact, as soon as he'd said those words, I'd forgotten what movie we were seeing in the first place.

He had to have done it on purpose. He'd obviously enjoyed me being spun up earlier, and he probably wanted me spun up when we got back to the room. As if he needed to work at it—just knowing I was spending all of tonight with him was enough to keep me at half-mast almost constantly.

Well, if I was going to be distracted, so was he.

I hooked a finger under his chin and turned him to face me. He didn't resist at all as I pulled him in, and when our lips met, my whole body tingled as if this were the first time I'd touched him all week. We'd fucked earlier? This was the first I'd heard of it.

His hand warmed my cheek. It stayed there, gently resting on the side of my face, and I hoped he didn't move it anytime soon.

He didn't. And we didn't move either. We ignored the

film and wrapped up in each other, exploring each other's mouths.

So this was what it was like to make out in a movie theater. Mentally, I was already dragging him into bed and tearing off his clothes. In reality, though, I intended to savor this for as long as I could. I'd never done it as a teenager because I'd been too afraid of getting caught. I'd never done it with him for the same reason.

Tonight, there was nothing to do except lose myself in Will's soft, sensual kiss. Had we been someplace private, we'd have had free rein to do anything we wanted. Here in a theater, kissing and touching each other over clothes was as far as we could go, and... I loved it. The creak of his leather jacket. The way my scalp tingled whenever his fingers combed through my hair. The heat of his hand through the denim on my thigh. As I snaked my hand between his jacket and his shirt, it was as hot as if I were touching his bare skin.

And, dear God, kissing for the sake of kissing was quickly becoming my favorite thing ever. The way his lips and tongue moved lazily with mine? Oh yeah, I could do this for hours if he was on board. I probably wouldn't be able to feel my mouth by the time we were done, but oh fucking well.

Will let a couple of daring fingers slip under my shirt, and when they grazed my side, I shivered, which pushed me closer to him. He grinned against my lips and slid his whole hand under my shirt and onto my back. How the hell could that be as erotic as if he were groping my ass or stroking my dick?

He started to draw his hand back, but I caught his arm.

"What's wrong?" he asked.

"Just..." I swallowed. "Don't want you to stop."

"I'm not doing anything."

"*Oh*, yeah you are."

He laughed softly, and his hand rested more firmly on my skin as he kissed me again, and damn if that hot point of contact didn't take this to the next level. It hadn't been more than two hours since he'd been balls-deep in me, and somehow having his hand on my back under my shirt was enough to make my pulse surge.

I ran my palm up his inner thigh. The quiet growl that rumbled against my lips gave me goose bumps, especially as his fingers curled into my back. When I ran the tip of my thumb along the very edge of his erection, he shuddered hard.

"Someone's turned on," I said.

"And you're not?"

"I didn't say that."

He took his hand out from under my shirt and guided mine all the way onto his cock. In a husky whisper, he said, "Maybe we should go back to the room."

"What about the movie?"

"What movie?"

I glanced at the screen and had absolutely no clue what was happening. I was still a little hazy on what movie we were seeing. Or not seeing, as it were.

"Good point." I kissed him again. "Let's go."

We almost stayed in control all the way back to the room.

Almost.

The walk out of the theater? No problem.

Getting from the theater to the hotel? Easy.

Crossing the hotel lobby? No sweat.

The second the elevator doors closed, though, Will

grabbed me around the waist, shoved me up against the mirror, and kissed me. There were probably cameras in here, and some security guard was getting a hell of an eyeful, and I didn't care. I clung to Will's leather jacket and ground my neglected hard-on against his as we made out like it had been months, not minutes, since his tongue had been in my mouth.

Then, with a low groan, he pulled my head back and started on my neck. I bit my lip, and when I opened my eyes, I had a better view than the city of Portland had earlier —Will, in jeans and leather, holding me there against the wall with his face buried against my throat like he was an insanely hot vampire.

I glanced at the numbers above the door. Fuck. Not even halfway to our floor. Could this thing move *any* slower?

Will flicked his tongue across my skin.

Would anyone notice if we hit the emergency stop and stayed in here?

I tilted my head to offer up more of my throat. "You serious about me being on top?"

"You better believe it." He kneaded my ass and rubbed his cock against my hip. "I just keep getting carried away and fucking you, but tonight? Oh yeah. I want you on top." He met my eyes and, with a wicked grin, added, "That, and I don't want you to be *too* sore this weekend."

I laughed. "Sore? Please. You'll have to try harder than that."

His eyebrow flicked up. "That a challenge?"

"Maybe. But later. I've been dying to fuck you."

"Why didn't you say so?"

"Remember that part about getting carried away with fucking me?"

He nodded.

"Yeah. That."

Will chuckled and drew me in for another kiss. He was about to say something else, but the elevator dinged and lurched to a stop. We separated, clearing our throats and tugging at our clothes as if either of us could hide our very prominent hard-ons.

Good thing the hallway was empty. That could've been awkward.

We walked as fast as a couple of erections allowed, and somehow I got the key card into the reader on the first try. The second we were in the room, it was just like those nights we hooked up at either of our apartments—door shut, dead bolt turned, deep kiss. No more worrying about someone else stepping into the elevator. No more holding back because another moviegoer might see us. We were alone, sealed in, and why the hell wasn't he naked yet?

He guided me toward the bed we'd already fucked in once tonight. As soon as my calves touched the mattress, he let me go, leaned toward the nightstand, and pushed a condom into my hand.

"What?" I smirked. "No foreplay?"

Will shrugged off his jacket and tossed it over a chair. "What do you think all that was in the movie theater?"

"Oh yeah. Good point." I unbuckled my belt. "I guess the elevator counted too."

He eyed me as he toed off his shoes. "You guess?"

I just grinned.

We both made quick work of getting out of our clothes, and he wasn't kidding about that condom.

"Put it on," he breathed between kisses. "I want you *now*."

I squirmed in his embrace, condom still in my hand. "I kind of like it when you beg."

He grabbed my hair tight enough to make it sting, and dear God, I hadn't thought I could get harder, but I'd been wrong, especially when he said in a husky whisper, "Put it on. And fuck me. *Sir*."

My knees shook and a moan escaped my lips. Nothing was filthier than the way he called me that when he was ordering me around. "Good... good idea."

He laughed softly. "Thought you might see things my way." Then, for good measure, he kissed me again. As he pulled back, he met my gaze. "So how do you want to do this?"

I thought about it as I tore the wrapper. I was tempted to come in from behind so I could ride him good and hard, or so I could put him down on his stomach and make him beg for it, but more than anything, I wanted to see his face.

As I started rolling on the condom, I nodded toward the bed beside us. "On your back."

Will didn't argue.

He lay back on the pillows, and as I knelt between his thighs, he hooked his hands under his knees, spreading his legs wide and offering himself to me.

I put plenty of lube on the condom, and used a couple of fingers to make sure he was good and slick too.

"Don't you dare fucking tease," he growled as I fingered him. "I want *you*, not your hand."

"I just don't—"

"Go slow at first. Trust me, I can handle it."

"And what if I *want* to tease you?"

He bit his lip and sucked in a sharp breath through his nose. Whether it was because of what I'd said or what I was doing with my fingers, I couldn't be sure. All I knew was that I fucking loved the sight of him getting all flustered because he wanted my cock. And as fun as it could be to tease him, I wanted to give it to him.

I slid my fingers free, and Will swore as I guided myself in. Or maybe I did. I'd been too turned on to think since we'd started kissing in the theater, and I was surprised my body wasn't literally on fire with anticipation.

The head slipped into him. He shivered. I groaned. I withdrew and pushed in again because I couldn't resist those shallow strokes. That moment of penetration when he yielded enough to take me—it was mind-blowing.

"Not that slow," he said through his teeth. "C'mon."

I grinned. "After all the times you've teased me and made me beg for it?"

Will glared up at me. Then he wrapped his legs around me, pressed his heels into my ass cheek, and pulled me forward, driving me deeper inside him.

"Oh God!" I caught myself on my arms. "Fuck..."

He chuckled and rocked his hips. "Don't make me put you on your back and ride you myself."

"Uh-uh." I regained my balance and thrust into him, which earned me a throaty, satisfying grunt. "That how you like it?"

"Oh yeah."

I did it again. In no time, I found a rhythm, and my head spun as I fucked him hard. I wanted to lean down and kiss him, to pick up where we'd left off in the elevator, but... this view. As if he wasn't sexy enough when he was on top, or when he was just lying there beside me, naked and satisfied. Seeing Will flat on his back with his legs apart, taking my dick into his tight hole while he stroked himself, was obscenely hot. *Why* hadn't we done this sooner?

"You look amazing like this," I breathed, withdrawing slowly.

"You're one to talk." He teased my nipple between his thumb and forefinger. "You are so—" He closed his eyes and sucked in a breath as I slid back into him. "God... so hot."

I dug my teeth into my lip to keep myself centered. Good thing this wasn't our first round of the night, or it would've been over way too fast. I wanted to savor this. Having him all to myself in a giant hotel bed, fucking him like I had in more fantasies than I could count—this definitely needed to last.

"Should've..." I bit back a moan. "Should've suggested this sooner."

"No kidding." His hands ran up my chest. Then to the back of my neck. As he pulled me down, he lifted his head, and then I was kissing him *and* moving inside him, and *holy fuck*. He was doing something with his hips—swiveling them? rocking them?—and kissing me like he always did when he was turned on. Deep and demanding, and I swore I could taste that dirty *sir* on his tongue as he forced his way into my mouth.

A shudder pushed me deeper inside him. I fucked him harder, and he moaned into my kiss, and suddenly I couldn't get deep enough inside him, so I broke the kiss with a gasp, sat up, and slammed into him as hard and fast as I could.

Below me, Will arched his back. He pumped his own cock, and the curses he released bordered on sobs. The cords on his neck stood out. His muscles tensed and quivered. He was absolutely the picture of almost there, and all because he was taking my cock.

"Oh God!" My orgasm came out of nowhere, and the force of it knocked me forward. Whatever he was doing with his hips, he kept doing it until I slumped over him, shaking and out of breath and dizzy as hell.

He wasn't done. He pulled me down into another kiss and kept pumping himself between us. I was still inside him, still hard, still blindingly sensitive from coming, and whimpered into his mouth as he clenched around me.

He broke the kiss but didn't let me go, panting hard as his grip tightened around my neck and his hole tightened around my cock. I rocked my hips a little bit, and that must've been exactly what he needed because he jerked violently and released the sexiest, most helpless cry as he came on both of us.

"Oh fuck…" His hand slipped off my neck, and he sank back to the pillows. Sweaty. Covered in semen. Fucking gorgeous.

I carefully pulled out, then sat back on my heels to let the room stop spinning.

"Anytime you want to do that again," he slurred. "Say the word."

"Yeah. Likewise."

I wasn't going to be able to move tomorrow. He probably wasn't either.

Oh well.

Worth it.

Something jostled me awake.

No, that wasn't quite right. There was movement and contact, but… jostling? Not really. It was so much gentler than that. More like… moving up against me.

Will.

Molding himself to me. Draping his arm over me. Lazily

pulling us back together after we'd drifted apart during the night.

Oh yeah. That was nice. His skin was warm against my back, and his breath was soft on the side of my neck. When he kissed below my ear, his stubble grazed my skin and made me shiver.

I smiled into the pillow. We'd done it. We'd gone to sleep in the same bed and woken up lying where we'd fallen. And it was exactly as perfect as I'd thought it would be.

We lay like that for a while. Not quite dozing, but not quite awake. We were both sporting some morning wood, but he didn't make any move to turn me on, and I didn't either. After last night, I suspected he needed a rain check as much as I did. Especially if we were going to be walking around today. As it was, my hips still felt kind of disjointed.

No regrets, though. Good God.

Eventually, I did need to break away from his embrace so I could take a leak. On the way back to the bed, I paused to stare at him.

He was partly on his stomach now, having shifted around a little after I'd gotten up. His bare torso was half covered by the sheet, but I could still see plenty. Stubble darkened his jaw, and his hair was as mussed as it could be when it was that short.

I couldn't help grinning.

So that's what you look like in the morning.

His eyes fluttered open, and he returned the grin. "You just going to stand around naked like that? Or get back in bed?"

"Well, if those are the options..." I chuckled, and he lifted the covers as I slid back into bed with him. Once again, he draped his arm over my waist and molded himself against me.

"We should probably get moving eventually," he murmured, lips brushing behind my ear. "But it seems like a damn shame to waste an opportunity to sleep in."

"I agree. We don't get to be lazy very often."

"Especially not together." He cuddled closer and kissed the side of my neck. "What time is it anyway?"

I craned my neck a little to see the alarm clock next to the bed. "Ooh, we're really indulging—it's almost *seven*."

He laughed softly and pressed another kiss to my neck. Holding me tighter, he whispered, "That just means we have more morning left to spend like this."

I laced my fingers between his on my stomach. "Sounds good to me."

It was almost ten when we finally got up, showered, shaved, and dressed. We grabbed breakfast downstairs, then headed out to see what Portland had to offer.

Without the Navy lurking nearby, Will relaxed. And I realized I hadn't seen him in casual clothes more than a handful of times. If we were lounging around and eating whatever takeout we'd had delivered, he'd put on a pair of gym shorts or jeans or something so he didn't have to answer the door naked, and I'd seen him in uniform, of course. I couldn't remember what he'd worn the night we'd fucked at the High-&-Tight. I'd been too caught up in seeing him at all to spare any synapses for his clothes.

Today, he had on a pair of jeans he'd probably had for years. The denim was worn in places, but they weren't fraying or full of holes. Just worn. And, good Lord, they sat perfectly on his hips and ass. I wouldn't have been surprised if this was a favorite pair—the ones he'd keep until the seams were barely holding themselves together, and he'd *still* look good in them then.

He'd paired the weathered old jeans with an equally faded black Pink Floyd T-shirt—"Another Brick in the Wall," of course—and the black leather jacket he'd worn last night.

And, as we stepped outside, a pair of wraparound sunglasses.

"Oakleys." I grinned. "Nice."

He chuckled. "They're Navy issue. I'd never spend this much on a pair of sunglasses."

"What? MAs get issued Oakleys?"

"Hey, our job has to have *some* perks."

"Fair enough, fair enough."

We headed out to explore Portland, and as we walked, I couldn't help myself—I kept stealing glances at him in the windows of shops and cars.

I had no idea where the line was between a guy trying too hard to look a decade younger, and a guy who could dress like that and get away with it. I didn't know what one thing or combination of things would tip the scales in either direction.

All I knew was Will landed firmly in the category of a guy who could not only get away with that look—he *rocked* it. He still looked his age, but not like he was having a midlife crisis. He wore leather and rock band shirts and weathered jeans and Oakleys because of course he did. What else would he wear? Khakis and a polo?

That thought made me snort before I could stop myself.

He glanced at me. "What?"

"Nothing." I shook my head. Before he could press, I

gestured at a café coming up. "That place looks like it could be good. You hungry?"

"Sure. I could eat." We stopped and perused the menu they had on display. It sounded promising, so we went inside.

At the table, Will shrugged off his jacket and hung it on the back of his chair. As he sat down, he set the Oakleys on the table. "So. Any ideas for the rest of the day?"

"Don't know." I thumbed the edge of the menu, but wasn't in a huge hurry to open it. "I'm not real familiar with this town."

"Neither am I. Did you see anything interesting on that rack of tourist stuff at the hotel?"

"The Japanese Gardens caught my eye." I felt a bit stupid suggesting it—a lot of guys seemed to roll their eyes at things like that. I wasn't obsessed with flowers or anything, but I found Japanese and botanical gardens relaxing as all hell.

Will smiled. "Sure, we could check it out. It's probably pretty empty and quiet this time of year, but..."

"It's worth a look." I shouldn't have been this relieved that he didn't think it was stupid. Or this surprised. "Assuming it's open."

"I'll check after lunch." He gestured with his phone. "Man, just thinking about going to a place like that brings back memories. I haven't spent as much time as I'd like in Japan, but I have been and I've loved it."

"Oh man, I want to go to Japan so bad. Have you been to Okinawa?"

"Oh yeah. Never for very long, though. I tried to get orders there a few times, but..." He shook his head. "Just had to enjoy it whenever my ship pulled in."

"I always heard that place was kind of a shithole."

"Yeah, me too. It's bullshit, though. The island is beautiful."

"So, why the reputation?"

Will shrugged. "Don't know. I mean, I guess a lot of the people who bitch about it probably never went farther than Gate Two Street."

"Meaning...?"

"It's the area right outside Gate Two of Kadena. That's where all the bars and shit are. If that's the only part of the island you ever see? Yeah, I could understand why it might be a shithole."

"Huh. So what's the rest of it like?"

"Lots of beaches. Some cool shops here and there. The food is *unbelievable*. And if you're into history, the island may be tiny, but it can keep you entertained for a while."

"Damn." I pursed my lips. "Now I do want to go. Is it true they hate Americans there?"

Will laughed. "Oh my God, no. I guess there's a protest outside one of the bases every time Japan's having an election. Some politician runs on the platform of booting the Americans off and reclaiming that particular base. Then as soon as the election's over, that's the end of it. Otherwise, everyone I know who's actually lived there has said the locals don't have a problem with us at all."

"Well shit."

"Right? I mean, our civilians pour money into their economy, and their civilians work on our bases." He shrugged. "I couldn't tell you how people in general feel about it politically, but as far as the economy goes, it seems to be a pretty sweet deal for everyone."

"Sounds like it." I flipped open the menu but didn't read it yet. "I keep wanting to take a military flight out there just to see it. If I can't get orders, might as well visit, right?"

Will nodded. "It's worth the trip."

I almost—*almost*—suggested it was something we could do together.

But something told me that would be pushing my luck with the Navy *and* with Will.

CHAPTER 15

WILL

WE SPENT most of the weekend doing exactly what I'd expected—enjoying each other's company during the day, enjoying each other's bodies at night. It was such a switch from our usual secrecy, and I reveled in being so relaxed and comfortable with him. Leisurely meals that hadn't been delivered to one of our apartments. Taking our sweet time walking through a couple of museums. Just being together.

I'd missed this. Vince and I had been open about our relationship for a long time, and I'd taken for granted being able to go out like straight couples did all the time.

But it wasn't that Brent was filling in a void my ex had left. Going out in public with Brent didn't feel anything like it had with Vince. Now that I'd gone out with Brent, and we'd walked the streets like a normal couple, I realized just how different we were from me and Vince.

Vince and I had been... comfortable. I'd loved him, and there'd been a strong attraction between us even to the end, but seeing Brent in the daylight took my breath away.

His light-brown hair had reddish highlights I'd never seen before. His blue eyes were more vivid in natural light, and his smile was... wow. Maybe he was extra relaxed being this far from the base and his job, or maybe he was letting his guard down since no one was going to catch us, but he laughed more easily, and every time I glanced at him, he'd smile that smile and make my knees weak.

When we'd first started out, every time I saw him, I wanted to be in bed with him. That hadn't faded at all, but when I looked at him now, all I could think was *I don't want to be away from you*. It didn't matter if we were naked. If we were out in public or cuddled up in the dark. If we were passing in the halls at work or falling into bed. I was as content to sit across from him at a table, sipping coffee while the afternoon went on around us, as I was to fuck him up against our hotel room window.

As long as you're here, I'm happy, no matter where here is.

I didn't remember ever feeling like this with Vince. Not this strongly, anyway. And, in fact, thinking about Vince didn't make me feel much at all now. Which was good—it meant I was getting over him. Or maybe I'd already gotten over him.

But it was dangerous too.

Because it meant something about how I felt about Brent.

And we couldn't go there. We just couldn't.

I stole a glance at him under the streetlights as we walked off an amazing dinner, and the light caught his eyes like it always did, and my heart fluttered.

Too late, fucker. Already there.

The next morning, I woke up first but didn't get out of bed

right away. I didn't wake Brent either. It was hard as hell to keep my hands off him, but I didn't want to disturb him quite yet. After today, there was no telling if we'd ever have a chance to wake up in the same bed again, and for a minute, I wanted to enjoy the view.

He'd been sleeping on his stomach for most of the night, but at some point, he'd turned onto his side. He was facing me now, partway buried in the hotel's obscenely fluffy pillows, and despite having longer hair than mine, he somehow still looked neat and put together. I could've sworn I'd disheveled the hell out of his hair last night. Now it was all lying the way it usually did, with maybe a few strands here and there that were slightly out of place.

The dusting of stubble on his jaw and across his top lip didn't do much to lessen his baby face. He was one of those guys who would always look a few years younger than he was, at least until he started getting some gray to even things out.

That mental image made my toes curl. If he was hot at this age, he was going to be jaw-dropping once he was closer to mine.

I glanced at the time. It was almost nine, so we still had a couple of hours before we needed to check out. I was pretty sure breakfast went until at least ten thirty. If not, there were plenty of other places we could eat.

As I faced him again... nope. Still couldn't disturb him. I wasn't normally one to stare at a man while he slept, but I normally wasn't involved with someone I couldn't risk spending a whole night with. Indulging this one time hardly seemed like it should be out of the question.

The longer I gazed at him, the more I saw. He had a little scar above his eyebrow. Maybe half an inch long, and so faint I only noticed because the light hit it just right.

There was another hiding below the part of his hair. Probably the souvenirs of a rough-and-tumble childhood. I had a few myself.

I also hadn't noticed how much tension he always carried until now. His face was completely relaxed, and I realized that his brow was usually furrowed like there was something stressing him out. His lips—parted slightly—almost always had a certain amount of tightness in them unless they were occupied.

A mix of guilt and concern tugged at me. How much of that tension was because of me? Obviously some of it predated our relationship—there were faint lines across his forehead and between his eyebrows where stress had worked itself into creases that were probably permanent.

A different flavor of guilt worked its way under my skin. It wasn't uncommon for those of us in the enlisted ranks to snark about how "rough" the officers must have it. We joked that Officer Candidate School and the Academy were finishing school for those too delicate to go to boot camp.

Of course I knew there was plenty of stress and loads of demands put on officers. I didn't envy them for the decisions they had to make, especially in combat situations. If I struggled with the idea of a couple of my young MAs walking into a volatile domestic call on my watch, I could only imagine what it was like to order an aircraft carrier and its crew of five thousand to sail into potentially hostile territory.

But still, there was a certain amount of animosity between their ranks and ours. We were the ones who got our hands dirty, did the grunt work, and got paid significantly less. In fact, even though I hadn't looked at the pay charts in a long time, I'd have bet good money that Brent—an O-3 with just a few years under his belt—earned significantly more than I did as an E-8 after damn near twenty years. A fucking *ensign* probably still earned more than I did.

So yeah, I'd long ago jumped on the us versus them bitterness bandwagon. But now I was sharing a bed with an officer. A young one. One who was still early in his career, long before he'd ever have to point an aircraft carrier into unfriendly waters or send a unit of ground troops into the line of fire.

The thought of him being in that position made me want to pull him into my arms, even if it meant waking him up. It was a weird feeling, suddenly being fiercely protective of a man who was a few levels above my paygrade. He wasn't a kid—especially not like my young MAs who were less than a year out of high school—but in a way, he was. Too young, I thought, to be carrying that much stress. And it would only get worse the further he went up the ranks. Didn't I know it.

Brent murmured something and burrowed into the pillow. His stubble hissed across the fabric. Then his eyelids fluttered, and as soon as they were open, his gaze fixed right on me. The sleepy smile that spread across his lips made my blood pump faster. How could someone be that simultaneously sexy and adorable?

As I stared at him, I suddenly understood why I was so irrationally protective of him—I wanted him to be happy. With his career, with me, with everything. Like no one else I'd ever been with, his happiness was almost painfully important to me.

So this is what it feels like to be willing to move mountains for someone.

He slid a hand up my chest. "Morning."

"Morning." I kissed his forehead. "Sleep well?"

"Oh my *God*, yeah. Like the dead." He yawned and scrubbed his hand over his face. "How long have you been awake, anyway?"

"Long enough to stare creepily at you."

Brent laughed. He slid closer and cuddled against me. "Better be careful doing that. You'll give yourself a boner that I'll have to take care of."

I guided his hand under the sheets. "Funny you should mention that..."

———

All too soon, we had to leave our comfortable bed and huge room. After one last long, sensual roll between the sheets, we went downstairs for a leisurely breakfast. Then we checked out of the hotel, but we still had several hours before we needed to head back to the coast, so we left our bags in our cars and the cars in the parking garage.

The day was chilly, but not unpleasant. Brisk and crisp, if anything.

Our walk took us past a few shops, and then a cab took us out to the Japanese gardens that we'd discussed on Saturday. They weren't in full bloom this time of year, and certainly not crowded, but it was a nice place to wander around. The grounds were meticulously groomed, and the hardier plants that could stand the wet chill of a Pacific Northwest November were green and robust.

"We should come back here when the cherry blossoms bloom," I said. "I've never been much of a flower guy, but I have to say—they're gorgeous."

"You've been here before?"

"Not here, no. But I went to a cherry blossom festival in

Japan." I chuckled at the memory. "If you ever get the chance, go to one of those. Like, in Japan. Not here."

"Oh yeah?" He glanced at me, eyebrows up. "What are they like?"

"They're something else. The parades get kind of wild, and the music is awesome. The street food..." I laughed, shaking my head. "Let's just say you want to be careful what you order."

"How's that?"

"Because you might think you're ordering a pastry with fruit in it, and realize at the last second there's a goddamned tentacle sticking out."

He burst out laughing, oblivious to what that did to me. "You're kidding."

"Nope. One of my buddies got what he thought was a pancake with fruit in it. Turns out it was, as he called it, an octo-pancake."

Brent wrinkled his nose. "Gross."

"Eh, he said it wasn't half bad. He just wasn't expecting it."

"Surprise tentacle," Brent said with a smirk. "It *is* another world over there, isn't it?"

"It is. I still have my fingers crossed I'll get orders there eventually. I'd love to actually live in Japan and see what it's really like."

"Yeah, me too." He glanced at me again, and his smile faded. So did mine. As if there weren't already plenty of things ready and waiting to separate us, there was one more —the reality that the Navy would eventually send one or both of us to another base.

I didn't want to think about that, though. Not today.

I cleared my throat. "I ever tell you about the time my

buddies and I ended up shooting pool with a bunch of guys we thought were yakuza?"

His eyes widened. "No way."

"Yep. Ironically, we weren't at one of the clubs that was off-limits because of yakuza activity. But one of my friends started shit-talking in Japanese to a couple of really well-dressed guys at the next pool table, and the next thing I know, we're having an informal tournament with them."

"How'd you figure out they were yakuza?"

"The one who did the shit-talking, he said he heard one of them say... I don't know, something. But he suddenly decided we needed to get the hell out of there." I rolled my eyes. "Except he'd already committed us to this stupid tournament, so we ended up staying another two hours until they'd beaten us."

Brent laughed. "Did you let them win?"

"Let them? Please. I was twenty-two and had the ego to go with it." I shook my head. "No, I tried like hell to win, but they were *that* good. When it was over, they bought us beers and then left. To this day I don't know if they were actually yakuza, or they were trolling us, but they were definitely intimidating."

"That's a hell of a sea story." He glanced at me, eyes sparkling. "Sounds like you have some good ones."

"Oh, I have a few."

"Yeah? Tell me."

I slid my hands into my pockets and took a deep breath of the crisp air. "Well, there was the time one of my friends got drunk and tried to take a stripper on the boat with him..."

We wandered for a while, Brent laughing as I regaled him with the wild stories of my time at sea. He had a few too, but he'd only done one shipboard deployment so far.

A comfortable silence settled between us, and we walked through the empty gardens for a while. As we were strolling along a path we'd been down twice already, Brent released a long breath, making a little cloud in the air. "This was nice. Spending the weekend up here."

"Yeah, it was." I tucked my hands into my coat pockets, as much for warmth as to keep them to myself. "I'm glad we did this."

He turned to me, and his smile sent a pleasant shiver through me. "If you want to come out here again or maybe hit up some other city..."

"I don't think you'll have to twist my arm."

"You definitely won't have to twist mine." We kept walking for a minute or so, but then he slowed and stopped. "Listen, um..." He dropped his gaze, but not before I saw the pink in his cheeks. "As long as we're in a city where we don't know anybody, do you, uh..." He swallowed. Then he looked in my eyes again. "Are you opposed to being... physical? In public?"

"Depends on how physical you mean." I grinned. "I seem to recall the first time I fucked you was in public."

Brent squirmed. "Yeah, but that was in a gay bar. And in the restroom. It wasn't quite"—he made a sweeping gesture at our surroundings—"*this* public."

I put a hand on his waist and pulled him a little closer. "It's always a risk, but right now, it kind of seems worth it."

He swallowed again and slid his hands up my chest. "Yeah. It definitely seems worth it." He held my gaze. I held his. Everything around us seemed to freeze in place while the air between us was damn near vibrating.

Finally, he wrapped his arms around my neck and I put mine around his waist, and the space between us disappeared.

His lips were cool thanks to the crisp morning, but they warmed quickly, especially as they parted to let my tongue slide past.

It was a deep kiss, a passionate one, but still somehow mellow. Like we both knew this wasn't going to end with sweat and orgasms, and we were both completely okay with that. We'd reached that point where we could kiss—really kiss—without being overwhelmed by the need to rip off each other's clothes and fuck each other senseless. Maybe because we'd already had so much sex this weekend. Or maybe because we both knew damn well we'd have plenty more.

Or maybe we'd passed the point of being fuck buddies, and a kiss like this one could exist all by itself. It wasn't foreplay—it *was* the main event.

Which didn't seem like it should surprise me that much. After all, hadn't I spent an inordinate amount of time this morning watching him sleep and wishing I could somehow protect him from everything unpleasant in the world? Because making him happy was suddenly absolutely critical?

I pulled back enough to meet his gaze.

Oh shit. I was right.

So much for fuck buddies.

CHAPTER 16

BRENT

NOW THAT WE were checked out of our hotel, my enthusiasm was definitely tempered by the slowly building disappointment. I didn't want this weekend to end, but it had to. Anything we did today was just delaying the inevitable.

I was happy to keep delaying it as long as possible, though. Even if it was a little tougher to work up the excitement like I had on Friday and Saturday, this still beat the hell out of the lonely drive back to Anchor Point and my empty apartment. Or my job.

I suppressed a shudder as I continued walking beside Will. We'd finished at the gardens, and now we were on the hunt for lunch. Neither of us was exactly starving yet, and Portland was a hell of a foodie town, so we were both enjoying checking out the seemingly endless options.

I had no idea where we were by this point. Portland wasn't a place I'd visited enough to really know my way around. Will probably didn't know it well either, but we had GPS on our phones, and push came to shove, we could grab a cab back to the hotel. Getting lost wasn't a big concern.

Halfway down some block or another, Will suddenly stopped in his tracks. "Whoa, I didn't know this town had a Chicken 'N' Fire."

I gave the red and yellow sign a wary side-eye. "Oh God. Not that place."

"You've had the pleasure, I take it?"

"Uh-huh. Their wing sauce is fucking brutal."

Will chuckled. "So, what you're saying is… you had your ass handed to you by some Chicken McNuggets?"

"Chicken McNuggets?" I sputtered. "Have you eaten here?"

His eyebrow rose. "I've done their hot wings challenge."

"Okay, but have you *beaten* the challenge?"

"Well." He cleared his throat. "Not quite. But I lived to tell about it."

"You ever going to try again? See if you can actually beat it?"

Will's eyes narrowed a little, and he grinned. "Is that…" He cupped his ear and furrowed his brow. "Is that the sound of a gauntlet dropping?"

"Maybe."

"Fine." He shrugged and met my gaze. "But you're doing it with me."

Oh fuck.

"Sure." I gave my best flippant shrug. "Let's do it."

Fuck. Did I really just sign up for this?

"You sure?" Will smirked. "If that sauce is too much for you, we don't have—"

"I'm good." I nodded toward the restaurant. "Game on. Loser picks up the bill."

He laughed. "Better have your credit card standing by,

then." He winked, then pulled open the door and gestured for me to go inside. "After you."

Me and my big mouth. I went into the restaurant, and my eyes started watering almost immediately. The fucking *air* was spicy. By the time we sat down, my neck was already beading with sweat, though I was pretty sure that was because I was nervous as hell about facing down their hot wing challenge. I liked hot stuff as much as the next guy. Hot sauce was sometimes the only way to make ship food palatable, so by the time my first deployment ended, I'd developed a serious tolerance. Right now, it was a question of whether my tolerance was high enough for the kind of hot that, according to the menu, separated the men from the boys?

Crap...

I wasn't sure I wanted to know the details of the challenge, but I flipped to the page anyway so I could see what I was up against. The Chicken 'N' Fire's hot wing challenge was pretty standard. You had a set amount of time to eat a certain number of ridiculously hot wings, and if you did it without getting sick, your name went on the wall of fame.

I searched the room and found the wall of fame in question. It was a huge bulletin board with paper flames, and there were Polaroids of all the winners.

All *nine* of them.

I was so fucked.

"Ghost pepper blend?" I rolled my eyes. "Why do they bother putting other spices and shit into something like that? Two seconds after it touches your mouth, all you can taste is pain anyway."

Will laughed. "If you're scared, you don't have to do it."

"Hey! I didn't say I was scared. I just don't understand why they bother flavoring it."

"Beats me. So are we doing this or not?"

My eyes were watering just thinking about it, but I could hear the undertone of his question. It wasn't *Are we doing this?* It was *Can you* handle *this?*

Pride goeth before the fall and all of that shit. "Yeah." I swallowed. "Let's do this."

It hadn't occurred to me that if I failed to finish the wings, I wouldn't be able to hide my shame. Not that Will would let me forget it, but I hadn't considered the other people in the restaurant. Not until the manager brought us our order.

"We've got two ghost wing challengers over here!" He made a grand gesture of setting the plates in front of us. "You boys ready for this?"

All around us, heads turned and people applauded in encouragement. My face was already burning and I hadn't even taken a bite.

I tried to ignore the small crowd, instead focusing on my nemeses—the wings slathered in sauce made of ghost peppers and whatever the fuck they'd been "blended" with.

The plates were surprisingly small, and the wings were arranged in semicircles. There was no celery or blue cheese in sight, either. Just half a dozen hot wings, smothered in a bright-red sauce that I was reasonably certain would actually glow if we shut off the lights.

Will grinned across the table and our wings. "You ready?"

It was only six wings. How bad could it be?

"Yep. I'm ready."

"All right, gentlemen." The manager held up a stopwatch. "You've got thirty minutes. Time starts..." He clicked the button. "Now!"

Will and I each grabbed a wing and dove in. If there

was one thing I'd learned with hot wings, it was that you bit in and started eating. You didn't bother adapting to the heat because it wasn't going to happen. Might as well swallow as much as possible before—

Oh.

Oh God.

Oh sweet Jesus, what had I gotten myself into?

Two bites in, and I couldn't feel the chicken now because my tongue was too busy burning with the fires of hell. Before I'd finished the first wing, a badly timed cough got some of the heat up into my sinuses. My eyes teared up so fast I almost—*almost*—forgot what I was doing and wiped them with my hand. That would've been a disaster.

Across from me, Will dabbed his eyes with the back of his wrist. His face was already red. Judging by the warmth in mine, I probably matched the demonic sauce that was currently chewing its way through my fingertips, soft palate, and sinuses.

Will dropped the first bone on the plate and reached for another. He took a bite, then paused and pulled in a breath through his mouth, probably trying to cool the fire. "Fuck..."

"What's wrong, Senior Chief?" I grinned. "Too hot for you?"

He glared at me, sweat gleaming on his forehead. "That's an awful lot of talk for a man who's still on his first wing."

"Fuck you." I dropped the bone on the plate and picked up a second. Like the first, I started eating it without giving myself a chance to think about it. How my pain receptors still worked at this point was a mystery, but the new wing meant a fresh barrage of flames. Allegedly there were some other flavors in there too. I was starting to think the "blend" portion of the sauce consisted of battery acid and hatred.

Otherwise it was just a waste of perfectly good spices that might otherwise be *tasted*.

We both finished wing number two, and the bones clattered onto the plates, much to the delight of our growing crowd of spectators.

Will ate the third so fast, I wondered if he'd said to hell with it and taken the bone too, but no, it dropped on the plate with the others, stripped of meat and torment. I was barely two pitiful nibbles into number three when he finished number four. Asshole.

He picked up a napkin off the stack and dabbed at his face. "One of my buddies did this, and..." He stopped to grimace and take a few more breaths as he mopped sweat off his forehead. "Said he wanted to lick the inside of the ship's reactor. To cool down."

"Uh. Yeah." I gagged. "I can relate."

We looked at each other, and I couldn't tell if it was endorphins or just the stupidity of the situation we'd gotten ourselves into, but we both burst out laughing. Maybe crying a little too. But mostly laughing. Because there we were, getting our asses kicked by tiny chicken wings covered in the sauce extracted from the surface of the sun, with sweat and tears streaming down our faces, and somehow this was supposed to be fun, and right then, all of that was hilarious.

"Fifteen minutes left," the manager helpfully pointed out.

My laughter died, and I cleared my throat. "Fuck my life."

Will chuckled. "C'mon. You can do it."

"Fuck you."

He just laughed and picked up another wing. The clock kept ticking. People kept cheering. Somehow—God only knew how at this point—we kept eating. I didn't bother doing anything about the tears now, even though I was irrationally worried they'd burn right through my skin.

Suddenly everyone was chanting, "Go! Go! Go!"

And I realized why—Will was down to his last wing. He was struggling—wincing between bites and pausing twice to gag like he was *this* close to puking—but damn if he wasn't killing it.

He threw the bone down so hard it nearly bounced off the plate, and he pumped his fists in the air. Everyone roared, and my face burned hotter. I was getting my ass kicked by the wings *and* him?

"Nicely done!" The manager clapped his back. "Grab this guy a beer."

"Yes, please." Will picked up a napkin and wiped it over his face. "Coldest one you've got."

All eyes were suddenly on me again. A whole different kind of heat rushed into my face.

To my surprise, though, the sudden pressure of everyone, including Will, watching me gave me a second wind. I finished the wing, dropped it, and picked up another. By now, the endorphins really should've been making this easier, but... no. The fifth was harder than the four before it. My stomach lurched a couple of times, and I had to slow down a little to keep from getting sick. Which, of course, meant "savoring" the "ghost pepper blend" for a few more agonizing seconds.

Somehow, though, while I was wallowing in how horrible it was and how there was no way in hell I could do this, I'd reduced the wing to bones.

I dropped it on the plate and exhaled, which only seemed to make the fire worse.

"Come on," Will said over his beer, which was already half gone. "You've got this. Just one more."

I glared at his plate through my tears. Yep. Nothing but bones. "How the fuck did you do that?"

"Same way you're going to—one bite at a time. C'mon. You can do it." He took a swig of beer. My mouth watered with envy. Which... made it burn more.

I shifted my glare to the one remaining wing. The dripping monstrosity of a chicken wing covered in glowing orange horror. I'd eaten five. I could eat one more.

When I picked it up, the sauce stung my fingers. They weren't raw, but they weren't far from it—apparently the wings were eating me right back.

Will sipped his beer. My mouth watered some more. The sooner I beat the little bastard on my plate, the sooner I could have a cold beer too.

Steeling myself, I tore into the wing and somehow managed not to curse. Or puke. Or stop.

When I tossed the bone on the plate, the whole place erupted into cheers.

"Two winners at one table!" the manager shouted. "That's a Chicken 'N' Fire first!"

"Beer," I croaked. "I really need a beer."

"Get this boy a beer." The manager handed us a couple of Wet-Naps and towels for our hands, and clapped my shoulder. "You boys want photos by yourselves or together?"

"Uh..." I cleared my throat, eyes darting toward Will as I cleaned off my burning fingers.

He'd suddenly sobered too, and shook his head. "How about just one of each?"

I tensed. So did Will. The manager eyed us, suddenly

visibly uncomfortable as if he'd picked up on the *oh shit* passing between us.

Will coughed. "Listen, I didn't just scarf a plate of hellfire and brimstone so I could share the glory with this jackass."

I laughed and elbowed him playfully. "Hey, fuck you."

That seemed to convince the manager there was nothing to worry about. He shrugged, led us over to the wall of fame, and took our pictures.

Afterward, Will asked, "Any chance we *could* get one of the two of us after all?" He smiled. "Not for the board—as a souvenir?"

"Of course." The manager motioned for us to stand close together. We did, arms around each other's shoulders like we were a couple of friends, and gave the camera a thumbs-up. After he'd taken two photos, he handed us the Polaroids, then went to check on our drinks.

Now that we were sort of alone, Will turned toward me. "Nicely done." His eyes were still red and wet. Mine probably were too.

I smiled despite the heat. "Thanks. The encouragement helped." I licked my burning lips. "Except now I feel like I just gave Satan a rimjob."

Will threw his head back and laughed. "That's not a description I've heard before, but... yeah, it kind of makes sense."

"Can't really think of a better one at this point."

"No kidding. And, thank God, here come our drinks."

We sat back down to cool off with our beers, and while we did, I watched the manager pin up our photos with the others who'd beaten the challenge. Will and I hadn't dared be in the same frame in the photos going on the wall of fame. Even separate photos was a little risky. If anyone saw our individual pictures and recognized us, we still had some room for deniability, though. We'd been with a larger group and were the only ones who'd succeeded. Hell, coincidence —someone had recommended Chicken 'N' Fire, and we'd both picked the same weekend to give it a try.

I rolled some cold beer around on my tongue, then swallowed it. My mouth and throat were on fire like they'd never been before. I couldn't take a breath without my eyes watering, and I was genuinely shocked every time I touched my lips and they weren't bleeding. Still, I was happy we'd done the challenge, and that we'd both beaten it.

Because even if it was only a couple of Polaroids on the cheesy fiery bulletin board of a hot wing restaurant, there was one place on this earth with evidence that we'd been there together.

I didn't think I'd ever been more disappointed to see my own car.

We'd put it off as long as possible. After killing the hot wing challenge, we'd stuck around the chicken place for a while, mostly to let some ice-cold drinks soothe the burn. Then we'd wandered around town in search of... well, anything. We'd even swung by a theater to try seeing that movie again—wasn't like either of us was in any danger of getting frisky—but we'd missed the matinee by twenty minutes.

And now it was time to call it a day.

As we walked through the hotel parking garage and the cars came into view, my heart sank. The weekend was over. It was time to go home.

I wondered if this was what it felt like to have a long-distance relationship. Wedging everything into slivers of time that never seemed like quite enough, and then having to face this—going home separately—every single time.

"Well." I sighed. "I guess I'll see you back in Anchor Point."

"Yeah." He smiled sheepishly. "I'd kiss you, but I, uh, still can't feel my lips."

I laughed. "Yeah. Same here. I can't feel anything in my mouth."

"Give it a few hours. Then you'll wish you couldn't."

Groaning, I rolled my eyes. "Tell me again why I let you talk me into that?"

"Me?" He put a hand to his chest and scoffed. "It's not like I twisted your arm."

"Would you have let me hear the end of it if I hadn't?"

"Absolutely not."

"Uh-huh. Exactly."

Will chuckled.

"Anyway. I guess we should go." I paused. "This was fun. We should do it again." I regretted the words as soon as they were out. The pinch of his brow said it all.

No. No, we absolutely should not.

We shouldn't have done it this time, and we'd be fucking idiots to do it again.

But he just kissed my forehead and said, "You're right. We should."

No, we shouldn't. But we definitely will.

Halfway back to Anchor Point, my lips were still tingling from those fucking chicken wings. The rest of my body ached and tingled from other things, though. Had we ever fit that much sex into that little time? I didn't think we had, and this had been while we went out and did other things too. Going out like a real honest-to-God couple.

I grinned despite the burning in my lips. When I'd suggested the weekend away, I'd thought maybe the shine would wear off. That when we *could* be open about dating, it wouldn't be quite as fun as we'd imagined.

Maybe one of these days, I'd figure out that when it came to Will, nothing ever played out the way I expected. I sure as hell hadn't expected us to cap off the weekend by diving face-first into a ridiculous thing called "ghost pepper blend"—seriously, what the fuck had I been supposed to taste besides fire and pain? But, hey, we'd both beaten it, and we'd laughed like idiots and had a surprisingly good time, all things considered.

If I had one regret about the hot wing challenge, though, it was that I couldn't pretend I could still feel the long kiss we'd shared at the deserted garden.

He'd been right that it'd been a risk. When two guys kissed in public, especially when it lingered past a chaste peck, there was always the chance that some homophobe would harass them. Or worse. And the whole time we'd been standing there, part of me had been tuned in to our surroundings. I was pretty sure Will had been too. He was a cop, after all.

But every part of me that hadn't been carefully maintaining situational awareness had been zeroed in on Will. On how much I loved the feeling of his body pressed against mine. Not in a sexual way. More like how it had been whenever we'd woken up together—just warm and solid and strong and *there*.

I sighed, resting one hand on top of the wheel and pressing the other elbow against the window. This weekend was everything that had been missing between us. Going out together. In *public*. Not watching our backs. Falling asleep in the same bed, and waking up next to each other. I finally knew what he looked like when he was scruffy and disheveled in the morning, and that sight hadn't been a letdown at all.

Nothing about the weekend had been a letdown except the part where it had to come to an end.

Up ahead, the highway curved, then straightened out, and my high beams illuminated an all too familiar sign.

Welcome to Anchor Point.

My heart sank. The weekend was definitely over. Now I had that feeling like I'd stayed too long at a concert. Long enough to see the lights come up over the empty stage and the deserted seating area covered in trash. If the weekend had been nonstop booze and partying, this was the part when the hangover would kick in without mercy.

I didn't regret it, though. I just wished it hadn't ended. Not so soon. Not at all.

It wasn't only the excitement of fooling around in a movie theater, or the thrill of fucking against the window above the city, or the exhilaration of having the audacity to go out together in public.

It was the lazy mornings. Waking up in the middle of the night and finding him there beside me, warm and softly snoring in the darkness.

For three days, I'd had Will, and for three days, the Navy hadn't existed.

Sure, we'd talked about places we'd been and some of the things we'd done on liberty. But there'd been no shop talk. No bitching about politics, promotions, or the day-to-day drudgery.

For one weekend, we'd *almost* been civilians. Just a

couple of guys enjoying some time together like there was no reason they shouldn't. Only looking over our shoulders because we were a same-sex couple, not because someone we knew might bust us.

Pity it couldn't last.

Tomorrow, we'd be back at work. Back to the grind. If we crossed paths, he'd be there in his blue digicams—same as what I'd be wearing, except with the bulky black police belt around his waist and the pistol strapped to his thigh.

Still, I couldn't help imagining him like he'd been today. The black leather jacket. The wraparound Oakleys. The "Another Brick in the Wall" T-shirt whose irony was suddenly not lost on me.

During the day, we were both generic blue-camouflaged drones doing our jobs.

At night, though, and on the occasional weekend we could slip away, that all disappeared.

In the quiet of my car as I followed the familiar road back to my apartment, I smiled. Well, I was pretty sure I did. Still couldn't feel much from my nose down.

The weekend was over, but Portland wasn't that far away. As soon as possible, I hoped we could take off again for some more time away from the Navy. More lazy, unhurried sex. More waking up in the same bed. More going out like a real couple.

But... maybe not another hot wing challenge.

CHAPTER 17

WILL

THERE WERE days I hated how slow and boring NAS could be. On a small base like this, there were only so many people around to do so many things that actually warranted police involvement.

Then there were days when I wished it were a little slower and a little more boring.

Days like today.

I'd advised my MAs to keep an eye on the house where that domestic had happened a while back. The one where the broken glass, scraped knuckles, and dented wall had added up to something we all knew but couldn't prove.

Noah had been in my office when the call came through for police and medics. Both of our radios had crackled to life, and when the dispatcher read off that address, our eyes had locked for a split second. Then we'd been on our feet and sprinting to the parking lot.

A patrol unit beat us there, and a local ambulance wasn't far behind. Minutes later, the slight blonde woman was being led out of the house in cuffs, screaming obsceni-ties the whole way while the neighbors watched from their driveways, and her husband, shaken and bleeding, stayed on the sofa.

Noah and one of the patrols went from neighbor to neighbor to find out who'd heard or seen what. Me, I got the fun part—staying with the man who'd finally taken enough of a beating to say enough was enough.

The living room and kitchen looked like a bar brawl had happened here. A glass end table had been shattered—one of my guys wisely surrounded it with police tape to keep anyone from stepping on a shard, even with boots on. The kitchen table was shoved up against the sliding glass door, the chairs on one side toppled like kids' toys while the others were pinned between the table and the glass. Blood was smeared on the wall above a dent I distinctly remembered reading about not long ego.

The EMTs glued a cut on the husband's cheekbone and another on his arm. The wounds weren't as severe as they looked, fortunately. They happened to be in places that tended to bleed profusely enough to be terrifying. Kind of like the cut on Brent's face the night we'd met.

The husband changed out of his bloody T-shirt, put on a gray Navy T-shirt, and returned to the couch to talk to my MA2 and me. "So what happens now?"

"We need to ask you some questions," I said as calmly as I could. "JAG is being notified, but for now, it's just us."

He nodded, wringing his hands. His knuckles were bruised and raw in places, but they looked mostly healed. Like scabs on top of scabs, bruises where other bruises had already been, and scars filling in the rest—pretty typical of the maintainers down on the flight line.

Those battered, discolored hands were trembling in his lap. He didn't look at me or MA2 Sanchez. From the way his cheek tensed, I suspected he was trying really hard not to break down. In his mind, he'd probably been humiliated enough.

The kindest thing we could do at this point was get the questions over with and leave him alone. Give him some time to catch his breath before he had to talk to JAG.

Clearing my throat, I met MA2 Sanchez's eyes and nodded toward the victim.

She gulped.

I gave her what I hoped was an encouraging smile. *You can do this.* I'd have said it out loud, but we had a shaken victim who didn't need to know the cop asking him questions was second-guessing herself. She needed the experience. If she couldn't do it, I'd take over so we didn't draw this out for him.

MA2 Sanchez sat on the couch a comfortable distance away from the husband. Petty Officer Swain, according to MA2's briefing when I'd joined them.

"Can you tell me what happened?" she asked him.

His jaw worked. Yeah, he was definitely trying not to cry, and I was trying almost as hard not to remember how it felt to be in his shoes.

Swain pushed himself up and started pacing across the floor. He was favoring his left foot slightly. Could've been an old injury. Could've been something from work. Could've been... neither of those things. I made a note of it.

He folded his arms across his chest, flinching when his finger brushed the freshly glued gash above his elbow. "I've had to work a lot of long shifts lately. We're short on manning. Got someone out on maternity leave, couple of people on light duty..." He hugged himself tighter as he kept pacing. "She always thinks I'm cheating when I have to pull extra hours. So I got home late this morning. I, uh, work nights. And... she lit into me, and we got into a fight."

"How did the injuries happen?" MA2's voice was calm and even, exactly as it should've been.

Swain absently touched the bruise that was slowly spreading across his left cheek. "I'm not sure, to be honest. When... when she gets really pissed, she loses it and comes at me. Fists. Feet. Whatever. I'm..." He stopped pacing, gestured at himself, and faced us with a broken expression. "Look at me. I'm twice her size. I'm afraid to defend myself because I don't want to hurt her. So I try to, you know, stop her. Keep her still until she runs out of steam." He exhaled, then came back to the couch and sank onto the cushion, shoulders sagging with the same defeat that filled his voice. "Today, we just... It just went on for so long. When she finally stopped fighting, there was blood everywhere. I don't even know what cut me where. I guess when we clipped the corner of the counter, or maybe when the end table broke. I don't know. But... man, I can't live like this. Not anymore."

"How long has it been going on?" MA2 Sanchez asked. "The physical violence in your marriage, I mean?" Her eyes flicked toward me, brow pinched as if needing reassurance, so I nodded.

You're doing fine.

"It's been going on since..." Swain sighed, rubbing the back of his neck and avoiding my gaze. "I don't know. A long time. At least since my last deployment, which three years ago."

Goose bumps sprang up under my uniform, and I tried not to visibly shudder. My ex had roughed me up periodically over the course of one year. Three? Fuck...

MA2 glanced up at me. *What else should I ask?*

I made as subtle a gesture as I could toward the dent beneath the blood smear on the wall. Her eyes tracked in that direction and stopped.

"Swain," she said gently, "can you tell me what happened there?" She pointed with her pen at the dent.

He didn't look. I suspected he didn't have to. Sighing, he leaned forward, elbows pressed into his thighs and fingers kneading his neck. "We got in a fight. A while ago. She came at me, and we both..." He motioned toward the dent. "Never got around to fixing it, I guess."

My stomach twisted. He and his wife had hit the wall hard enough to dent it, and he was worried about fixing the damage to the plaster. Fuck.

Been there, done that, buddy.

It was a good two hours before Noah, the patrols, and I all returned to the precinct. I debriefed the patrols, mostly to make sure they were coping okay. Cops were supposed to be desensitized to this stuff, but domestics fucked with the best of them. Especially when we'd been called out to the same house enough times—it was easy to drive ourselves insane wondering if we could have prevented today.

At least it had been relatively minor. Everyone was alive. Injuries weren't severe. It could have been so, so much worse.

After I'd made sure my younger MAs were steady on their feet, I swung by Noah's office to check on him. This was hardly his first domestic, and he'd seemed solid at the scene, but I always worried about him. The job took its toll, and every once in a while, I worried something might make him relapse and start drinking again.

"Hey." I stepped into his office. "You going to be okay?"

He looked up from his computer and nodded, lips taut. "Yeah. I... think I might get out of here, though. Anthony will be here soon, and I..." He didn't finish the thought. He didn't have to. God knew I understood fully.

"Me too," I said.

He held my gaze. "You going to be okay on your own? I know this stuff doesn't, uh, sit well with you."

"I'll be fine."

With any luck, I won't be alone either.

"Okay." He gave another nod. "You know where to find me if you need me."

"Likewise."

We exchanged a look, and then I left his office. We'd both taken each other up on that offer quite a few times over the years. Me when an abuse case hit too close to home. Him during the first few months he'd been getting sober.

In my own office, I closed the door and took out my phone to text.

It's been a hell of a day. Please tell me you're free tonight.

In seconds, Brent replied, *If I wasn't before, I am now. See you as soon as I can.*

And for the first time since that call had come through, I released my breath. Tonight couldn't come soon enough.

Brent didn't ask any questions. The second my door was closed behind us, he grabbed on and kissed me, and I held on to him like my life depended on it. Kind of felt like it did.

I couldn't get Swain's face out of my mind. After my own abusive ex-boyfriend, and then Vince, I knew what it was like to be with someone I couldn't trust. To second-guess everything they said. To flinch every time they made a sudden move.

Brent was... the opposite. Ironically, since being with

him at all was dangerous in its own right, there was safety in his arms. After being in other relationships where I had to keep my guard up to a certain extent, it was amazingly liberating to let that guard down. Not that I had to let it down. As soon as he was here, it was down. Gone. Forgotten.

"Tell me what you want," he breathed.

You. All I want is you.

I kissed him and held him closer.

Brent broke the kiss and touched my cheek. "We should go in the bedroom. Get out of these clothes."

"Good idea."

And good thing I had a small apartment, so we didn't have very far to go. Just a few feet down a short hall—littering it with clothes as we went—and we were there.

Brent dropped his boxers on top of his jeans and turned to me. Grinning, he stroked himself slowly in one hand and reached for my neck with the other. "Tell me what you want," he repeated. "Anything you want tonight."

I pulled him close, sucking in a sharp breath when his arm grazed my erection. "This is exactly what I want. You. Naked. In my bedroom."

"I'm here. I'm naked." Brent licked his lips, making that slow gesture into something deliciously obscene. "What are you going to do with me?"

His hand slid up the shaft of his dick, and his knuckles grazed my stomach. I looked down, watching him touch himself between us. The sight of his cock—thick and hard and ready—made my mouth water.

Without a word, I went to my knees, held his hips in both hands, and took his cock as far into my mouth as I could. Brent whispered profanity, cradling the back of my head as I deep-throated him.

My own cock desperately needed attention, so I stroked

it slowly to take the edge off. Mostly, though, I concentrated on Brent's. On making him shiver and gasp.

"Oh fuck, Will," he murmured. "You like having your mouth fucked, don't you?"

The dirty talk drove me wild coming from him. I moaned an affirmative and licked around the head to be sure he understood. He responded with a low, helpless sound and raked his fingers through my short hair.

"*God.*" He rocked his hips, just pushing my gag reflex. "Oh fuck, yeah... oh yeah..." A shudder rippled through him, and I glanced up in time to see him look down at me with heavy-lidded eyes. He licked his lips again. "I want to fuck you tonight."

I let him slide out of my mouth, and slurred, "Yeah. Please."

"You want that?" It was a playful taunt, like he wanted me to beg, but with a subtle note of uncertainty. Even with his pupils blown from arousal, his eyes were still full of the same question he'd had when he'd arrived—*What do you want me to do?*

"Fuck me," I whispered, and as soon as the words were out, I couldn't have him soon enough. "Please fuck me."

He held out his hand. I clasped mine around his forearm, and with a little help from him—and an audible protest from one knee—I stood. He threw his other arm around my waist and kissed me deeply, kneading my ass cheek as his tongue played with mine.

When we came up for air, we were both out of breath, and he nodded toward the bed. "Now."

Oh hell yeah.

He grabbed a condom and lube from the drawer, and we both got on the bed. Once he had on the condom, he knelt behind me. Slick fingers teased, then probed. I was worried he'd spend half the night fingering me to drive me insane, but he didn't do it for long. Just enough to lube me up and stretch me a little.

After he'd withdrawn his fingers, he nudged me all the way down onto the mattress. His knee gently pushed my thighs apart, and I closed my eyes as his weight settled over me.

He slid the head of his cock back and forth along my crack, stopping now and then to press against my hole before he continued teasing.

I gripped the edge of the mattress. "C'mon. C'mon. I want..."

He stopped again, giving me just enough to make me think he was going to push in this time.

"Brent... God... I need—"

Everything blurred as the head slipped past the tight ring.

"That what you want?" he taunted in a husky voice.

"Uh-huh."

He withdrew, then slid back in. He could've easily forced himself all the way to the hilt without hurting me, but he took his time anyway, steadily working his cock deeper. And, holy fuck, I loved it. The stretch, the invasiveness, the warmth of his body covering mine, the hot huffs of breath rushing past my neck—it didn't get any better than this.

"You feel so good," he purred in my ear as he took a slow, deep stroke. "Jesus, Will."

I closed my eyes, pressing my forehead into the pillow and arching up to touch as much of him as I could. "So... so do you."

He nuzzled my neck and exhaled. "Fuck. I could do this

all night, but... not gonna last." The faltering restraint in his voice made my balls tighten.

"Same." I tried to rock my hips—not that I could do much in this position—and my head spun as my dick rubbed against the sheets and his slid across my prostate. "Ungh. Brent..."

"Don't come yet," he panted in my ear. "I want..." He shuddered. "I'm gonna come, and then I'm going to... suck you off."

"Oh God." Not coming was suddenly a lot easier said than done. "You're gonna make me come like this."

"No," he whispered, lips grazing my neck. "I'm right there. I want..." He shuddered again, driving himself into me so hard we both grunted. "Not yet." The line between begging and commanding were impossibly blurred, and the desperation in his voice was unbearably sexy.

So was the low, crescendoing moan he released as his body started to tremble. He was all the way inside me, and his hips jerked as if he thought he could still get a little deeper, and his fingers dug into my arms as he buried his face against my neck and came.

With one last shudder, he sank on top of me and exhaled cool breath across my skin. His weight, his heat, his breathing—he was on me and all around me, and I was distantly aware of something that had made me desperate for all of this, but the only thing I could focus on was right now. I couldn't remember why I'd needed relief, only that I had it. That he felt so good I was halfway to tears.

Brent lifted himself up and pulled out. I wanted to protest even though I knew he had to, but then he said, "Turn over. On your back."

I rolled onto my back, and Brent didn't waste any time. He tapped my thigh so I parted my legs, and he settled between them. Electricity crackled along my nerve endings —fuck, I was so close to losing it already, and the anticipation of his mouth had me hovering on the brink. Then he pushed two fingers into me in the same moment he swallowed my cock almost to the base.

"*Oh* yeah," I moaned, stroking his hair as he worked his magic on me. "God, yeah, you're gonna make me..."

Instead of backing off, he must've taken that as a challenge, and he gave me everything he had. The fingers inside me curled just right, and his lips and tongue relentlessly teased my cock, and my neighbors—hell, *his* neighbors—had to have heard me when I cried out with the force of my orgasm, and he didn't quit. He fingered me and sucked me until I made a pitiful pleading sound that somehow translated to S*top, no more.*

He lifted his head and slid his fingers free. I collapsed back on the bed—apparently I'd arched up off it—as he rose up to kiss me. He only stayed for a second, just long enough to let me taste the salt on his tongue, before he left to take care of the condom.

I didn't move. I was too comfortable. Too fucking blissed out and relaxed and perfect. The only thing that could make this better was him pressed up against me, and I wouldn't have to wait long for that part. After he'd put me through the delicious wringer, fucking the stress right out of me before capping it off with a short, spectacular blowjob, I was too spent to be impatient.

I was right—he didn't keep me waiting long. Or maybe I just dozed off for a minute. Whatever the case, I opened my eyes as he was sliding into bed beside me, and *now* everything was perfect.

He pushed himself up onto his elbow and gazed down at me. He trailed his fingers along the side of my head like he always did when I'd recently had my hair cut. "You okay?"

I nodded. "I am now."

That was the extent of his questions. I liked that about him—he knew I'd speak up if I wanted to, but he didn't dig. Especially not while it was obviously still raw.

I cupped his face and looked in his gorgeous eyes. "Thank you. I needed this."

Brent smiled. "Good. Glad I could help." He leaned in and kissed me.

This was so perfect. Especially after the day I'd had, but also in its own right. I was never more relaxed and content than I was when Brent was lying next to me.

I stroked his hair.

I might be stupid for dating you at all.

In fact, I am stupid for dating you at all.

I pressed a tender kiss to the top of his head.

But I'd be a fucking idiot not to fall for you.

CHAPTER 18

BRENT

NIGHT AFTER NIGHT, I found myself in bed with Will. I didn't think I'd ever spent more time naked than I had since I started seeing him. It had long since become normal, though. The whole day could be chaotic or painfully boring, and I could be at the end of a fraying thread, ready to lose my shit completely, and then... ah. There. Tangled up with his warm, familiar body under either his sheets or mine. It was like hitting the reset button on my brain. Something told me that if we just climbed into bed together and didn't have sex, it would have the same effect. It wasn't the sweat and orgasms—it was *him*.

But we probably wouldn't be testing that theory anytime soon. Once I was in bed with him, sex was pretty much inevitable. I couldn't get enough of him, and he wasn't showing any signs of getting tired of me either. For all he joked about getting old and not being able to keep up with a young guy like me, he did *just* fine.

Tonight was like any night. Sort of. We were at his place, comfortable and satisfied together, but he'd been a little distant earlier. Not standoffish, and definitely not far enough away to turn down my playful come-ons, but there'd been something else there. And I had a feeling I knew what it was.

I turned on my side and lifted myself up on my elbow. Draping my arm across his chest, I said, "You okay?"

He nodded and absently played with my hair. "Just a long day. Well, long week. But..." He smiled, genuinely if a little sleepily. "I'm okay."

"Good. And I, uh, meant to ask, but how are you doing? After the other night?"

Will shrugged, and I had the distinct impression he was trying not to shudder. "Better."

"Glad to hear it." I ran my fingers along the shaved side of his head. He had a severe high and tight, so he must've had his hair cut in the last day or so. The back and sides were shaved to the skin, and the top was just long enough to almost mess up when we were fooling around. I loved it like that. I liked the way the sides gently abraded my fingertips when I ran them across.

We were quiet for a little while, but I couldn't let go of the thought about the other night. It had really shaken him, and even now, it didn't seem like it had gone away.

I rested my hand on his chest again and studied him, trying to read him. "I'm curious about what happened. I mean, if you don't want to talk about it..."

His eyes lost focus. I thought for a moment he'd tell me the bedroom wasn't where he wanted to think about that shit, but then he quietly said, "We had a domestic. I mean, we get those all the time in base housing. Difference was that this call was... one I've been expecting for a while."

"Expecting? How so?"

"The couple seemed like a time bomb. My guys have been called out to their place several times, and it kept escalating. Husband and wife were both really good at coming up with excuses for dents in the wall or broken glass or whatever."

I grimaced. "Holy shit."

"Yeah. This time, I guess it was finally bad enough for him to press charges against her."

"Oh, it was the wife beating him up?"

Will nodded. "Happens more often than you think. Doesn't get reported as much, but we see it a lot." He shifted uncomfortably, gaze still fixed someplace else. "When it's repeat incidents like this, we're always afraid it's going to get too far out of control before we can actually do anything."

"Like someone's going to get killed?"

The shudder answered the question well enough.

"Does that happen?" I winced at my own stupidity. "I mean, on base. Do you ever see murders and things like that?"

"They're rare on bases, especially smaller ones like Adams, but they happen."

"And you've... been to them?"

Will nodded again. Then, slowly, he took in a breath. "Remember how I told you I hate domestics?"

"Yeah?"

He swallowed. "Years ago, there was a couple in base housing. We kept getting called out to their house, and we all knew what was happening, but we couldn't prove it. And as long as we didn't see anything and she wouldn't press charges..." He sighed. "What could we do?"

I studied him, then laced our fingers together. "What happened?"

"We got called out. Again. Neighbor heard something and called us." His eyes were distant, and he was silent for a long moment. "My partner and I were the first on the scene. We..." He paused, then met my gaze. "We were the ones to call into dispatch and report that our domestic was now a homicide."

My heart dropped. "Oh my God."

"They train you for that stuff, you know? They tell you over and over that eventually, it's going to happen. You're going to be the first to show up at a crime scene." Shaking his head, he said, more to himself, "They can train you for decades, but nothing really prepares you for it."

"I can't imagine anything could."

His Adam's apple bobbed. "No. So, ever since then, whenever we get a domestic—especially when it's a house we've been to more than once—I go right back to that day."

"Has it ever happened since then?"

"Not on my watch, fortunately, but yeah... it's happened." He didn't elaborate.

I studied him for a moment, then whispered, "How do you do it?"

"What do you mean?"

"I mean, I have to psych myself up every day to face a desk and paperwork. You come to work and... shit, you never know what you're going to deal with."

"If I don't do it, who will?"

"I know someone has to do it," I said. "I just... How do you stay sane?"

He absently trailed his hand up and down my arm. "Because sometimes you can keep it from happening. The day I met you, that whole thing could've gotten ugly if my MAs hadn't intervened. Yeah, they needed backup, but in the end, everyone calmed down, and nobody got hurt."

I swallowed, remembering all too clearly how sure I'd been that Jenna's husband was going to rip my head off once the two of them had finished their screaming match. I'd never in my life been more relieved to see the cops, even if I'd been scared the report would hurt my career.

"That's the kind of thing that keeps me going," he said. "Knowing that we sometimes keep the really bad shit from happening."

"I guess I can see that. Feeling like you're actually doing something."

He nodded. "And, really, even with the bad shit, this is what I want to do. I like my job. I like the Navy. I like being a cop. It's hard as fuck, and there are days that keep me awake at night, but it's definitely my calling."

The words prodded at me in a weird way. When he talked about his job being his calling, even after almost twenty years and with all the horrific crap it threw at him, there was an undercurrent of passion in his voice. It wasn't just a path he was following because it was the path laid out in front of him. It was who he was.

I should have been able to relate to that. I should have been able to nod along and say, *Yeah, me too—I know exactly what you mean.*

But where that passion should've been? Nothing. Not a goddamned thing. And it wasn't a void that could be filled with my usual platitudes about paying my dues or getting there eventually. What the fuck?

"Hey." He touched my cheek. "You're spacing out on me."

I shook myself. "Sorry. Just..." *Wondering when I stopped knowing who the hell I am.* I cleared my throat and smiled. "I'm good."

"You sure?"

I had a dozen assurances on the tip of my tongue. Mostly bland shit about being all right, just thinking, being distracted, whatever. But looking at him now, realizing that for all I was bored and frustrated with my life these days, that predestined Navy path had led me here. Maybe my job sucked right now, but it seemed like a small price to pay for nights like this.

For him, the horrific parts of his job were worth it whenever he could defuse a situation and keep people safe. When he got to be that thin blue line that meant the difference between someone getting hurt and not.

For me, right now, the boring, demoralizing, and seemingly endless drudgery of my job seemed worth it when I came home and landed in bed next to him.

Smiling for real this time, I trailed my fingers along the shaved side of his head. "Yeah. I'm good."

Then I leaned in and kissed him, and no one asked any more questions that night.

———

As much as I loved winding up in bed with him most evenings, I had to admit that, especially after our trip to Portland, the bedroom walls were closing in. Now that I knew what it was like to be out with Will, I wished like hell we could actually *date*. It would be nice to have a change of scenery and go somewhere besides one of our apartments without having to dash off in separate cars to another city. Maybe eat something that didn't involve tipping a driver. This was the reality of dating him, though, so I sucked it up.

But it wasn't all bad. Having the same scenery over and over wasn't a *horrible* imposition when that meant spending a lot of time under the sheets.

Sprawled across his bed, I wiped some sweat off my

forehead. "I don't think I've ever had this much sex in this little time."

Will laughed. "I can't remember the last time I had this much *good* sex."

A pleasant shiver ran through me. "Ditto." I circled his nipple with my nail, grinning when he pulled in a sharp breath, and added, "We should go back to Portland. Like, stat."

"I know. Definitely." He paused, then frowned. "Except my next off weekend is Thanksgiving weekend."

"Thanks— Aw, fuck. Is that really coming up already?"

"Yep." He groaned. "Under two weeks now, and I am so not looking forward to it."

I laughed humorlessly. "Sounds like you're about as enthusiastic about it as I am."

"Yeah?"

"Yep." I trailed my fingertips through his dark chest hair. "So why don't you want to go?"

"Because I hate pretending to be straight."

The answer—not to mention the bitterness coating it— made my stomach flip. "Your family doesn't know you're gay?"

"Oh, they know I'm gay." He sighed. "They just refuse to acknowledge it. So we agreed a long time ago that I'm gay except in their house."

"How the hell does that work?"

"Basically, I don't discuss boyfriends or dating with them, and they don't ask me when I'm settling down with a woman."

I studied him, trying to proceed with caution. "Didn't you have a boyfriend for a long time, though?"

"Six years," he said quietly, absently sliding his hand up

and down my arm. "And I never once said his name to them."

"Wow. I can't imagine."

"It sucks." He cleared his throat and turned toward me. "So why is Thanksgiving such a drag for you?"

"Besides traveling to the East Coast during the busiest travel week of the year?"

"Besides that, yeah."

I pushed out a breath. "Because the conversation will revolve entirely around my job and my brother's job. So... the Navy. Like, I don't mind discussing my job, you know? But give it a *rest* once in a while."

Will nodded. "I can totally understand that. It sounds exhausting. And I'm not looking forward to it either."

"Yeah?"

"Yeah." He exhaled. "For the opposite reason—what I *won't* be able to talk about."

"Which is?"

Will looked in my eyes. "You. I'm used to not being able to talk about you because of our ranks. But it'll be weird to have to keep quiet because..." The sadness in his eyes made my throat tighten. He brought our hands up and pressed a kiss to my knuckles. "Because you're a man."

My heart sank. Fuck. It was hard to imagine not being able to tell my parents I had a boyfriend. Then again, I wasn't so sure I could tell them about this one. Not without very carefully omitting a few details.

He gently freed his hand and caressed my face, lightly callused fingers scuffing across the stubble on my jaw. "I wish I could tell them about you."

Forget sinking—my heart wanted to break. "They'd probably remind you that we're technically fraternizing." *Really, Brent? That's where you went with that?*

But Will sighed. He slid his hand up into my hair, drew me in, and kissed me softly. "Is it weird that half the time, I completely forget we shouldn't be doing this?"

"So it's not just me, then."

"No. Definitely not."

I drew back again so we could see each other. "I know this is still a bad idea. I know we should have stopped before we started." I touched his face, fingertips hissing across his five-o'clock shadow. "But I also know I don't want to."

"Neither do I. I mean, I…" Will pressed his cheek against my hand. "I thought we were just fooling around, and maybe we were, but it doesn't really feel like that anymore."

I swallowed. "No, it doesn't."

It hasn't for a long time.

Since at least before we went to Portland.

Oh God. I am really in over my head, aren't I?

I trailed my fingers along the side of his head. "How long before the novelty wears off and the secrecy gets old?"

"The secrecy got old a long time ago. And I figured when it did, I'd want to jump ship." He sighed as he slid his palm up my arm. "But I don't. I'm just frustrated that I've met someone like you, and I can't breathe a word about it to anyone."

My stomach fluttered. He had a hell of a knack for saying exactly what I was thinking but hadn't been able to put into words, and hearing my own thoughts on his lips was both a rush because he felt the same, and heartbreaking because what the hell could we do about it? At the end of the day, the secrecy wasn't negotiable. We either did this in the dark or we didn't do it at all, and that second part had stopped being an option somewhere in that space between fucking in a bathroom stall and waking up together in Portland.

"Maybe we *do* need some time away again," I whispered. "After we both get back from seeing our families."

Will nodded. "I don't think there's any *maybe* about it. I need to kick out the rest of the world and just be with you. After I've been with my family?" He whistled.

"Yeah. Me too. Especially the family part." *Especially the "just be with you" part.*

A tired smile played at his lips. "Well, we've still got another week or so before we have to run off for the holidays." The way his hand was drifting down toward my hip made me squirm.

"You're right." I pressed against him as my cock started to stir. "What do you think we should do with it?"

"I think you know."

He lifted his head, pulled me in, and we both sank to the bed in a kiss that very quickly went from sweet to *oh fuck yes*. There was a renewed sense of urgency too. Not the frantic need for sex because we'd been pretending not to know each other all day, but the need to exploit every single second we had at our disposal before we had to be apart for a long weekend. Holding him closer, kissing him harder, I needed us to be sweating and panting and fucking, but more than that, I needed us to be *here*.

Oh yeah. I'm in way over my head.

And I don't care if I drown.

CHAPTER 19

WILL

I'D KNOWN Noah long enough to be able to read him like a book. We were cops too, so picking up on things sort of came with the territory. He'd tried his damnedest to keep his cards close to his vest, but I'd always seen right through him. Maybe I'd been in denial for a good long time because I hadn't wanted to admit my best friend had a serious drinking problem, but even the subtle signs hadn't escaped my notice.

So it really wasn't a surprise that it cut both ways. Especially these days when Noah was sober.

It was two days before Thanksgiving, so the precinct was utterly dead. A lot of people were on leave, and I was heading out myself at the end of shift. Noah had taken last Thanksgiving off, so he was working over the holiday, though I suspected Anthony would get a pass to join him on-base for dinner.

For the moment, though, it was only him and me. He was lounging in a chair in front of my desk, and his full attention was fixed right on me. "What's going on?"

"Hmm?"

Noah rolled his eyes. "C'mon, dude. Playing stupid never worked on you, and you know damn well it's not going to work on me either."

I blinked, something cold slithering through my veins. How much did he know? "You want to at least tell me what I'm playing stupid about?"

He smirked. "You're getting laid, and you haven't said two words about him."

"Oh. That." I laughed, trying to play it cool, and hoped he bought it. "I told you—it isn't just one guy. I'm playing the—"

"Nuh-uh. Not when you keep spacing out and wandering around with that grin on your face."

Oh crap.

"Come on." He thumped his knuckle on the desk. "We've compared notes on pieces of ass for years, and you couldn't stop talking about He Who Doesn't Deserve to Be Mentioned Anymore when you met him. But now you're being awfully cagey." Noah inclined his head. "What's the deal?"

I chewed my lip, avoiding his eyes.

Noah inched his chair closer to the desk and lowered his voice. "Hey. What's going on?" The teasing in his tone was gone, replaced by concern. "Whatever it is, it stays between us."

I lifted my gaze and searched his.

His forehead creased as his eyes widened. I could only imagine the scenarios bouncing around in his head.

"I, um..." Sighing, I rubbed the back of my neck. "This doesn't leave this room?"

"Of course not." He came closer, so his knees were probably right up against the front of my desk. "Is everything okay?"

"It's fine. I mean... kind of. It's..." I swallowed hard. "It'll be fine as long as no one finds out."

Noah's lips parted. "Finds out... what, exactly?"

Well, if I couldn't trust Noah, I couldn't trust anyone. "That the guy I'm seeing is a lieutenant."

His eyebrows climbed higher. "You're shitting me."

I shook my head. "No. I'm not."

He whistled. "An officer. Wow. And a younger one." He paused. "I mean, unless the guy got his commission later or—"

"No. No." I shifted in my chair. "He's... definitely younger. Twenty-seven, twenty-eight, I think."

"You think?"

I tried not to roll my eyes. "I haven't checked his driver's license, thank you."

"Okay, fair. But how did you even hook up with this guy?"

"I..." Heat rushed into my face.

Noah sat up a little. "Okay, you'd damn well *better* tell me now."

"What? Why?"

"Because if you're this twitchy over how you met, there has got to be a story behind it, and I want to hear it."

"Sadist," I muttered. "Fine. I... actually met him on a call. A domestic."

Noah's jaw nearly hit the desk. "Don't tell me he's *married*."

"No! For fuck's sake."

"Hey." He put up his hands. "I figured if you'd already said to hell with worrying about the whole officer-enlisted thing, you might've decided adultery wasn't such—"

The pen I threw at him missed his head by about three inches, but only because he ducked.

"I'm just saying!" He laughed. "I mean, you do know you're playing with fire, right?"

I glared at him. "No, I had no idea. That's why I've been keeping it under my hat, even from you."

He smirked. "I figured. I just really, really couldn't pass up the opportunity to call you out for doing something stupid. You know, finally returning the favor after all these years."

"That any way to talk to someone of higher rank?"

Noah snorted. "That going to be the name of your sex tape?"

"You want me to tell you how I met him or not?"

"Right." He cleared his throat and schooled his expression. Sort of. "So you were on a call..." His eyebrow rose again.

"Yeah. Turns out the woman he was hooking up with was married, and her husband busted them. After it was all said and done, I gave him a lift back to where he'd parked his car. And before you get any ideas, that was the end of it."

"*Was* the end of it."

"Well. Yeah. But to be clear, I did not bang a guy right after responding to a domestic."

"But you met him on a domestic and you ended up banging him."

"Eventually."

"Eventually." He nodded. "Got it. Go on."

"*Anyway*." I rolled my eyes again, but couldn't help chuckling. If Noah was still willing to crack jokes about this, then maybe it wasn't as big of a crisis as I'd built it in my head. It was absolutely career threatening, and something that *could not* get out to the chain of command—Brent's or mine—but maybe if we kept it on the down-low like we'd already been doing, it would be fine. "So, I couldn't stop thinking about him, and decided to go hit up that place where you met Anthony. The High-&-Tight. And... he showed up."

Noah held my gaze for a long, uncomfortable moment. Voice still low, he said, "So you knew he was an officer, and he knew you were enlisted. Before you ever hooked up."

I nodded.

"I can't decide if that makes you fucking stupid or fucking ballsy."

"Probably a bit of both. Funny thing was, we both figured it was worth the risk for a one-time thing. Fuck once and call it a day. I don't think either of us thought we'd wind up doing this regularly."

"Isn't that usually how it works? I mean, Anthony and I only meant to hook up while he was in town, and now he's moving here, so..."

"Guess I should've kept that in mind."

"Would it have stopped you?"

I wasn't sure how to answer that.

"Come on, Will." He smiled knowingly. "I know you've got your head screwed on way straighter than I do, but the dude obviously does *something* for you that makes you reckless."

Goose bumps prickled my back and shoulders, and I forced myself not to shiver. I wasn't giving Noah the satisfaction.

"So, is this serious?" he asked. "Or are you guys fuck buddies?"

I gnawed my lip. "That's a good question."

To my surprise, he smiled. "I figured as much. You've had that look for a while that you only get when you're really into someone. And it's good to see you happy again."

He sobered and held my gaze. "Just be careful, all right? You've busted your ass too long to get force-retired over something like this."

"Yeah, I know." I laughed dryly. "Think I should tell my parents about him?"

Noah snorted. He knew all too well how my parents felt about this kind of thing. "At least wait until after dessert. No point in missing your mom's pumpkin pie over something like this."

"Good point."

If I was thankful for one thing this year, it was my family's lifelong obsession with football. We were all gathered in my parents' living room, glued to the TV as we lived and died with every catch and fumble. Mom and Dad were kicked back in those old matching recliners that shrieked whenever they sat up. I shared the sofa with my younger brother, Jason, and his girlfriend, Nicole. Everyone was perched on the edges of their seats, decked out in matching jerseys and waving beer cans at the TV. It would not have surprised me in the least if the refs could actually hear us when we protested a stupid call. And there was no shortage of stupid calls during this game. Jesus Christ.

During commercial breaks and timeouts, Mom or Dad would jog into the kitchen to check on the turkey, making us all shudder as ancient recliner mechanisms squealed into motion.

This was a family tradition—shitty recliners and all— and I loved it. Especially this year. As long as we were screaming at the refs, we weren't talking to each other. That meant I didn't have to think about everything I *couldn't* talk to my family about.

In theory, anyway.

Even more than I'd realized, I'd gotten used to having Brent next to me. Sure, I spent plenty of time without him—our days off didn't line up as much as we would have liked—but even then there was always the promise of seeing him later that night. At worst, the next night. This weekend would be the longest stretch of time we'd spent apart since we'd slept together the first time. And it was driving me *insane* because I was with people who didn't want to know he existed. Not because he was an officer, but because he was a man. What we had and what we were wasn't welcome here. Probably never would be.

On the screen, the timer went off, announcing the second quarter was over. Everyone was immediately on their feet. In this house, the halftime show was our cue to refill the chip bowls and beer mugs, so everyone moved into the kitchen.

As I poured some Cool Ranch Doritos into a bowl, Dad asked, "So how are things in Oregon?"

I opened my mouth to speak, but hesitated. Pretending to be focused on carefully closing the bag and clipping it shut, I chose my words carefully. "It's, uh..." *I met someone.* "Work is keeping me busy." *He's amazing.* "As always." *I just want to tell you guys his name.*

"Well, I'm glad they're not keeping you busy this weekend." Mom grabbed my face and kissed my cheek. "You're right down the coast, and I never see you!"

I forced a laugh. "You know how it is. Never any time off."

Guilt prodded at me. I hated lying to my parents. On the other hand, they'd all but *told* me to lie to them twenty-some-odd years ago, so what else could I do? Tell them I didn't come visit because my boyfriend and I were taking off to Portland so no one caught us together?

It was a double-edged sword, being stationed so close to my parents. I'd avoided coming home for the past several months because I'd still been dealing with my breakup. Coming back to a place where I couldn't acknowledge that I'd *had* a boyfriend didn't seem like it would help me grieve the fact that he was gone.

With the holidays in full swing, there'd been no avoiding a trip home. Not without causing a *conversation* with my family. But since the sting of losing Vince wasn't so intense now, I'd figured this would be okay.

Except it wasn't.

Now that I was with my family, that sting came back full force. Not in the sense that I was pining after my lying philandering whore of an ex-boyfriend. I'd been happy with Vince. Not that last year or so, but for a solid half a decade? Definitely. I'd loved him. Watching him drive away in that U-Haul had crushed me. I'd broken down on Noah's shoulder right there in my front yard. I'd been so fucked up over it, I hadn't been interested in dating or getting laid until recently.

Until Brent.

God. *Brent.* Just thinking about him made my heart speed up in a way that I couldn't recall it ever doing with Vince.

"Will?" Mom's voice shook me out of my thoughts.

"Hmm? What? Sorry."

She eyed me. "You okay, honey? You're awfully distracted today." The slight upward flick of her eyebrow reminded me that there were limitations on how much I could divulge.

"I'm fine." I forced a smile. "Just, uh..." I cleared my throat. "You know, I'm going to grab some air before the game gets back in full swing."

I didn't wait for a response, picked up my beer, and went out onto the back deck.

The day was crisp but comfortable. Typical Seattle in November. Alone, I leaned my forearms on the railing and stared out at the park across the street from Mom and Dad's place. I'd played there as a kid. Back before they had the shiny metal playground equipment that didn't have sharp edges or rusty rivets. Before the plastic benches replaced the rotting wooden ones. Definitely before they'd put in a Frisbee golf course.

I took a deep swallow of beer, the cold making my teeth ache. Every time I came back here, this place felt a little less like home, and not just because the city kept modernizing that old park.

The house itself would always be the home I'd grown up in. It had barely changed since I'd left for boot camp damn near twenty years ago. But every time I came home...

Maybe that was it. Every time I came home, I left more and more of myself behind. There was more and more I had to keep to myself. Yeah, I could come home, but not all of me.

Noah had said he liked seeing me happy again, and the more I thought about it, the more I realized he was right—I *was* happy again. Stressed, of course. Worried the wrong person might find out I was with Brent. But happy.

And I couldn't say a word. Not here. Not today.

That had been part of my reality since I'd come out ages ago, but it hurt more now than it had in a long time. It was two-pronged—I couldn't tell them Vince had stomped on my heart because that meant telling them he existed, and I couldn't tell them I was stupidly happy right now because that meant telling them *Brent* existed. The two most significant men in my life for the past ten years were completely erased from reality as soon as I walked into my parents' house.

I closed my eyes and sighed into the cool air. It would have meant the world to me to be able to say his name inside the house, and nothing drove home how much I felt for Brent more than not being able to tell my parents about him. The same thing had made me realize how serious I was about Vince. When I'd desperately wanted to tell them his name and that we were moving in together and that I was madly in love with him. With other guys along the way, I'd been more annoyed than anything that I'd had to appease their homophobia. It was the principle that had pissed me off.

When Vince had come along, it had become more infuriating and more painful because he'd been such an important part of my life. We'd lived together. We'd planned a future together. There'd been conversations about rings and even *kids*.

And then he'd been gone. He'd stomped on my heart, made me feel lower than I'd ever felt before, and... left. With someone else.

I wanted to tell my parents he'd been there, that he'd left, and that I'd found someone else who made me want to hunt Vince down and thank him for getting the fuck out of my life. For making room for Brent.

My throat tightened. Every time I thought I was used to hiding my sexuality from my family... I wasn't. I didn't think I'd ever really get used to it. Especially not now. It hurt like hell that I couldn't tell my family I'd lost the man I'd fully expected to marry, and it hurt so much more that I couldn't say a word about the man I was definitely falling for. As if I weren't already struggling with keeping him a secret at work. Hiding him from my family too? Fuck my life.

Behind me, the sliding glass door opened. I bristled as I turned around but then relaxed.

Jason stepped out onto the deck. As he shut the door, he glanced over his shoulder as if to make sure we were alone. "So, uh, how are you doing? After that asshole left?"

"Better." I paused. "I actually met someone new. Pretty recently, actually."

"Really?" He turned to me. "How's that going?"

Despite my gloomy mood, I couldn't help smiling. "So far, so good. He's a little younger than I usually date, but..." I shrugged.

"How much younger is 'a little younger'?"

"Late twenties."

He gestured dismissively with his soda can. "Eh, that's not bad. You're both adults." He smirked. "Well, I don't know about you, but—"

I elbowed him. "Shut up."

He snickered, but as he turned serious again, he gave my shoulder a gentle squeeze. "I'm glad to hear it, by the way. Really."

"Thanks." I paused, glancing back in the kitchen window. "Is it pathetic that I wish I could tell Mom and Dad about him? I mean, I'm pushing forty. I shouldn't—"

"No, it's not pathetic." Jason shook his head. "I don't know how you keep your shit together, to be honest. I mean, Vince was a big part of your life. Sounds like this new guy is too." He scowled. "I can't imagine not being able to *mention* Nicole. And if we ever split up, and I couldn't say anything? Fuck. How *did* you deal with it?"

"Did I have much choice?"

He seemed to consider it. "I guess not."

"Yeah. So that's why I've been avoiding coming home since Vince and I started having problems. And now that I'm here, all I can think about is how much I wish I could tell them about Brent."

Jason grimaced. "Man, that's rough. The fucked-up thing is, I think they know."

"What do you mean?"

"Mom's asked me a few times if you're doing all right. Said you'd been kind of distant and seemed depressed. I told her she should ask you, but she got all evasive about why she wouldn't."

"Yeah," I muttered. "She knows."

With a grunt, my brother nodded. Neither of us spoke for a moment, but then he broke the silence again. "It's messed up, you know? Being so hung up on how much you don't like people being gay that you can't even listen to why your son's having a rough time." He turned to me. "I ever act like that with Aiden or Breanna, please kick my ass."

"Oh, I will. Believe me." As it was, my niece and nephew had already been told in no uncertain terms that if they had questions about gay people—or if they thought they might be queer themselves—and they were too embarrassed to talk to their parents, they could come to me. Jason and Nicole had instilled that in the kids as soon as they were old enough to have the slightest inkling of what being gay meant, and it was understood that anything they said to me was strictly confidential unless I thought one of them might get hurt.

Aiden was thirteen now, a year older than I'd been when I realized I was gay, and I envied him. It was entirely possible he and his sister—who was eleven—were straight, but that safety net was there anyway and always would be.

What I wouldn't have given for that kind of thing when I was a kid. Even if my parents had simply said *they'd* been the ones who were uncomfortable, and given me someone else to go to. Something other than leaving me to twist in the wind because I was something they couldn't cope with.

At least I had my brother and his family in my corner. At least someone here knew. About Vince. About Brent. About *me*, for God's sake.

I cleared my throat as a sudden wave of emotion almost threw me off-balance. Jason didn't notice, fortunately, but I sure did.

Come on. Get it together. Just a couple more nights, and it's all over.

I can do this.

It wasn't only my family's obsession with football that had me feeling thankful this year. It was that the holiday was almost over, and before I knew it, I'd be with Brent again.

Is it Monday yet?

CHAPTER 20

BRENT

THE FOOTBALL GAME wasn't holding my attention. My team wasn't playing, and I was pretty sure my heart wouldn't have been in it even if they were. Sitting back in one of the recliners in Dad's rec room, I kept letting my gaze drift away from the TV and over to the various military relics on the walls and shelves.

I'd never really noticed how much my parents' house was like a Navy museum until after I'd moved out. Every time I came back, though, it was obvious. The walls had more photos of ships, submarines, and aircraft than people.

My mom insisted on tasteful furniture in the living and dining rooms, and the office and man cave had nice leather chairs and hardwood bookcases. In the garage, though, were several drab metal shelves and a desk-turned-workbench that could only have come from a base. The Navy sometimes jettisoned furniture like that when an office was renovated or a department had moved, but I imagined a few pieces had also been "reappropriated" during Dad's active-duty years.

There was probably enough maritime memorabilia in the house to open an actual museum. Attached to the front of the bar was a wood and brass helm that had been a gift to Dad after he'd retired. On either side of it, a pair of brass artillery casings stood to almost midthigh on me. I shuddered at the memory of one of those tipping over and breaking eight-year-old me's toe.

Along the far wall of the rec room were four of the huge hardwood bookcases. There were tons more pieces of Navy memorabilia on the shelves. Even the bookends were all military themed. A pair of cannons from the crew of his first ship after he transferred. The bow and stern of an aircraft carrier. Red and green navigational lights. And, of course, all the books between them were Navy related. Dad must've had every book Tom Clancy had ever written, plus dozens of books on great military leaders, naval battles, World War II, and the history of the Navy. He even kept a handful of old copies of the *Manual for Courts-Martial* from both his era and my grandfather's.

I wonder what those versions say about officer-enlisted hookups.

I squirmed. It had always been forbidden, and I'd known it since I was a kid. My grandparents had both been in the Army during World War II, and Grandma wouldn't date Grandpa because he wasn't an officer. If he hadn't gotten his commission while stationed there—thanks to a battlefield promotion after his commander was killed—I literally wouldn't exist.

They'd both be spinning in their graves if they knew about me and Will.

I shook that thought away and scanned Dad's familiar Navy memorabilia. Every time I came home, I realized how much I'd truly been living and breathing the Navy since the day I was born. When I'd reported to my first shipboard command, the smell of the ship—a distinctive combination of metal, rubber, diesel, and seawater—had taken me back to my childhood like the smell of beer and hot dogs takes most people back to baseball games and county fairs.

The football game wasn't holding my interest at all, so I got up from my recliner and made a slow path around the room to scrutinize all the things that had surrounded me since I was a child.

The colorful framed certificates from Neptune's Court and the Order of the Blue Nose were as familiar to me as my parents' wedding photos. Things I'd seen on the walls but hadn't completely understood until I was older. As a child, it had never struck me as odd how normal the Navy was to me, or that kids in civilian families really didn't understand Wog Day or know what a shillelagh was. When I'd crossed the equator for the first time myself, I'd been as ready as anyone ever was for the traditional hazing, and though I'd never admit it out loud to my old-school dad, relieved as hell that the shillelagh really had been banned for good. The thought of getting beaten with a three-foot chunk of firehose had never held much appeal.

I shuddered at the memory and kept wandering the room. Every room in my parents' house had at least one shadowbox in it, usually with examples of knots or with some small trinkets Dad had picked up overseas. Of course the one over the mantle was *the* shadowbox—the one with Dad's medals and the last official portrait of him before he retired. I couldn't count how many times he'd proudly told me I'd have one of those myself someday.

I stared up at that shadowbox. It had been impressive when I was younger, but it was intimidating now. I was proud of what few promotions and medals I had so far, but comparing them to

Dad's gold oak leaves, the rows of medals, and all the bars on his shoulder boards... it was like wearing a Little League uniform to a Major League game. Same sport, drastically different level.

Maybe it would've been easier if Dad had still been on active duty when I'd been commissioned. Like when my brother had gone in ten years before me. Dad had retired between my sophomore and junior years in high school, but my brother had already made lieutenant commander and had a couple of combat deployments under his belt. I wondered if it had intimidated him, being the son of a decorated captain when he'd still been at my level, or if it'd made it easier, knowing Dad was still in and still busting his ass commanding an aircraft carrier.

Now that Dad was retired, his perspective had changed. Everything was filtered through rose-colored glasses, and he couldn't imagine why my brother or I were stressed or frustrated or sometimes legitimately wanted to quit and go back to being civilians. The minute he'd retired, he'd forgotten all about how much he used to snarl and complain, and how many times Medical had threatened to recommend a medical retirement if his blood pressure didn't come down.

I wondered if that was what Will had meant when he'd talked about remembering where I came from. If I really would put on a pair of oak leaves and forget there'd ever been a time when I'd been anything other than a leader who was to be respected and obeyed.

My mind didn't drift toward my future as a leader under those oak leaves, though. Or whether I'd remember where I came from.

It went right to Will.

I pulled my attention away from Dad's shadowbox and took a deep swallow of beer. I missed Will. How was he holding up, anyway? My family drove me crazy sometimes, but his sounded downright toxic, at least as far as his sexuality was concerned.

With a glance over my shoulder to make sure Dad was still glued to the game, I took out my phone and texted, *How is your Tgiving going?*

He responded in under a minute. *Would much rather be with you.*

Same here. Going ok with your folks?

Good as it ever does.

Well, that was something. No screaming matches or anything, I guessed. I was about to send another reply when my brother, Dan, materialized beside me.

"Hey." He held out a bottle of beer. "Looked like you could use a refill."

I glanced down at the bottle in my hand and realized it was nearly empty. I quickly drained it, put it in the recycling bin behind the bar, and took the one Dan had offered. "Thanks."

"Don't mention it." He clinked the neck of his own against mine. "So how are you liking NAS Adams?"

There was not enough beer in this house.

Channeling every reserve of patience I possessed, I met my brother's gaze. "It's all right. It's fine."

"What do you think of—"

"Dan." I sighed and shook my head. "Dad's going to grill me up one side and down the other about work once the game is over. I really just want to relax."

He nodded. "Yeah, I can understand that. But, uh... fair warning?" He tilted his beer bottle toward the living room. "My new XO is the son of one of Dad's old buddies, and a guy he went to Annapolis with just took command of the

East Coast fleet. So, that's probably going to be dinner conversation."

I groaned. There was definitely not enough beer in this house.

I'd never know how Mom did it, but she timed it so dinner was ready right when the game was over. We all sat down—my parents, my brother and his wife, and me—said grace, then dug in.

"So how are you liking that base?" Dad asked as he poured gravy on a slab of turkey.

Jesus. Can I eat first?

"It's all right." I focused on scooping some peas onto my plate.

"How long do you figure you'll be there?"

"Two more years."

He scowled, and I cringed. Wrong answer.

"You shouldn't stay there longer than you have to," he said. "Those landside commands are fine and good, but if you really want the boards to take you seriously—"

"I know, Dad." I tried to keep some of the frustration out of my voice. "But I've already spent three-quarters of my career on a ship. Spending a couple of years on shore won't kill my chances of getting promoted."

He shook his head. "You don't want to think about what might hurt your chances. You need to think about what will *improve* your chances. It's going to start getting competitive before you know it, and you'll need every advantage you can get."

The food on my plate looked and smelled amazing, but my stomach suddenly wasn't interested. Still, I chased a few peas into the gravy and took a bite so Mom wouldn't worry. To Dad, I said, "The commander I work for is helping me make connections. It's a small base, but he knows people."

"Oh good. Good." He gave an approving nod. "That's what you need."

No, what I need is to eat, and then get back to Anchor Point and my boy—

"So they still have you working in admin? Or did someone finally give you a real job?"

It wasn't going to stop, was it?

I exhaled. "Yes, I'm still in admin."

"You don't belong there. You went to Annapolis, for God's sake!"

My brother chuckled. "Tell them to put you somewhere where you're not doing grunt work."

"At least it's just paperwork," Dad muttered. "Anything else is what the enlisted ranks are for, son. Somebody's gotta do the shit jobs."

I gritted my teeth. There might've been a time when I would've laughed along with him. In fact, I realized now how much contempt I'd been raised to have for those who enlisted. They were there to do the dirty work while the rest of us rose to the top, and they should be grateful for everything we officers bestowed on them.

The fact that it took dating an enlisted guy to make me see how fucked up that was? Yeah, that made me feel like a piece of shit, but better late than never.

"Well, what you need to do," Dad continued, "is talk to your commander about working at a joint command. Offutt is in Nebraska, and it's not great, but it's good for your career."

I chased a glob of stuffing along the edge of the gravy.

The nonstop Navy hadn't bothered me as a kid, but now it was exhausting. Fuck, I needed a *break*.

"Dad." I put up a hand. "I know you're trying to help, and I appreciate it, but I'm on leave. I want to leave work at work for a few days."

He laughed. "Kid, that's one thing you need to learn sooner than later—you might be on leave, but you're never *not* in the Navy."

I ground my teeth. "I get that. But it doesn't mean every conversation needs to focus on it."

"You need to stay focused, Brent."

"During Thanksgiving dinner?"

He started to speak, but Mom broke in with, "Are you meeting anyone there? Making some friends?"

You could say that.

I hesitated. "A few, yeah."

"No girlfriends?"

"Nope. No boyfriends either."

She smiled, but I could *feel* my dad's scowl even before I turned his way.

He put his fork down and sighed. "Son, I know they've changed the policy, but that doesn't change everybody's minds. When you get higher up, you're going to be relying on congressmen for your promotions." He shook his head. "Not all of those guys are keen on—"

"Dad, I'm aware of the political situation," I growled. "Times have changed."

"Not as much as you think," he muttered.

"Ron." Mom's tone was laced with warning, which she didn't direct at him very often. "Brent said he doesn't want to discuss the Navy. Can we please let it drop?"

Dad scowled harder. Wisely, though, he didn't push.

When Mom put her foot down, he knew better than to keep at it. We all did.

After a moment, he exhaled and turned to my brother. "So I hear Frank Hayes just transferred to your base. You met him?"

My brother nodded. "Yeah, several times. You know he's a two-star now?"

Well, it was still a Navy conversation, but I could tolerate hearing about my brother's career more than I could tolerate discussing mine, so I quietly ate while they talked.

Between dinner and dessert, I helped Mom clear the table, and on the way back from the kitchen, stole a second to check my phone.

Half an hour or so ago, Will had texted: *Is it Monday yet?*

I laughed. *Never thought I'd say this, but I wish.*

LOL Soon, right?

Yep. Soon.

The texts from Will made me smile, but also added some apprehension to my gut. I cut my eyes toward Dad as I took my seat at the table again. Pocketing my phone, I reminded myself there was no way my parents could possibly know about him. I hadn't dropped any hints about seeing anyone. Mom always asked, and she hadn't seemed to suspect anything when I'd given my standard *Nope, still single* response.

It wasn't like telling them I actually *had* a boyfriend—rather than casually reminding them a boyfriend was an option—would turn Thanksgiving into a disaster. My parents didn't have anything against gay people, and though they didn't entirely understand bisexuality, they had nothing nasty to say about it. Nothing they'd said to my face, anyway, and neither of them had ever been inclined to hold back if they disapproved of something.

The problem was that the military had not been historically queer friendly, and my dad wouldn't let go of his fear that being out would damage or kill my career. He still wasn't completely sold on the idea that DADT was truly gone, and he was convinced I'd never make rank if I was openly queer. He'd given me crap tonight, and it was *so* not the first or last time.

"You like women," he'd said last Christmas, *"so find one and marry her, and then you won't have to worry about losing out on a promotion or getting your own boat because the board finds out you're queer."*

If he knew I was dating an enlisted guy, he would lose his fucking mind.

And an unusually rebellious part of me wanted to tell him. I wanted to look my father in the eye and tell him. Not only that my boyfriend was enlisted—he was *career* enlisted. Dad could grudgingly accept someone enlisting long enough to get the GI Bill so they could pursue a respectable civilian career.

Enlisting for twenty years or more? That was a joke as far as my father was concerned. Never mind that the Navy would fall apart without the people in the senior enlisted ranks. A coal mine wouldn't get very far without miners, but that didn't mean Dad respected them.

A weird feeling settled in my stomach.

Was I dating Will to rebel against my father?

Except... no. No, I could definitely say that I wasn't. Maybe in the beginning. He'd been attractive as hell from the moment I'd laid eyes on him, but it was entirely possible his enlisted uniform had had something to do with it. In the *beginning*.

I thumbed the label on my beer bottle. If there'd been any rebelliousness at all, it was gone. I wanted Will. My momentary temptation to tell Dad about him? That was gone as quickly as it had come. Thinking about him now made me want to call the airline and see about moving up my flight home. I missed him.

I swallowed. God. I really did miss him. Like, a lot.

No, really. Is it Monday yet?

CHAPTER 21

WILL

I COULDN'T REMEMBER the last time I'd been this squirrelly. It had only gotten worse since Brent texted me to let me know his plane was on the ground, and again when he'd left the airport to head for Anchor Point. Of course it was almost a hundred miles from there to here, so there was nothing for me to do except wait for him and try not to twitch to death.

I'd driven back from Seattle late last night. He'd left Norfolk early this morning.

Soon. Not soon enough, but... soon.

He texted me again: *Stopped for gas. Be in A.Pt in 10 min.*

I barely kept myself from groaning out loud, both in frustration and anticipation. Ten minutes out of Anchor Point meant another five to eight minutes to my front door.

If I hadn't been losing my mind before, I sure as hell was now. I paced the living room. Wandered through the kitchen I'd already cleaned three times since breakfast. Checked the bedroom to make sure the condoms and lube I'd bought last night hadn't magically disappeared.

I was too wound up to focus on anything except *being* wound up. After the better part of a week without him, I was too restless to handle another fifteen minutes apart. I was sure there'd been a time when I'd been this hungry for Vince or someone who'd come before him, but those memories had faded pretty sharply with time. Assuming they'd existed at all. *Had* I ever been this desperate for anyone besides Brent?

I didn't know, and it didn't matter, because I was this desperate for him, and he was almost here.

Closing my eyes, I slowly released a breath. He was on his way. He'd be here. Ideally before something caught on fire, but he'd be here.

Not a moment too soon, Brent pulled in. His car wasn't that distinctive—no massive engine that could be heard from down the block—but every vehicle had its own purr, and I could pick his out from a mile away.

I closed my eyes.

The engine turned off. The car door shut. Footsteps. God, yes, footsteps.

My heart pounded as he came up the walk, and before he'd reached the bottom step, I opened the front door.

Our eyes met. His smile made me shiver, and it was all I could do not to grab him and kiss him right there on the porch. Thank God we had all that practice with restraint.

I moved aside, and he quickly slipped inside. I closed us in, and somehow had the presence of mind to turn the dead bolt, and then? Then I was all his.

The second the door was shut enough to block out any potential voyeurs, we collided in a breathless embrace, and... fuck. Yeah. The world was back on its axis. Maybe this meant I was addicted to him, that I needed him more than I should, but right about then, I couldn't have cared less. If this was an addiction, it wasn't one I had any intention of fighting anytime soon.

"God, I missed you," I growled between kisses.

"Me too." He pushed his hands into my back pockets and squeezed my ass. "Been losing my mind since I left."

"You and me both." I rubbed my rock-hard dick against his, and groaned at the friction. After too many days of hiding his existence and my feelings for him, I needed to make up for lost time. I wanted him. Craved him. Damn it, I needed him to know that even though I couldn't mention him, I sure as fuck hadn't forgotten him.

You were there the whole time, and I am so glad you're here now.

He pushed his hand between us. I shivered hard enough to break the kiss, and he went straight for my neck, letting his lips skate up and down as he struggled with my zipper. Then his hand was around my cock, and everything went white for a couple of seconds. After needing him so badly for the last few days, having him was overwhelming. His soft lips. His hot and cool breath. His strong, warm fingers around my dick. It was too much, and I wanted *more*.

I licked my lips. "Get on your knees, sir."

Brent whimpered softly against my throat, and it was like his knees just buckled out from under him. He sank to my feet, running his hands down my body as he went, and he'd barely settled on the floor before he took my cock in his mouth.

God, that was a beautiful sight: Brent on his knees, eagerly sucking my dick. I kept a hand on the back of his head and fucked his mouth. He moaned, digging his nails into my hips, and took every thrust I gave him. I was careful not to gag him, and my hand was only resting lightly in his hair, but the forcefulness always seemed to turn him on as much as it did me.

And if he turned me on much more than he already had, this would be over before it started. I fully intended to go more than once tonight, but why rush it?

"Get up," I half ordered, half begged.

Brent stayed on his knees a few seconds longer, long enough to tease the head of my cock and almost get me off, before he finally stood.

I gripped his throat—not enough to choke him, but enough that he *knew* my hand was there—and he moaned into my kiss. I used my body to pin him to the wall, and he slid his hands up my sides as we kept right on kissing. How the fuck had I gone more than one night without tasting him? Jesus.

"You know," he panted, "I can see why this is considered conduct unbecoming a gentleman."

"Yeah?" I met his gaze. His gleaming, lust-filled gaze. "Why's that?"

He gripped my ass cheeks, digging his nails in, and grinned. "'Cause there is nothing gentlemanly about sex with you."

I rubbed my cock against his thigh. "Doesn't sound like you're complaining?"

"Not at all." He kneaded my butt again. "This is how I like it. And I fucking missed it while I was gone."

"You and me both." I leaned down and flicked my tongue in the divot where his collarbones met, and he sucked in a breath.

"God..." He shuddered, then blurted out, "I want you to fuck me. Been... thinking about it all day."

Oh yeah. Fuck yeah. Somehow, I played it cool. "Do you?"

"Uh-huh."

I nipped his neck. "How do you want it?"

"Hard."

Couldn't argue with that.

In the bedroom, I quickly relieved him of his clothes. As soon as mine were off, he grabbed a condom and put it on me, and I wasted no time shoving him over the bed and pushing his legs apart with my knee. He gasped, arching as he clutched at the sheets.

I'd barely teased his hole with my cock when he moaned, "Harder."

Laughing softly, I teased him more mercilessly. "I'm not even in you yet."

"*I know.*" He looked over his shoulder and leaned back against me. "Come *on.*"

Well hell. Who was I to argue with a man who wanted my dick inside him?

I worked myself in, and his desperate little whimpers drove me wild. As I picked up speed, he only got louder, and so did I. Every sound either of us made was primal and hungry. Low, throaty groans. Ragged curses. Grunts that were probably equal parts pain and pleasure.

He was right—there was nothing gentlemanly about this, and I loved it. I loved the sheer raunchiness of it. How he didn't just *let* me throw him around, he *reveled* in it.

The only downside? I couldn't see his face, and I wouldn't get to watch him come. So I pulled out and nudged his hip. "Turn over. I want to see you."

Brent pushed himself up, wobbling a little, and turned onto his back on the edge of the bed. He spread his legs wide, offering his hole to me again and exposing his cock and balls. Oh yeah. Oh yeah, that was exactly what I wanted.

As I slid back in, his face was the picture of pure bliss—lips apart as he moaned, eyes squeezed shut, skin flushed. I couldn't resist, and pulled all the way out before taking the long, deep stroke inside again.

"C'mon," he pleaded. "Hard."

Groaning with pleasure and exertion, I gave it to him hard, knocking cries and grunts out of him every time I slammed home. How I hadn't come already, I had no idea. Turned on as I was, losing my mind as I thrust into this beautiful, horny man, I should've come three times already.

"*Fuck.*" He squeezed his eyes shut and arched under me. "You feel so good."

"So do you." It didn't get any better than this. Here in my bed, naked and debauched and making each other sweat and tremble, buried to the hilt inside Brent, I was...

I was...

Why does this feel more like home than the place I grew up?

His eyelids slid open, and he looked up at me with blown pupils. Grinning, he reached for my face. His fingertips on my cheek sent a shiver through me.

Because he's here. That's why.

I leaned down as much as I could, and he pushed himself up to meet me halfway, and I kissed him. He returned the kiss hungrily, slinging an arm around my neck for support, and we moved together and breathed together, and it didn't feel like we'd been on opposite sides of the continent a few hours ago. Of course we were here. We'd always been here. Or at least it felt that way. If we hadn't been, we should've been, and we were now, and it was perfect.

With a strangled cry, Brent broke the kiss and dropped

back onto the mattress. "Yeah. Just like..." He bit his lip and rocked his hips. "Fuck, Will. I'm so close."

I gritted my teeth and gave it to him hard and fast, just the way he loved it, and my head spun as I watched him fall apart below me. His breath came in rapid, uneven gasps. His nails dug into my arms. He screwed his eyes shut and bit his lip so hard I was amazed it didn't bleed, and then—

"Oh *yeah*." His hips bucked up, nearly knocking me off-balance, and that first jet of cum on his stomach set off my orgasm. I thrust into him, nearly shoving the mattress right off the bed frame, and the sound that escaped my throat didn't begin to convey the pleasure surging through me, but I couldn't get enough air for more than a soft whimper.

Then everything was still. I leaned over him, holding myself up on shaking arms since my legs were this close to useless, and he wrapped his around me.

"I seriously missed you," he murmured before kissing me softly.

"Me too." I met his gaze. "Hope you're game to go more than once tonight."

Brent's lips pulled into a sexy, almost drunken grin. "Bring it."

We both laughed. After we'd shared one more lazy kiss —okay, three more—I carefully pulled out, and we made a clumsy effort to clean ourselves up before collapsing on top of the covers together.

Ahh, this was what I'd been missing for the last few days—lying here naked in bed with Brent half against me, half draped over me.

I pulled him a little closer. It was a damn shame we couldn't keep doing this without sinking both of our careers.

Except not doing this had stopped being an option. Somewhere along the way, in between sneaking in and out of each other's apartments under the cover of darkness, this had turned into something else. If it had started out as something neither of us could walk away from, then God knew what it was now, but walking away sure as shit wasn't an option.

I closed my eyes and savored being beside him.

I can't believe how much I missed you.

The weekend we'd spent in Portland had made me wonder. The holiday I'd spent with my parents had driven it home.

Fact was, there was no way in hell I wasn't falling for him.

I *couldn't* fall for him. Absolutely couldn't.

But God help me, I also couldn't stop myself.

CHAPTER 22

BRENT

ADMITTEDLY, it was good to be back at work. I still hated the drudgery of my job and the endless bland gray of the base, but being back at the office meant I was back in Anchor Point. It meant the occasional sext with Will wasn't just something to jerk off to later—he was here in town, and tonight, one of us would be in the other's bed.

The phone on my desk rang. Commander Wilson's extension came up on the caller ID, so I didn't bother with the generic greeting.

"Yes, sir?"

"Lieutenant, could I see you in my office?"

Always something. "Yes, sir. On my way."

I got up and headed down the hall. Chances were, he had more work for me to do, but that was fine. A visit with Commander Wilson usually meant a new project, and a new project meant more to keep me busy. That would make the day go by faster.

Whatever you've got, Commander, sign me up. Nothing is killing my good mood.

His office was open, so I paused in the doorway. "You wanted to see me, sir?"

"Yes." He gestured at the chairs in front of his desk. "Shut the door and have a seat."

My gut clenched, but I figured it was a knee-jerk reaction. The deep-seated childhood response to Mom or Dad saying, *I need to talk to you*. Besides, conversations behind closed doors weren't *that* unusual here. His tone was a little weird, though.

With the door shut, I sat down and tried not to look too wound up.

Wilson shifted in his own chair, a flicker of pain tightening his lips. How he dealt with that every fucking day was beyond me.

When he finally seemed to be as comfortable as he was going to get, he looked at me across the desk. "I need you to be honest with me about something, Lieutenant."

My *oh shit* gut clench came back with a vengeance. "Uh. Okay?"

His eyes narrowed slightly. He opened his mouth like he was going to ask a question, but hesitated. Lips quirked, he stared at his desk for a moment, then started again. "You're aware of how small and incestuous a base like this really is, aren't you?"

I tried not to fidget. "Yeah?"

"It's not like Norfolk or San Diego. It's a safe bet most people here are separated by two or three degrees at most." His eyebrows rose. "Am I right?"

"Yes, sir." *What the hell?*

He drummed his fingers on the desk. "For example, did you know that my husband's ex-brother-in-law is moving to town to live with his boyfriend, and that his boyfriend is active duty?"

I had no idea where he was going with this, but I was nervous as fuck. "Uh. No. No, sir. I didn't."

He looked me right in the eye. "His boyfriend is Chief Jackson. A master-at-arms."

Oh fuck...

"I see, sir."

Do you really? his eyes asked.

He let me squirm for a moment before he spoke again. "How long did you think you and Senior Chief Curtis could keep this a secret?"

I cringed. "Uh..."

He exhaled. "Damn it. I was really hoping you were going to tell me I was wrong."

"Would you have believed me?"

"Considering I'm just going off rumors?" He shrugged. "Maybe?"

"What rumors, anyway? Did Chief Jackson say something?"

"No, I was making the point that it's a very small world on a base like this. The rumors... I couldn't tell you where they started. Someone apparently saw you leaving Curtis's apartment at two in the morning." He inclined his head. "On three separate occasions."

Shit. One camera phone picture and we were fucked.

I had no idea what to say.

"I'm not judging, Lieutenant." Wilson's tone was surprisingly gentle. "And I get it—these things happen. I've told you before about my best friend. The old CO on this base who retired so he could be with the man he's now married to. So don't think I'm taking this lightly. I'm not unsympathetic, and I know it isn't easy. But... the UCMJ is very clear."

I nodded. "I know it is."

"I'm also not going to ask if you knew he was enlisted before you started seeing him, or..." Wilson shook his head. "Look, the fact is, you're one of the best young officers I've worked with in a long time. You're bright, you're committed—hell, I've seen you throw yourself into work that we both know you hated, because that's your work ethic. You probably have more potential than even you realize." He made an apologetic gesture, and his wedding ring caught the light. "I don't want to see you throw that away."

The words *fuck my potential* were closer to the tip of my tongue than they'd ever been. It was irrational, and I knew it. I was frustrated and didn't want to acknowledge that Will and I were screwed no matter what.

"I understand, sir." I paused. "Does it make sense to you, though?" I struggled to hold his gaze. "You and your husband work down the hall from each other, and no one bats an eye. I'm dating someone who doesn't even work in this building or in my chain of command, and it's enough to kill my career."

Wilson pursed his lips. "Yeah. I know. Believe me. And to tell you the truth, I don't know why that particular fraternization rule still exists. But as long as it *does* exist, you need to be careful."

"Guess I can't argue with that."

"I'm going to trust you to do what needs to be done." His lips tightened into a subtle grimace. "But if this continues, and someone besides me finds out, there isn't much I'll be able to do to help you."

I nodded. "I know. Thank you, sir."

"Dismissed."

I got up, left his office, and numbly headed back to my office. There, I shut the door behind me, sank into my chair, and let my elbows *thunk* onto my metal desk. Groaning, I rubbed my temples. Shit. This was bad.

We'd been discreet, though, hadn't we? Hell, I didn't think it was possible to be *more* discreet. We'd never stayed at the other's place overnight. We never spoke at work unless we could convincingly hide it under official business. We sure as fuck never went out in public together unless we were in another city. What more could we have done?

Talk about missing the point. Wilson hadn't confronted me so I'd be more careful and work harder to keep things with Will out of sight. He'd confronted me so I'd do the smart thing. If another rumor came his way, or someone actually caught me or Will with a smartphone as we tiptoed out of the other's apartment, or that kiss we'd shared in the Japanese garden in Portland appeared in the background of some viral video of a pigeon doing backflips...

Shit.

I was lucky he was giving me this much slack. He was putting his own neck on the line by letting me correct the situation instead of having me hemmed up. If it came out that he knew and didn't do anything, he could be in deep shit right along with us.

I wished like hell those rumors had made it to my commander a lot sooner. Before I'd let myself get in this far over my head. It was one thing to know we were breaking the rules. It was another to realize that someone with the power to fuck up my career was onto us.

But this wakeup call had come way too late in the game.

Walk away from Will? I hadn't been able to do it back when it was just sex.

How the hell was I supposed to do it now?

CHAPTER 23

WILL

IT WASN'T unusual for Brent to collapse and be a little quiet after we'd fucked, but this was different. He'd gotten up to get rid of the condom, and ever since he'd settled into bed again, he'd been someplace else. Not rejecting my touches, but not exactly welcoming them either. Which, after he'd been so voracious a few minutes ago, was weird.

I lifted myself up on my elbow and trailed the backs of my fingers down his chest. "Hey. You still with me?"

He shook himself. As he met my gaze, he smiled, but it wasn't very convincing. "Sorry."

"What's wrong?"

He opened his mouth like he was going to insist everything was fine. Then he exhaled and rubbed his eyes. "My commander's onto us."

My throat constricted. "Uh, come again?"

"He..." Brent sighed, lowering his hand. "He knows about you. Not just that I'm seeing an enlisted guy. *You*."

I stared at him in horror. "How?"

"Rumors. I guess someone saw me leaving your place in the middle of the night."

A chill ran through me. There were a few service members in this complex, but I hadn't realized any of them knew me or Brent. "Shit."

"Yeah. And, I mean, he knows, but he's not going to do anything about it. Not right now, anyway." He swallowed. "He was basically telling me that if someone *else* finds out, there's nothing he can do."

I grimaced. That sounded distinctly like something I'd told Noah back when his drinking had been out of control. Who knew I'd be eating *those* words? "So what do we do?"

Brent slid his hand over the top of mine. "I don't know. I mean, I don't want to stop doing this. I know we should, but..."

"Yeah, I know the feeling." I avoided his eyes but didn't pull my hand free. "I won't lie. I'm... not sure if I can keep doing this."

Brent sighed heavily. "Yeah. The secrecy is exhausting."

I winced. I wasn't surprised he'd agreed with me, but hearing him say it was harder than I'd expected. Maybe I'd thought he'd come up with some solution that only an optimistic kid could think of—and an older jaded guy needed to hear—and we could make this work after all. Because I *wanted* to believe we could still make this work.

Knowing he was as tired as I was? And that his commander was onto us? My own optimism was taking on water, and fast.

This was the point when we both should've gotten up, gotten dressed, and moved on like we should have the first night. I'd always played things by the book because my career was everything to me. Making master chief would be a pipe dream if I kept sneaking into Brent's bed.

But damn if I could help myself. He was everything Vince wasn't. Even in the early days when Vince and I had been as in love as Anthony and Noah were now, it hadn't felt like this. If things had been half as risky with Vince as they were with Brent, we wouldn't have lasted a month. Brent and I were still hanging in there, though, because despite all the risk and frustration, it was worth it whenever we found ourselves like this. Every time I was lying next to him, my body aching and satisfied, everything seemed right. Like this was how it should be, UCMJ be damned.

Except...

I sighed.

Brent met my gaze. "Doesn't seem like we have a lot of options, does it?"

"No." I carded my fingers through his hair. "But we'll figure something out. If anything, we'll just find a way to be more discreet."

Brent searched my eyes.

I leaned in and pressed a kiss to his lips. "I'm not going anywhere."

I wanted him to believe me. So, so bad.

But deep down, I was pretty sure we both heard the unspoken *yet*.

When we were in bed together, it was easy to tell myself we could make this work. As soon as the clothes were on and we'd gone our separate ways until the next time, reality was a little harder to ignore.

As I tried to go about my day, I could still feel everything we'd done the other night. Not just the sex. *Everything*. The phantom weight of him resting against my side and on my shoulder was still there, though I knew that was just my imagination. The conversation we'd had in bed had settled into some very uncomfortable places behind my ribs, in my stomach, and somewhere in the back of my head.

It didn't help that I hadn't slept. All of that had kept me awake, and the fatigue was making it all worse. I was getting way too old to do this job on that little sleep.

Not that I had a choice. The Navy didn't do sick days, and they sure as hell didn't do mental health days. In fact, as if out of spite, this was one of those days when I needed to have my shit together and not look like I was about to pass out. Captain Carter's daughter and one of the maintenance guys from the flight line had been busted making out in the lot behind the Exchange, and most of my morning had been spent explaining that it didn't matter if "she said she was eighteen" was a legitimate defense. That would be up to JAG, not us. And then, of course, Captain Carter and his wife had come to pick up their daughter, which meant a lot of yelling, threatening, and warning—all directed at me, since if I valued my career, I would make sure the man went to Leavenworth and the daughter's name never appeared on anything, since it would damage the captain's reputation. All the while, he and his wife completely ignored their daughter because they still hadn't figured out that her rebellious streak—which was getting to the point of seriously damaging people's military careers—was a desperate plea for her parents' attention.

By the time the Carter family had left and the security officer had taken over with the man—who by now was a terrified mess—it was almost three in the afternoon, and I was exhausted. I felt sorry for both of the kids who'd been caught. The guy was nineteen, and between her makeup, fake ID, and genes, Captain Carter's daughter really did look eighteen. She could've easily passed for twenty-one. He'd seemed genuinely horrified to find out she was sixteen.

She'd looked devastated on the way out because, once again, her father was more concerned about his career than about her.

And since the family would likely be focused on how she was hurting her dad's career, it would be just about time for her sister to act out. I gave it two weeks tops before we were bringing her in for pot possession again. I just hoped like hell that she never escalated to selling. Or if she did, that we never caught her. There were some charges her father could magically erase, but distributing drugs on government property was not one of them.

With that debacle—or at least my participation in it— finally over, I returned to my office to wallow in my tired, distracted, depressed state of mind.

Cursing under my breath, I sat down at my desk. Not that I could get comfortable. I was used to the bulk of my police belt, but today, it was annoying. Everything was. Especially the stiff, uneven cushion on the back of my desk chair. The Navy wasn't exactly known for stocking its ships and offices with the latest and greatest in ergonomic furniture, and this particular chair had probably been in the Navy as long as I had. It would probably still be here after I retired.

Especially, I thought bitterly, *if I end up retiring sooner than later*.

The worst part was that, as much as it made me feel like a gigantic asshole, I was beginning to resent my relationship with Brent. There was an ultimatum in place, and though it wasn't his fault, it was there, and I wasn't keen on being forced to choose between a man or my career again.

I tried to tell myself I wasn't being fair. Brent wasn't pressuring me, but I could hear echoes of Vince in all this.

Even if it hadn't started souring our relationship, it would. Inevitably.

Either you give up and retire, or things are going to go to shit.

Fair or not, I hated that I had to be the one to make the decision. Brent was too early into a promising career. I was on the cusp of retirement eligibility. If someone quit, it was going to be me, and damn if that didn't sound a hell of a lot like, *If you loved me as much as you say you do, you wouldn't even have to think about this.*

I also hated keeping any part of my life a secret. The repeal of DADT had been a massive thing for me because I didn't have to hide who I was from the Navy anymore. My parents still had their own version of DADT in effect, but I spent more time around the Navy than my family anyway. Being able to be openly gay was... fuck. *Huge.*

Dating Brent was like reinstating that fucked-up policy all over again. It was like going back to the days when I could do whatever—and whoever—I wanted, but if the Navy caught wind of it, I was done.

And as I sat here and thought about it, I decided I *was* done. I'd devoted too much of my life to the Navy to kiss it goodbye over a relationship with a younger man who I'd only known for a little while, and who'd probably get bored of me eventually anyway. I wasn't stupid—he was in his twenties. How many twentysomethings had I watched get divorced over the years? That wasn't to say he was nearly as immature as a lot of the younger Sailors and officers I'd worked with, but he was still a kid to some extent.

A knock at my door startled me out of my thoughts. Fortunately, it was the one person whose presence I could tolerate right now—Noah.

He stepped in with a high stack of folders on his arm

and shut the door behind him. "It's your favorite time—eval time." He put the stack of evaluations on my desk with an emphatic *thump*. "You know the drill."

I glared at the stack. Yeah. I knew the drill. Read them. Sign them. Send them back. Or read them, kick them back to be unfucked, then read them again, and hopefully sign them. I'll get to them." I nudged them aside. "Probably by the end of the day."

"Fine by me." He paused. "You look like shit. What's going on?"

"Besides a long afternoon dealing with Captain Carter and—"

"Yeah. Besides that." Noah took a seat in front of my desk. "You were dragging ass long before patrol brought in those kids."

Couldn't get anything past him. Didn't know why I tried.

I sighed. "Just... things with Brent."

"Like, things between you guys? Or the reasons you probably shouldn't be with him in the first place?"

"Column B."

"Ouch. I mean, I'm glad things are good between you. But you know what I mean."

"Yeah." I chewed the inside of my cheek. "I don't know how long things are going to stay good between us, though. Because of all of that."

"Damn. That's rough."

"Yeah. Something has to give, and... I'm pretty sure I know what that something is."

Noah studied me. "Yeah?"

"Yeah." I sank back into the stiff cushion, rubbing a hand over my face as the chair's aging mechanism shrieked into place. The uppermost part of my police belt bit in between two vertebrae. Not enough to hurt, but enough to prod and annoy. I shifted a little, but it didn't help.

Just going into this conversation made me a hundred times more exhausted. "There's no way we can keep doing this. His boss is onto him. Master Chief Holloway will catch on to me eventually. It's..." I sighed and pressed the heel of my hand into my forehead, making slow, useless circles. I dropped my arm onto the wobbly armrest and met Noah's gaze across the desk. "Either one of us gets out, or we both get caught and get booted out."

Noah grimaced. I caught myself wishing for a smug *I told you so*, but it didn't come. The situation was too serious for even him to make a joke, and that did nothing to loosen the knot in the pit of my stomach.

He pressed his elbow into the armrest and absently rubbed the backs of his knuckles along the edge of his jaw. "I'm guessing when you say 'one of you,' you mean you."

"I don't see how it could be him. If he gets out, then he's wasted all that time and effort he spent with the Academy and getting to where he is, and he'll have nothing to show for it. If I get out, at least I have my retirement and benefits."

"Yeah, but I give it six months before you start resenting the hell out of him."

What could I say? He knew me well.

"I'd be surprised if it took that long." I let my head fall back against the chair, wincing when a piece of cracked plastic dug into my neck. "I think I already *do* resent him." I winced again, this time from my admission. "God, I'm such an asshole."

"No, you're not." Noah sounded uncharacteristically serious. "You both have really, really strong ambition, and you're not going to compromise everything you've worked for."

"I seem to recall Vince making some comments along those lines when he was on his way out the door."

"Will." He sighed. "Vince wasn't cut out for being a military spouse. Everyone knows they have to be willing to put up with a lot of shit from the Navy to pull off a relationship like that. And let's face it—Vince was a lying, cheating asshole who deserves to be attacked by one of those little fish that swim up your dick."

A laugh burst out of me. "Jesus. Tell me how you really feel."

He shrugged. "Just saying. You deserve better."

"I know. And I... Fuck, I swear I've found better. He's just not someone I can have."

"That sucks, man. And seriously, he's not someone you can have. If you and Brent were both officers or both enlisted, then it could work out fine. But you're not. It's not his fault, and it's not your fault—it's the way the chips fell. I don't think anyone can hold it against you if you're not willing to cut your career short for a guy you've only known a few months."

I couldn't muster up the energy to tell him how I felt about that guy I'd only known a few months. It didn't matter, so why bother?

He must've seen something in my expression, though, and asked, "What if you'd given up your career when Vince asked you to?"

I shuddered. It was possible Vince would've stayed faithful if we'd both been civilians. Or maybe he'd still have cheated, but he would've had to come up with some other excuse for it besides blaming my job for keeping us apart.

"I don't know if he'd have cheated," I said. "But I'm pretty sure I'd be resenting the shit out of him right now."

"You would have. Guaranteed. And if you retire over this kid, you're going to resent him too."

"I know. Even if I did retire so we could stay together, that'd still be a year away. Someone's bound to find out about us." I let my head fall back against the chair. "Staying with him means losing my career one way or the other."

"And you'll hate yourself for it."

I nodded.

It hurt like hell, but there weren't any options here. Fact was, sooner or later, this relationship would be over. The only question at this point was whether our careers—one or both—would be a casualty.

The sound of Brent's car pulling up outside turned my stomach. I wasn't ready for this, but there was no avoiding it.

I hadn't slept for shit last night because I'd known tonight was coming. All day long at work, I'd been a step above useless, but not a very big step. Thank God for Noah —he'd run interference as much as possible, and handled anything he could. I owed him big time.

As Brent came up the walk, I opened the door. "Hey."

"Hey." He smiled, though it was weak, and slid his hands into his pockets. Neither of us said anything as he came in and I shut the door. Even after the dead bolt was in place, neither of us made a move to touch each other.

I cleared my throat and gestured for him to follow me into the kitchen. My mouth had gone dry, and I desperately needed to do something about that before we went any further. I offered him a beer, but he went for the same thing I did—coffee. I wondered if that meant he expected to be driving in the very near future. Maybe this wouldn't take long.

The coffee did little to settle my stomach, but at least my tongue wasn't sticking to the roof of my mouth anymore.

"Listen, um..." I set the cup down. "We need to talk."

He took a deep breath and pushed his shoulders back. "Okay."

Silence. Long, uncomfortable silence. A million different approaches ran through my head, but ultimately, there was no point in anything but the direct one. Pussyfooting around it wouldn't do either of us any good.

"I'm sorry," I finally said. "I... can't keep doing this."

I swore I could feel Brent's heart drop. Or maybe that was mine.

He shifted his gaze away.

"I want to," I said. "Believe me, I do. But..."

"I know." He looked at me again, and the hurt in his eyes cut right to the bone. It just confirmed what I already knew.

I should've cut you loose a long time ago so I wouldn't have to hurt you now.

I should've let you go before I fell this hard for you.

My own thought made me wince. Every time I admitted to myself that I was in love with him, doing the right thing got exponentially harder.

"I'm sorry," I said again. Because I was, and because I didn't know what else to say.

Brent nodded. "I know. Me... me too." His jaw worked, and I wondered if he was trying to hold himself together. "I guess there isn't much more to say, is there?"

"Not really, no."

We held each other's gazes. Never in my life had I imagined wanting a knock-down, drag-out, screaming-match type of breakup, but I wished for one right now. It was so much easier to let someone go after we'd spent an hour saying all kinds of shit we couldn't take back. Those fights usually hurt, and so did the breakups, but at least it was more like *Don't let the door hit you on the way out, asshole.* By the time it was over, we'd want nothing more than to be as far apart as possible.

Calmly, quietly, sadly calling things off with Brent hurt in a way I hoped I'd never experience again.

Brent broke eye contact first. "I'll, um... get out of your hair, then."

"Okay." I didn't know what to say, so for lack of anything better, I added, "Take care of yourself."

"Yeah. You too." On his way to the door, he paused. Slowly, he turned back to me. "For the record, I don't regret this."

I wished I felt the same. I'd already hurt him enough, though. "Neither do I."

Something flickered across his expression. His lips tightened, and then his eyes darted away from mine. I wondered if he saw right through me.

If he did, he didn't say a word. He just continued toward the door, and a moment later, he was gone.

Alone, I sat back on the couch and closed my eyes. I didn't want to regret it. The sex had been amazing, and the time we'd spent together in between had been... Oh fuck, when was the last time I'd enjoyed another guy's company like that? Brent and I came from two different worlds—we still *lived* in two different worlds—and yet we'd somehow fit together. First, physically. Later, so much more than that.

I ran a hand through my hair and cursed into my empty

apartment. Watching my live-in boyfriend drive away after over half a decade together had been hard. Who was I kidding—it'd been hell. I'd been devastated, and I'd broken down on my best friend's shoulder because watching that U-Haul disappear around the corner had torn something in me.

We'd gone down in flames. The fighting had been nonstop for too long. The cheating had been unforgivable. Nothing in the world could make me take that man back, but watching him go had still been one of the hardest things I'd ever done. A relief in some ways—we'd finally put out the trash fire that our relationship had become—but hard because at one time, I *had* loved him.

Letting Brent go was harder for entirely different reasons. We both *wanted* to be together. There was no anger. No fighting. No side pieces. Nothing but an ironclad regulation that said we couldn't.

I'd never even had a chance to tell him I loved him, and that was a good thing because it would've made this hurt more. For both of us.

I regretted dating him because I'd known from day one that it wouldn't last. The only variable had been when it would blow up and how much it would hurt. Dragging it on for as long as we had, giving things a chance to turn into something so much better, had been an exercise in masochism.

On the bright side, the pain of my other breakup was long gone. I could think about that relationship objectively and without getting choked up.

So, Brent had definitely helped me get over Vince.

Now I had to find a way to get over *him*.

CHAPTER 24

BRENT

DRIVING onto the base was torture. Even my evenings were miserable. I couldn't go anywhere in Anchor Point without thinking about Will because I couldn't go anywhere in this town without being face-to-face with the goddamned Navy.

When Saturday finally rolled around, I was out of bed before the sun came up, and got the hell out of town. I didn't have a destination. All I needed was to get as far away from the Navy as I could, so I drove down the coast until there was no chance of seeing a ship or one of the harbor security boats. With any luck, I wouldn't even see the Coast Guard. I supposed I could have gone inland instead of staying near the water, but then my dumb ass would probably have wound up in Portland, and I'd have had a complete breakdown when I saw the hotel we'd stayed in or the Chicken 'N' Fire or that fucking garden.

So I stuck to the coast.

Eventually, I parked in a deserted gravel lot with a trailhead leading down to the beach. Once I'd reached the sand, I walked as aimlessly as I'd driven.

Of course, my mind wasn't so aimless. It hadn't been far from one particular subject since the night I'd left Will's apartment.

We'd done the right thing and called it quits. Now I could continue with my Navy career, with at least eleven— probably more like twenty-one—years between me and retirement.

I wanted to fucking cry. I damn near did. If I'd had a little bit more energy, I probably would have. Because I was done. I couldn't cope anymore. It didn't feel like a straw had broken the camel's back. More like my back had broken a long time ago, and I'd only just gotten around to noticing.

Slowly, the truth sank in. The tears I was fighting back weren't because Will was gone. I missed him so bad it hurt, but what I was feeling right now was something completely different.

The thought of doing another eleven years in the Navy was excruciating. Twenty-one?

Fuck. I'd rather spend it in prison.

I wiped at my stinging eyes. Kind of felt like I *was* in prison. Like I'd been there for the last nine years, and there was no parole in sight for at least that long.

Except that was stupid. No one ever said life in the lower ranks was a walk in the park.

I'm paying my dues so I can get where I want to go. That's all.

Right?

So why didn't those higher ranks feel like such an appealing carrot on a stick anymore?

I found a huge piece of driftwood and sat down. Staring out at the ocean, I tried to muster up the enthusiasm I'd had for my career. I'd... I'd *had* some, hadn't I? I'd been proud when I'd been accepted into Annapolis, and prouder still

when I'd graduated. Even then, as my family had congratu-
lated me and taken dozens of pictures of me in my uniform,
there'd been a distinct feeling of *That's it?*

I wasn't sure what I'd been expecting. If I'd suddenly
feel like I'd made it after all that hard work, or what. Of
course the hard work had been just beginning, and I'd
known it, but as I sat here now on a beach, trying to escape
the base where I was stationed, I couldn't remember when
this disillusionment had started. Or if it had been there all
along and I'd written it off as being tired or annoyed by the
shit cadets and ensigns had to do.

I tried to think back to a period of my career when I
hadn't been miserable. I'd had my moments at the Academy.
Port calls were fun. Couldn't complain about the pay even
at this rank.

But all along, there'd been this distinct feeling of *Get
through this part, and it'll get better.*

And... had it? *Was* it better than my days as a cadet or
an ensign?

I couldn't say. All I knew was that throughout my childhood, the Navy had been gleaming brass, but at some point,
that brass had tarnished.

And not only did I not know how to bring back the
shine, I wasn't so sure I wanted to.

I tapped gently on Commander Wilson's office's doorframe.
"Sir?"

He looked up from some paperwork. "Hey, Lieutenant.
What can I do for you?"

"I, uh..." I hesitated. "Do you have a minute? To talk
about something kind of personal?"

His eyebrows flicked up a little, and his lips tightened. I wondered if he thought this was about Will.

If he did, he didn't say anything. Instead, he put his pen down and sat up, wincing slightly. "Sure. Have a seat."

I shut the office door behind me and took one of the chairs in front of his desk. "When you were a lieutenant, were you... I don't know... Did you *like* being in the Navy?"

He seemed to mull it over for a second before he shrugged. "It's been a long time. But I was a pilot, so..." He cracked a smile. "Yeah, I enjoyed my job."

"Oh. Do you ever regret your career?"

He thought about that too, then shook his head. "No. Do you?"

I gnawed my lip. "I... I don't know."

Wilson studied me. Then he folded his arms on the edge of the desk and watched me intently. "What's going on?"

I swallowed and stared down at my wringing hands.

"Is this about Senior Chief Curtis?"

I flinched. "It... Kind of."

"You're not thinking of giving up your career for him, are you?"

"Not exactly."

"You either are or you aren't." There was a hint of warning in his voice, kind of like when my mom was letting my dad know he needed to watch his step.

I sat up a little. "Permission to speak freely? Off the record?"

He nodded. I still had the distinct feeling I was on thin ice over hot water, but if there was anyone in this building I could trust with this conversation, it was him.

Sitting straighter, I pulled in a deep breath. "I know dating him is against the UCMJ. And I'm not asking you or the Navy to overlook that. The reason I'm in here right now is that I think dating him has... put a few things into perspective. About myself. And... my career."

Wilson cocked his head, offering no reaction except curiosity.

"It's not that I want to throw away my career over a man. But I've..." I chewed my lip as I tried to pull my thoughts into some semblance of order. Finally, I looked Commander Wilson in the eye. "I guess being with him has gotten me thinking about my career and if this is what I really want. Or if..." My throat tightened, and I coughed to push some air through. "The thing is, I don't know if I'm just disillusioned because what I'm doing now isn't what I envisioned myself doing in the Navy, or if maybe joining the Navy is the biggest mistake I've ever made."

The words tumbled out, and as soon as they did, a weight slid off my shoulders. The thought had been bouncing around in my head for a while now, but saying the words was beyond liberating. Like now that they were out there, I couldn't take them back if I wanted to, and I *didn't* want to. They weren't necessarily true, and I wasn't necessarily going to resign, but at least I'd fucking admitted it was a possibility.

A little slower now, maybe a bit more collected, I went on. "The Navy is all I've ever wanted to do." I swallowed hard. "Just like it's all my brother ever wanted to do. And part of me is wondering if I ever actually decided it was for me, or if..."

"Or if your father decided it was."

Exhaling, I nodded. "Yeah. So every time I think about resigning, I freak out about what my family will say and how disappointed they'll be. Not... not about what I'll do next, or how much I'll regret it if I don't stick with this."

"Do you think you would regret resigning?"

I was surprised by the lump in my throat and the hint of a sting in my eyes. Why the fuck was I getting this emotional?

Avoiding Wilson's gaze, I shook my head. "I don't know. And I guess the decision would be easier if he wasn't in the picture. Will, I mean." I paused. "Senior Chief—"

"I know who you mean," he said softly.

"Right. But, I mean, that way I'd know if I'm thinking of resigning for me or for him." I rubbed my eyes. "Except he's the reason I started thinking about this, so... I don't fucking know."

Wilson was quiet for a long time. I couldn't tell if he was waiting to see if I had more to say, or if he was pulling his own thoughts together. Eventually, he folded his hands on the desk and spoke.

"I've been doing this for a long time. I'm proud of what I've done and where I am, but I won't blow smoke up your ass—it's been hard as fuck, and it's taken a toll. There will never come a time when I'm not in pain. My husband and I will both have PTSD for the rest of our lives. Our jobs have cost us each a marriage, strained our relationships with our kids, and—hell, my *kid* even has PTSD as a result of my job."

I gulped. "Whoa."

"Yeah. Do I regret it? No. Because I wanted to fly, and I wanted to be in the Navy. For *me*." He leaned in a little closer, inclining his head. "This isn't a job you can do for someone else. It's going to be hard, and it's going to be fucking miserable at times. Sometimes for a long time. If your heart isn't in it, it's going to be a lot worse because you're not getting anything out of it except a paycheck. You're smart and a hard worker—there's no reason you can't get a damn good paycheck in the civilian world if you decide this job isn't for you."

"But what if I get out and there isn't anything on the civilian side that's any better?"

Wilson shrugged. "That's a risk you have to take."

Damn it. He was supposed to have answers that made me feel better.

I rubbed my forehead. "I don't know what I should do right now."

"Right now, I think you need to take a good long look at your career and what you want. Not what your father wants for you or the rest of your family expects of you. What *you* want."

"I know." I sighed. "You said the old CO retired because of his husband, didn't he?"

Wilson nodded. "His situation was a bit different from yours, though. He'd probably gone as far as he'd ever go in his career." He paused. "On the other hand..."

I watched him for a moment. "On the other hand, what?"

"One of the things he told me after he put in for retirement was that choosing between his man and his career made him realize just how much his career had already taken from him. And after over twenty years of that, he decided he wasn't willing to let the Navy take Sean from him too. He'd had enough." Wilson's eyes lost focus for a few seconds before he looked at me. "I think what you need to consider right now is how much you're willing to give the Navy if you want to eventually make captain or admiral. Because your boyfriend isn't the biggest thing this job is going to take from you—just the first."

I gulped, startled by his candidness.

Wilson went on. "At this juncture, you're not deciding

between the Navy and your boyfriend. You're deciding between the Navy and *you*. Which I guess means you're kind of at a crossroads. Are you throwing away the last decade of your life by resigning? Or are you throwing away the next one by staying?"

I pushed out a breath. "I don't know."

"Well, I think that's what you need to think about. If this really isn't what you want to do, then with every year you spend doing it, it's only going to get harder to justify leaving. You're young and you're bright. If you stay in, I have no doubt you'll be an amazing leader. If you get out, I'm completely confident you'll find your way."

What I wouldn't have given for his confidence.

But I just nodded. "Thanks for the pep talk, sir."

"Anytime." He smiled. "Good luck."

Yeah. I was pretty sure I was going to need it.

CHAPTER 25

WILL

"HOW YOU HOLDING UP?" Noah's brow was creased with sympathy as he sat down across from me at the E club.

"Still making it to work every day." I thumbed the edge of the menu I'd long ago memorized. Nothing sounded appetizing. I needed to eat something if I was going to make it to the end of the work day, but damn if just the thought of eating sounded like way too much physical effort.

Noah sighed. "I'm really sorry about how it played out."

"Me too." I laughed bitterly. "Guess I shouldn't be surprised, right?"

He offered a subtle shrug. "Doesn't make it easy."

"No, it doesn't." I pushed the unopened menu aside. "The thing that kills me is that this shouldn't hurt worse than it did to lose Vince. But it does."

"Nah, I'd say it makes a lot of sense."

"Why's that?"

"Because getting rid of Vince was a long time coming, and letting go of Brent was..." He paused. "I mean, Vince treated you like shit. Brent didn't *do* anything except get his commission."

I rubbed my eyes with my thumb and forefinger. "Yeah. That's a good point. Fuck."

"And, I mean, I know it's not much of a consolation, but you did the right thing."

"I suppose eventually it'll feel like I did. Right now... it feels all wrong."

"I believe it. I'm sorry, man. I wish there was more I could say."

At least he spared me the lecture about how stupid I'd been to get involved with an officer in the first place. With as much hell as I've given him for his drinking problem, any other guy probably would've seized the opportunity to turn the tables and enjoy his time on the moral high ground.

Noah wasn't like that, though. And right now, I was more grateful than ever that we'd wound up on the same base again. Without him to lean on, I'd have probably lost my mind already.

The waitress came, and I forced myself to eat enough to carry my sorry ass through the rest of the day. After lunch, Noah and I walked in silence back to the precinct. The whole way, I kept my gaze down, inspecting the sidewalk and the dirt path like I was checking a runway for debris that might get sucked into an aircraft engine. That wasn't my usual MO, but I was irrationally sure if I looked around, I'd see Brent, and I couldn't cope with that right now.

It wasn't all that irrational, really. If this were Norfolk or San Diego, we could easily coexist without ever crossing paths. Here? Not so much.

Thank God I'd be up for orders soon. I was stuck at NAS Adams for at least another eighteen months, but after that, I'd go overseas again. It was a perk of being an MA—instead of going back and forth from sea to shore, we went back and forth from stateside to overseas. I didn't know yet where I'd be going, but I couldn't get there soon enough.

A knock at my apartment door raised the hairs on my neck.

It was almost nine thirty, and no one ever came to my apartment besides Noah. He would've texted unless it was a dire emergency. Or he was drunk, and that had been a nonissue for months now.

Which left either a neighbor or...

I warily approached the door, and when I looked through the peephole, I swore. Then I turned the dead bolt, opened the door, and waved Brent inside. "Come on." I looked around in case anyone was watching.

He kept his gaze down and stepped past me.

"What's going on?" I dead bolted us in and turned to him. "You can't be here. We'll—"

"I know." He put up his hands. "I won't stay long."

I gritted my teeth. I was about to shoo him out and be done with it, but he pushed his shoulders back. I didn't think I'd ever seen him this bold and determined before, and it gave me pause.

"Listen, I know I shouldn't be here and..." He exhaled. "I'll go. But before I do, can I say something?"

I didn't want this to drag out longer than it had to. It was risky to be in the same place, and besides, I already hurt enough from trying to move on after letting him go. Why pour salt in the wound?

But I couldn't ignore the earnestness in his eyes.

"Okay." I swallowed. "Go ahead."

He set his jaw. "I'm resigning my commission."

I nearly choked. "You're *what*? Brent, are you—"

"I've made up my mind. And… it's happening whether we stay together or not."

I stared at him. "What the hell?"

"I can't keep doing this. I just can't."

"Brent, you've got your entire career ahead of you. You're an Annapolis grad, for God's sake. You've got so much potential to—" I shook my head. "I don't want you giving that up for me."

"I'm not." He looked me right in the eye. "I'm giving it up for *me*."

I blinked. "What?"

He pushed out a breath, and that confident, borderline confrontational posture melted to something much less so. No, that wasn't it. It wasn't a lack of confidence. Shoulders sinking, hip resting against the counter like he needed help staying upright, gaze down—he looked fucking *tired*.

"What's going on?" I asked.

"What's going on is that being with you made me realize what I want. Or more to the point, what I don't want." He lifted his gaze enough to meet mine. "And I don't want this career."

"But… you've been working at it for years. Since you were a kid."

"I know. Because everyone *told* me this was what I wanted." He paused as if he needed to collect himself. "You remember when you asked what I'd be doing if I hadn't joined the Navy?"

I nodded.

"When I said I didn't know, I meant it. Not because I always wanted to do this, but…" He hesitated. "I was *told* this was what I was doing. That's how it's been from the time I was too young to even think about my future. And I just accepted it because… because, fuck, I was a kid, and I wanted to make my parents proud." He ran an unsteady hand through his hair. "You know when all the other kids were talking about being astronauts and firefighters? It was all Navy, all the time for me. I wasn't allowed to think about doing anything else. The one time I ever brought up the idea that I might want to be something other than a Navy officer, my dad tore into me for an *hour*. You want to know how old I was?"

Mute, I lifted my eyebrows.

"Nine." He closed his eyes. "I was fucking *nine*." Brent was silent for a long moment, and I was too stunned to speak. After a while, he rolled his shoulders, met my gaze, and went on. "So it's never been an option, you know? Doing something else? But now... I still don't know what I want to do, only that this isn't it."

I cleared my throat. "And you happened to figure this out right when we had to split up?" I tried to keep my tone gentle and without any accusation.

Brent sighed. "Look, I have no idea when I would have figured it out if I hadn't met you. All I know is that when I had to choose between you and the Navy, it was a no-brainer because I only *want* one of those choices."

"So you—"

"I don't want this career. I never did. I went along with it because it's what was expected of me, and because even when I was a kid, I wasn't allowed to consider anything else. After that time when I was nine, I never *once* stopped to think about if it was really what *I* wanted." He swallowed like it took some serious work, and his voice wavered as he said, "Not until it was standing between me and something —someone—I *do* want."

"But... I can't be the reason..." I was still too shocked to put my thoughts in any kind of order.

Brent had it closer to together than I did, though. "Yes, you're the reason I figured it out. I won't lie. When I met you and realized I couldn't have you because of the Navy, it made me take stock of things. Of everything. And the fact is, I've been miserable all along. I thought it was because my career hadn't picked up steam yet and I was still paying my dues, but that's not it at all. I mean..." He clenched his jaw like he was trying to keep himself composed. "Remember when you said that the horrible parts of your job are worth it when you can keep other people safe?"

Suppressing a shudder, I nodded.

"That got me thinking, and I realized the silver lining of my job was that I had you. I met you because of the Navy, and we're both in the same town because of it. But then the Navy is also the reason I can't have you. And without you..." He shook his head and released a long breath. "The fact is, at the end of the day, I hate the Navy. I hate this job. And..." He met my gaze. "And I love you."

My heart somersaulted. I stared at him in disbelief.

Apparently, for longer than I thought, because he sagged against the wall and exhaled. "That's it. That's all I came to say. If you want me to go, then..." He made a weak gesture toward the front door. "I'll go."

"Let's get one thing clear right now." I stepped closer and cupped his face. "I have never once *wanted* you to go."

Then I kissed him.

And sweet Jesus, it was like coming home.

Brent stiffened for a split second before he wrapped his arms around me. His lips parted for my tongue, and we let this slow, languid kiss linger. Funny how our first kiss had been in the back hallway of a gay bar, and our first kiss after finding our way back to each other was in the hallway of my apartment. This one couldn't be any more different from that one, though. The first time, we'd been needy, demanding, and horny. Now, it was just as needy, but tender and... relieved. We'd been winding each other up back then so we could go fuck. Now, like that kiss we'd shared in the Japanese garden in Portland, this could stand all on its own. It was a relief more than a prelude.

That wasn't to say this wouldn't lead to something else —the heat building between us couldn't be ignored forever —but not yet.

Brent broke the kiss with a shiver. "I missed this so much."

"Me too." I caressed his face. "I didn't think there was any way..."

"I know. Neither did I." He swept his tongue across his lips. "I should've figured it out sooner. This is the first career decision I've ever made for myself, and I'm sorry you had to get dragged along while I got my head together."

"I don't care. I have you back—that's all I can think of right now." I tipped up his chin and smiled. "And, hey, on the bright side, if you hadn't gone into the Navy, I never would've met you."

He laughed. "Yeah, I guess that's true."

I chuckled, but it quickly faded. "Being with me means being with the Navy, though."

"I know. And I'm fine with that. I was a Navy brat, remember? I just don't want to be the one in the Navy. If you are, then... that's fine. That's great. In fact, I *want* you to make master chief and retire at thirty years. Because it's what you want." He cupped my cheek. "And I want to be there with you when you do."

"But what will you do?"

Brent shook his head. "Like I said, I don't know. I

honestly don't. I..." He chewed his lip as he avoided my eyes, and some renewed tension tugged at his features.

"What's wrong?"

He exhaled. "To put it bluntly?" He met my gaze. "I really have no idea what I'll do next because I have no idea who I am. The Navy was such a foregone conclusion for me from the time I was a kid, I've never given serious thought to doing anything else. Now that I have that opportunity?" He swallowed, and I swore there was the subtlest gleam of tears in his eyes. "I have *no idea*."

I gathered him in my arms. "Jesus, Brent. I didn't realize how much this had consumed your life."

His whole body seemed to go slack between mine and the wall. Not like he was breaking down, just that he was tired of holding himself up. That was fine—I had no problem letting him lean on me right then, especially with as close as I'd come to pushing him away.

As I stroked his hair, he quietly said, "The Navy has been my whole life. I will be so glad when that's over. And..." He sighed heavily. "I know this has been hard on you. Dating me on the sly and all. I'm sorry."

"Don't be." I held him a little tighter and pressed a kiss to the top of his head. "I wanted to be with you no matter what the Navy said about it."

"Me too."

For ages, we stood there, holding on and letting the truth sink in. After being so convinced there was no way we could make this work... here we were. I had no doubt we'd be dragging each other into the bedroom before too much longer, but for now, we let the moment be.

After a while, I combed my fingers through his hair. "So what happens now?"

"Now I start looking for a job."

"How much time do you have?"

"I have a solid thirty days of leave on the books, so... a month?" He grimaced. "Not that the economy is great, and I can't imagine there's a whole lot of work in this town, but I'll find something. And I don't know how it'll look on a résumé that I went to the Academy and then quit after less than ten years, but..." He waved a hand. "I'll figure something out. I've got enough in savings to keep me going for a while."

"I think you'll be fine. If I can help, say so."

"Thanks. I'm nervous, but... God, it's a huge relief just to say it. I'm resigning." He smiled up at me. "No more living the life someone else decided for me, and I get to be with you. What's not to love?"

I smiled back and wrapped an arm around his waist. Touching my forehead to his, I whispered, "I love you, Brent."

"I love you too."

I kissed him once more, then met his eyes. "You know, as long as you're here..."

His eyebrows rose, as did the corners of his mouth. "Hmm?"

I glanced toward the bedroom.

So did he.

And neither of us had to say another word.

CHAPTER 26

BRENT

I'D BARELY LANDED on Will's bed before my back was arching off the mattress. I couldn't help it—with his hot, naked skin against mine, and with the way he kissed up and down my neck, I was coming unglued. It wasn't even that I was getting close to coming—I wasn't yet—just that it felt like forever since I'd touched him, and now I wanted to drown in him. Every time I'd been with him, I'd wanted him so bad it'd threatened to drive me insane, but none of those times held a candle to the way I needed him right now.

It wasn't like makeup sex after a fight. We hadn't fought. Someday we definitely would, and then I could find out what makeup sex was like with him, but not tonight. This was something completely different, and... not. It was less *Let's fuck now that I can stand you again* and more *I didn't think I'd ever have you again.* It wasn't even the same as when we'd been apart for a few days at Thanksgiving. We'd known that was a finite separation. This time, not so much.

The way we touched was gentle and subdued, but with

an undercurrent of need that reminded me of the night we'd fucked in the bathroom at the High-&-Tight. Like if we'd waited another minute to get undressed and into bed, something would've caught on fire. Or it still might.

He dove for my neck. "I missed you so much. I've been going crazy."

"Me too." I dragged my nails up his back as he kissed along my throat. "Fuck, I want you so bad."

"You have me. I'm not going anywhere."

This time, I believed him a hundred percent. He wasn't going anywhere and neither was I, and there was nothing else to do tonight except turn each other on and make each other come.

I pushed him onto his back, and he groaned as I climbed on top of him.

"I like where this is going," he murmured before claiming a demanding kiss.

"Me too." I rubbed my erection against his. "Think one of us should put on a raincoat, though."

Will moaned against my mouth. "Yeah. Definitely agree."

"Any preference?"

"Don't care." He squeezed my hips as he pressed our cocks together. "Long as we're fucking, I really don't care."

"Mmm, I like the way you think."

Except we weren't getting any closer to putting on a condom. His hands were all over me, and our bodies were moving like they didn't need any input from either of our brains, rocking together like one of us was already inside the other.

Will finally broke away and panted, "Condom. Now."

"Good idea." Still straddling him, I leaned toward the nightstand. On paper, it was a simple set of tasks—open the drawer, get a condom and the lube, and come back to Will—but damn he made it difficult. How was I supposed to operate a drawer or my own fucking fingers when he was kissing up my side, teasing my balls with his fingertips, nibbling my skin...

I shivered, still fumbling with the drawer. "You're a bastard."

He laughed as his finger drifted from my balls toward my hole. "You really think that's going to discourage me?"

"No, because you're a bastard."

"Fair enough." He teased my ass with a fingertip. "But I like making you squirm, so... sorry not sorry."

I groaned. Then I shoved the lube into his grasp. "Hold that." At least that would keep one of his hands busy.

It didn't help. He only needed one to drive me crazy, and he took full advantage. The tip of his finger pressed into me in the same moment I pulled the box of condoms from the drawer, and when I shuddered, I lost my grip. Of course they couldn't tumble back into the drawer—instead, they bounced off the drawer and onto the carpet.

"Damn it," I muttered.

Will craned his neck. He slid his finger out and started to reach toward the floor. "Actually, I think I can reach—"

"Fuck 'em." I turned his head and kissed him again as I pried the lube from his hand. "Don't want to wait."

"You... want to go bareback?" He didn't seem entirely opposed to the idea, but not completely sold on it either.

I shook my head. "Not yet. We'll get there." I winked as I poured some lube into my palm. "But there's plenty we can do without rubbers." I coated our cocks in lube, then pressed against him and closed my hand as best I could around them both.

Then Will added his hand, so I thrust into our grips.

His wasn't as slick as mine, and the hint of friction was dizzying.

"Like that?" I asked.

"Uh-huh." He arched under me. "Oh yeah, that feels good." Before I could respond, his free hand grabbed the back of my neck, and he pulled me into a kiss, and *now* it was perfect. Oh Christ. It was hard, sloppy, hungry kissing, both of us taking sharp breaths through our noses because no way in hell were we coming up for air. I fucked against him, into our hands, and he pushed back, the underside of his cock sliding back and forth along mine.

Our hands and bodies moved faster. My head spun faster. Everything seemed to be happening faster and faster and faster, and I finally *had* to come up for air so I didn't pass out, and Will moaned my name as he arched off the bed, and *Fuck yeah, don't stop, don't stop...*

"I'm gonna come." I shuddered. "God, I'm gonna—" Will picked that moment to slide his finger over the head of my cock, and I lost it.

As my cum landed on his stomach, Will grunted and jerked, and his cock stiffened against mine a second before he came too, adding his own semen to the mix. I tried to keep thrusting for as long as possible, but I was too far gone for that kind of coordination.

I shuddered one more time, and then my elbows buckled, and Will pulled me down on top of him.

"In case it wasn't abundantly clear," I mumbled, "I missed you."

He laughed, combing his fingers through my hair. Man, I'd missed that too. I'd missed all the little things he did that he probably didn't realize I noticed. Things like kissing my forehead and playing with my hair and looking at me like he was already mentally fucking me before we'd even taken off our clothes.

"We should get cleaned up," he said after a while. "All this lube and cum everywhere..."

I chuckled. "That just an excuse to get me into the shower so we can get started again?"

"Do I need an excuse?"

"Not really, no."

We pried ourselves apart and took a long, lazy shower, spending more time kissing and holding on than actually soaping or scrubbing. Neither of us was quite ready to go again, though, so we climbed back into bed under the covers.

Wrapped up in his arms, I closed my eyes. For the last few days, I'd been asking myself over and over if I was *sure* I wasn't giving up my career for him. If that decision had really been for *me*. I knew the answer was yes. The Navy wasn't for me, and I was done.

But when I was pressed against him like this, warm and satisfied, I could definitely concede that this was a damn nice bonus.

"How long did you say your terminal leave was?" he asked after a while.

I shifted around a bit so I could look at him. "Thirty days. Would've been longer, but I burned a few days over the summer."

"I'm not going to complain that it's shorter."

"Yeah, same here." I touched his face and smiled. "I can't wait until it's over."

Will kissed my palm. "No kidding. But we'll still have to be discreet for a while."

"I know. I can live with that if you can."

Will brushed his lips across mine. "I can definitely live

with it. In fact, maybe we can sneak in another trip to Port-land in the meantime."

"I like that idea." I grinned. "Let me know when you have another three-day weekend, and you're on."

He kissed my forehead. I loved when he did that. "I definitely will," he said. "And hey, I heard Chicken 'N' Fire has a new hot wing challenge."

I groaned, and he burst out laughing. "Asshole," I muttered.

Still snickering, he gathered me in his arms and held me against his chest. I sighed happily as I closed my eyes and nestled against him. I couldn't stay all night in his bed quite yet, but it wouldn't be much longer before I could. We couldn't go out in public together yet, but... soon.

All we had to do was get through my terminal leave, and we'd be home free.

The hard part was almost over.

EPILOGUE

Brent

THIRTY DAYS Later

My dad didn't take the news well.

I called him the day I went on terminal leave. I'd considered waiting until my actual separation date, since I could still withdraw my resignation and come back off terminal leave, but decided to get it over with. The decision was made. Dad wasn't talking me out of it. Nobody was.

The conversation had been long and loud. I'd been to the *Academy*. I'd graduated near the *top of my class*. Officers like me—especially Jamesons—didn't *resign*. I was a disappointment, and it was a damn good thing my grandfather hadn't lived long enough to see this, and what the hell was I going to do with myself as a civilian?

Truth was, I didn't know the answer to that. After a month of terminal leave, I still didn't know what the future held for me professionally. I'd never had this freedom before. My course had been plotted out since I was a kid, and up until recently, there'd never been any question that I'd stay that course.

For the time being, I'd found a part-time job renting out pleasure boats and fishing tackle down at the marina, and another as a cashier at the grocery store downtown. They weren't glamorous, and I was way overqualified, but they were low-stress and gave me something to do while I caught my breath and figured out what came next. Fortunately, my apartment was cheap, my car was paid off, and I had plenty of money in savings, so the pay cut didn't hurt as much as it could have.

Of course I was looking into other more permanent career paths, but so far, I had no idea what direction I wanted to take. I still had the GI Bill, so a master's degree was a possibility once I figured out what to major in. I was considering a second bachelor's to start with, just so I had some time to take a few random classes and see if anything piqued my interest.

For now, I wanted to get my feet under me. Maybe even resolve things with my parents. I'd tried to call them a few more times, but Dad still wasn't ready to speak to me. Maybe he hoped the silent treatment would convince me to pull my head out of my ass and unresign. Or maybe he really was that pissed. Mom was a little cagey either way— she'd chat with me, but wouldn't give me a straight answer about Dad's state of mind.

Hopefully he'd be over it by Thanksgiving or something. If not, well, Will and I could spend it on our own or with friends, since his family wanted me at their table about as much as mine currently did.

It was weird to have so many things up in the air, and to have so much tension with my family. More than once, I'd questioned my decision. Twice, I'd debated rescinding my resignation, but both times, realized I was just scared of the unknown. I'd be all right. Scared beat miserable, after all.

Today, there would be no turning back. Today, my terminal leave was over, and it was time to surrender my ID card. When I left the base, I'd be a civilian. For the first time in my life, I wouldn't have a military ID—dependent *or* active duty. Not even inactive reserve.

Commander Wilson met me at the gate. After I gave him my ID, he shook my hand. "It's tough to see you go, but I think you're doing the right thing."

"Thank you, sir."

He smiled. "You're a civilian now, kid. Call me Travis."

"You're a civilian now."

Good God, it was like an incantation that made the invisible anchor I'd been dragging around just disappear.

"Thank you, Travis," I corrected.

We talked for a few minutes. He'd been curious about my future plans—or lack thereof—and had a few suggestions, but he wasn't pushy about it.

As we stood there, I glanced around the gate. There were a few MAs hanging around. Sentries, mostly, plus a dog handler with a German Shepherd at his side, and a chief who was probably checking on everyone. They watched our exchange, but no one said anything.

I didn't have to look to know Will was not with them. He probably wasn't anywhere near this corner of the base, and thank God for that. If we were seen together once I'd left the base, it wouldn't be a big deal, but he didn't need someone catching wind that our relationship had started *before* I separated from the Navy. As long as no one had proof we'd been dating already, we were free and clear.

Even my parents didn't know I had a boyfriend, never

mind that he was enlisted or that he'd had anything to do with my decision to resign. Not that I'd been able to get a word in edgewise, but I wasn't planning to tell them until long after Dad cooled down. Still, I doubted I'd tip my hand about how our relationship had influenced my decision. Dad would probably be too busy sneering at Will's rank to hear me anyway.

His loss. This was my life, my career, and my boyfriend. Dad's opinion was no longer needed.

Travis and I shook hands one more time, and then I walked off NAS Adams.

On the way to my car, I took in a deep breath of the salty air. I'd done it. I was free. I was a civilian.

For the first time in my life, the future was mine to decide.

It was torture, but I waited until well after dark to go over to Will's place. To be on the safe side, I parked my car in a guest spot on the other side of the building.

As he shut his front door behind me, he said, "So, that's it? You're done with the Navy?"

I nodded. "Yep. I am officially a civilian."

"How do you feel?"

"Like there's no more pressure. I can be with you."

Will smiled. "More like now you can be *you*."

I exhaled. Someone had said it. My parents wouldn't understand anytime soon, and there would be plenty of people out there who thought I'd thrown away a perfectly good career, but Will got it. I couldn't think of much else that mattered. "Yeah. Kind of feels like it's *my* life now."

"That's because it is. And it's about damn time." He ran

his fingers through my hair. "You going to grow this out now?"

I thought about it, then shrugged. "I don't know. Maybe? What do you think?"

"I think it'll look good either way."

"What if I shaved it bald?"

The upward flick of his eyebrows suggested there were limitations on *either way*.

I snickered. "I'm kidding. I like having hair, thank you."

"Good. Because I like having something to hold on to."

"Oh fuck..."

He chuckled. "I think we understand each other. Don't we... sir?"

I rolled my eyes. "You know, I'm really glad the rest of the world is going to stop calling me that, but if you want to keep using it when we're naked? You go right ahead."

"Oh, I was planning on it."

"Dirty bastard."

"Mm-hmm."

"Just one more reason why I love you."

He grinned, then kissed my forehead. "I love you too."

I lifted my chin and indulged in another long kiss because... fuck, because I could. After tonight, there was no reason not to. There would be no more looking over our shoulders. No more worrying that someone might find out about us. Maybe not flaunting things at the Navy Ball or the Christmas parties because that meant *going* to those damned things, but we could eat dinner or go to a movie or walk through the grocery store together.

"By the way," he said after a moment. "I'll be negotiating orders in the next year and a half or so." He smoothed my hair. "Probably going back overseas for three years."

I swallowed. The Navy hadn't taken long to throw a

shiny new monkey wrench into this, had it? "We'll find a way to make it work."

"I know. I was, uh..." He hesitated. "I was thinking that might be enough time to decide if we want to... if we should make you my dependent. So you can come with me."

My heart skipped, and I lifted my eyebrows. "Is that a roundabout way of asking me to marry you?"

He chuckled, blushing as he broke eye contact. "Well, kind of a roundabout way of saying it's something we should consider." He met my gaze through his lashes. "So we can stay together when I transfer."

I smiled, trying not to look quite as excited as I suddenly was. "I like the idea of considering it."

Will grinned. "Is that a roundabout way of saying yes?"

"What do you think?" I cupped his face and kissed him. "Any idea where they might send you?"

He shrugged. "The detailer owes me a favor or two. I was thinking I might see if there's a billet available on Okinawa."

"If you get stationed on Okinawa, we're driving to Vegas, like, *yesterday*."

"So you're marrying me for my orders."

"And your insurance."

We locked eyes, both trying to keep a straight face, but we finally burst out laughing.

He wrapped his arms around me, and I rested my head on his shoulder. God, this felt good. It was going to be weird, moving forward together without the Sword of Damocles hanging over us. I suspected we'd both get used to the idea pretty quickly.

"You know," he said, "a transfer like that might be a good thing for you in terms of career too. There's a university on base, so if you do decide to work on a master's or something, you'd be all set."

"I hadn't thought about that. But... yeah, you're right. I guess it's something to look into. I mean, once I know what I'd actually study."

"You'll figure it out." He traced his thumb along my cheekbone. "There's plenty of time. Right now, you just get to enjoy being a civilian."

"A civilian who can actually go out in public with his boyfriend."

Will's smile made my pulse soar. "I'm definitely looking forward to that part too."

I pulled him in and kissed him, and we let it linger.

It was tempting to suggest going out to dinner tonight, but I knew it wasn't a good idea. We'd already agreed to wait a little while before we let anyone see us out in town. A couple of weeks, at least. And I was okay with that. Knowing the secrecy only had to hold out for a short time—and that it was only a precaution—was a hell of a lot easier than keeping this under wraps indefinitely.

"Well, since we can't go out in public quite yet," I said with a grin, "I guess we'll just have to stay in for the night."

"I guess we will." He returned my grin, and it was that amazingly sexy look he'd given me a hundred times before, usually right before he fucked me into some unsuspecting piece of furniture. Sliding his hands into my back pockets, he added, "Any ideas about how we should spend it?"

"I'm sure we can think of something."

"Hmm. I might be able to think better if you weren't so..." He looked me up and down. "Dressed."

"Seems like when I'm naked, you can only think of one thing."

"Huh." He nudged me back a step, inching toward the

bedroom. "Guess I know how we're spending the evening, then."

I laughed, and we kissed and touched all the way down the hall until we tumbled into his bed. And we kept laughing, kissing, and touching. Just like I had a feeling we'd be doing every night for the foreseeable future.

I still couldn't believe we'd made it here. I couldn't believe how any of this had played out, or that for the first time, I didn't feel the weight of too many people's expectations on my shoulders while I secretly lived the life I really wanted behind the scenes.

I was a civilian now. I had the most amazing boyfriend on the planet.

And my future—my life—was finally *mine*.

For more books by L.A. Witt, please visit

http://www.gallagherwitt.com

Romance * Suspense

Contemporary * Historical * Sports * Military

ABOUT THE AUTHOR

L.A. Witt is a romance and suspense author who has at last given up the exciting nomadic lifestyle of the military spouse (read: her husband finally retired). She now resides in Pittsburgh, where the potholes are determined to eat her car and her cats are endlessly taunted by a disrespectful squirrel named Moose. In her spare time, she can be found painting in her art room or destroying her voice at a Pittsburgh Penguins game.

Website: www.gallagherwitt.com
    Email: gallagherwitt@gmail.com
    Twitter: @GallagherWitt